Two Wrongs

CW00522388

Two Wrongs is the fo
Crime Thriller series. D
keen to progress her police career but is struggling
to shut down the current criminal turf war. Strong
looks to help, unaware that DI Campbell and others
have their suspicions on his methods of working,
and are watching him closely.

Other books by Ian Anderson:

Jack's Lottery Plan

This is the funny and moving story of Jack Burns.
One day he finds out that a friend has secretly won
the lottery and he embarks on a clandestine plan to
get a share. But his plan goes hopelessly wrong
impacting Jack and his friends in ways he would
never have imagined.

Jack's Big Surprise

Jack Burns is planning a surprise proposal for his
girlfriend Hannah. But as is usually the way with
Jack, things don't go to plan. Instead he finds
himself hopelessly involved in a series of hilariously
funny and unfortunate incidents. This is the sequel
to Jack's Lottery Plan and finds Jack just as chaotic
as always.

Other books by Ian Anderson (cont.):

The Anniversary

In the first book of the DI Strong crime thriller series, Andy Austin's family are killed in a road accident. With a sense of injustice, he becomes obsessed on seeking revenge. He befriends DI Strong and uses him to help carry out his plan. As the police get closer to catching him, it becomes clear that there are a few people with guilty secrets.

The Deal

Detective Inspector Strong hatches a plan to use Andy Austin, a wanted murderer, to help him deliver justice to serious criminals he just can't convict. As Strong gets more and more confident with his scheme, he begins to make mistakes and leave himself exposed to a greater risk of being caught and ruining his career. This is the second great book in the DI Strong crime thriller series, following on from The Anniversary.

Other books by Ian Anderson (cont.):

Loose Ends

This is the third book in the DI Strong Crime Thriller series, following on from The Anniversary and The Deal. DI Strong has been bending the law to get the justice he can't achieve through conventional police methods. But is Strong taking too many chances and arousing suspicion? Too many people are becoming involved, too many loose ends, which Strong knows he will have to do something about.

For more information, please visit my website at:
www.ianandersonhome.wixsite.com/ianandersonauthor

Or find me on Facebook at:
www.facebook.com/IanAndersonAuthor

Two Wrongs

Two Wrongs

By

Ian Anderson

Author website:
www.ianandersonhome.wixsite.com/ianandersonauthor

Facebook:
www.facebook.com/IanAndersonAuthor

July 2022

Two Wrongs

Chapter 1

Detective Constable Laura Knight was feeling worried, which was very unusual for her. She got up from her desk and walked across the office to the Ladies toilet. There was no-one else there and she stood by the wash basins, looking at herself in the mirror. She brushed back her long dark hair with the back of her hand and smiled, the corners of her mouth rising slightly to show a set of bright, white teeth. She ran her hands down the side of her body, smoothing her jacket and skirt, and reassuring herself that she was still an attractive woman.

Throughout Laura Knight's career so far, she had always been seen as a very confident police woman and that was one of the reasons she'd made it to the level of detective constable at the relatively young age of twenty nine. But the last few months had been difficult. The toughest she'd experienced as a police officer so far.

The strange thing was that it had all started because the head of a criminal gang, an OCG, an organised crime group, as they were officially known, had been killed. Tony Fleming had been a violent man. He'd built a criminal empire, eliminating anyone that got in his way till he reached the top. He was a big man in every sense of the word and he headed up a series of criminal businesses covering drugs, prostitution, extortion – you name it. If there was illegal money to be made then Tony Fleming was probably involved somewhere. The police couldn't get to him though. They knew he was the main man, their number one target, but he was clever and he made sure that there was no direct connection back to him on any of the illegal activities. He'd also had a very smart lawyer, Max Murray, and between them they'd known every trick in the book. They always seemed to be one step ahead of the police and so there had never been enough evidence to successfully charge him with anything.

But then he'd been killed. Not by a rival gang leader though as you might expect. The killer was just a normal, young guy, with no history of violence. Someone you would just pass in the street without noticing. A nobody, you might even say. His name was Dylan Hughes and in a strange twist of fate DC Knight knew his mother, Marsha. She worked in the same building as DC Knight, as part of the police administration support team. Dylan had also died at the scene, in what was a strange set of circumstances, but Knight and her boss, Detective Inspector Strong were very happy that Fleming was off the streets and so they didn't spend too much time investigating the exact details of what had actually happened. They simply concluded that it was a drugs related dispute between two men who had ended up killing each other. This seemed to suit everyone, although DC Knight and DI Strong knew it wasn't exactly what had happened.

Laura Knight had joined the police after a brief stint at college doing a marketing course. She hadn't enjoyed it. She couldn't take it seriously and quickly ended up losing interest in the course. The whole marketing thing was too fluffy for her. It was all about slogans and images and colours. She didn't get it. Laura needed something real, something practical and exciting, with a bit of danger thrown in. She'd always been a bit of an adrenalin junkie. Sky dives, bungee jumps, abseiling, she'd done them all. One of her friends, Joe, had joined the police and he persuaded Laura to apply.

'I think you'll like it. Once you get past the initial bit, learning all the stuff you can and can't do, they put you on proper investigations. Things that have a real impact on people's lives. After my first year I worked on some real hard line stuff, the sort of things you see on TV, but it's in real life. You come across some interesting characters and you have to learn on the job.'

So Laura had applied and got accepted. At first it was like Joe had said. A lot of training, a lot of administration, lots of rules and regulations to learn and follow. But she stuck at it and after a year or so she started to get involved in more interesting cases. Just a bit part player to begin with, but gradually doing more and more. She worked hard at it, often at the expense of her social life, and started to build a reputation for herself as a good police officer.

Two years ago she had applied for a position in the Serious Crime Team and, to her surprise, she had been successful. After a three month probationary period she was finally given the position of Detective Constable. Her mother had been so proud that day when Laura had told her.

'Oh my God,' she'd exclaimed. She ran forward and threw her arms around her daughter, giving her a big hug. 'A detective. I knew you could do it. I knew it.' she repeated and she squeezed Laura even tighter, if that was possible.

Laura was an only child and had always been very close to her parents. They'd done a lot for her over the years and she appreciated it, even though she knew she hadn't always shown that at times. She'd gone through the usual teenage rebellion phase, but thankfully without too much damage. A bit of smoking, quite a lot of drinking, but no drugs. Laura's mum worked in the local supermarket and her dad was a car salesman in a garage not far from where they had lived, where Laura had grown up. It was a three bedroomed semi-detached house, built in the post-war fifties, in a nice tree-lined street. Laura remembered it as being a quiet, peaceful street where she could play with her friends from neighbouring houses. But when she went back to visit now, the street was always busy with cars parked bumper to bumper on both sides of the road. There were no children to be seen playing in the street now.

One of the things Laura's parents had taught her was to be independent, to look after herself, and when she was twenty two she had moved into a rented flat, sharing with two other people, about half an hour's drive from her family home. Her mum had been upset when she'd moved, but she'd managed to contain it, knowing the time had come and it was the best thing for Laura to do. If you love them, let them go.

Since that time, Laura had progressed up the property ladder and was now the proud owner of her own two bedroomed flat in the same area of town where she'd first rented. She lived there on her own, although there had been a number of boyfriends over the years, two of whom had temporarily moved in, only to move out again a few months later. Or a few days later in the case of one of them. That had been a mistake. Laura was undoubtedly attractive to men, but even so, she hadn't had that many boyfriends, three proper ones according to Laura's counting. It wasn't that Laura was frightened of relationships or commitment of any sort, it was more to do with her job. Being in the police meant that it wasn't a straight-forward nine to five job. Laura enjoyed her police work and she took it seriously. She really believed she was doing something good for the world, or at least for the area where she worked. If that meant working long hours, or at weekends, then she wouldn't think twice about doing that. Criminals didn't operate to a daily work pattern. There was no nine to five for them and Laura had quickly learned that she would have to be prepared to work whenever was required if she was going to catch them.

So Laura was now single and almost thirty, with no obvious prospect of a serious relationship on the horizon. All the men she met seemed to be a bit immature, always joking or talking about some upcoming sports event. It wasn't that Laura didn't like a laugh or watching sports, but she also wanted someone she could have a serious conversation with too. Someone with a bit of substance.

The lack of a boyfriend did worry her a bit, and it worried her mum even more. Although her mum was proud of how well she'd done in the police, she also wanted to see her settled down, married with a nice man and kids. What mum wouldn't? How wonderful it would be to have a couple of grandchildren, but time was moving on and Laura was nearly thirty now. Her mum knew women tended to have children later in life nowadays, but she couldn't wait for ever. Time was passing by. The clock was ticking. Maybe she'd find Mr Right soon.

Tony Fleming had headed up a large, and constantly expanding, criminal business empire covering a number of illegal activities. When he first went missing, the businesses largely carried on as normal. It was a smoothly run operation and managed to stay clear of the courts largely due to Fleming's long serving lawyer, Max Murray.

Things began to change though when, a few months later, Fleming's body was found in a remote farmhouse. As news of his death got around, some of his lieutenants saw it as an opportunity to take over parts of his empire. There was no overall natural successor to Fleming and his businesses began to falter and stall. Small breakaway groups started to form, siphoning off bits and pieces of the criminal activity and the dirty money that went with it. At the same time, a criminal group from Eastern Europe, mostly Romanians, began to emerge and started to try and take over Fleming's business, bit by bit. They were regularly causing problems in what had been Fleming's clubs and bars. It looked like their plan was to disrupt the incumbents operations so that their overall structure fell apart. When people weren't getting the money they had been used to, it didn't take them long to switch allegiances. Detective Constable Knight had heard that a couple of men who had been in Fleming's mob were now working with the Romanians. But it was in no way a done deal. Fleming's lieutenants were still running the vast majority of the business and Knight feared there would be more trouble and bloodshed before it was all sorted out.

In short it had become a bit of a mess and Knight feared that, as the lead detective on this, it would begin to reflect badly on her abilities as a detective. If it wasn't already doing so. She desperately needed to do something, and quickly, to get a cap on the ongoing violence, and restore her credibility as a detective.

Chapter 2

It was pouring down. Yet again. The weather had been like that since the beginning of the month. Was it ever going to stop? Some places up North and in Wales had been flooded. Rivers had burst their banks. It had been all over the news. But, despite the rain, the bins still needed emptying.

Harry Kane had been a Bin-Man for ten years and he'd heard all the jokes about his name. There were no new ones. There hadn't been for the last five years and he was sure there never would be now. Just the same old ones. He'd learned to accept it, put up with it, smile and just get on with his life. His mum and dad could never have foreseen that their little baby boy would have the same name as the future England football captain. Unlike his namesake, Harry the Bin-Man had never been any good at football, or indeed any sport. They didn't look remotely alike either. Harry the Bin-Man was shorter than his namesake. Chunkier too, and he had curly ginger hair. He had sleepwalked through school and somehow landed a job at the local council in, what was then known as, the Refuse Department. Harry had started off in an administrative post. Assistant accounts payable clerk which mainly involved sorting out supplier invoices, making sure they had been paid, then filing them away in black lever arch files, sorted alphabetically in a set of wooden cupboards along the back wall of the office. When the council decided to outsource much of the Refuse Department's services, they were re-named to become the Waste and Recycling Department and, with Harry's job having been transferred to Bangalore, he was offered the position of a Waste and Recycling Assistant Officer. More commonly known as a Bin-Man.

Although it didn't have a great reputation, you didn't get many kids aspiring to be a Bin-Man when they were at school, Harry thought its downbeat status was very unfair. He actually quite liked the job. It was much better than what he'd been doing before, stuck in a dingy office, filing boring invoices. The guy in Bangalore was welcome to that, as far as Harry was concerned. Harry enjoyed being out in the fresh air, being part of a team and meeting people. It was surprising how many people he met on a daily basis as he went about his work and most of them were very friendly to him. The job could also be quite rewarding at times, it was amazing what you could find in people's bins. Harry had read about a Bin-Man in Motherwell who had found a sports bag full of cash, about ten thousand pounds they'd said, and when no-one claimed it after a while, he was allowed to keep it. Harry could only imagine that amount of money. What he'd do with it. Maybe buy himself a car or go on a big holiday? Or even finally leave home and get a place of his own. But so far Harry hadn't found any cash himself. The best thing he'd come across had been a screwed up lottery ticket which, after he'd managed to smooth it out with his mum's iron, had returned ten pounds when he took it to Mr Patel's corner shop. He'd celebrated his win by buying a fifteen pound case of beer and drinking it with his dad and two brothers at the weekend.

But, despite his lack of success in finding anything more valuable than the ten pound lottery ticket, Harry still enjoyed his job. Except when it was raining. Like today. And yesterday and the day before. The rain was really trying his patience. It was probably the only thing that put him off his job. He just didn't like getting wet. The rain would make his hair go really flat, making him look like he was wearing a red beret. And he hated having wet clothes. He'd only just got his overalls dry from yesterday's soaking when he'd had to put them back on again this morning. His boots were still a bit damp and he could feel it creeping through his woolly socks. It wasn't a pleasant feeling.

There were four of them on the bin lorry as always. As per the councils rules and regulations. The driver, Bert, and three bin collectors, Rav, Hitesh and Harry. Rav and Hitesh were related in some way, Harry thought they might be cousins, but he wasn't sure. When the two of them were together they spoke quickly to each other in a language Harry didn't understand, but they would switch back to English as soon as Harry or Bert appeared. Bert was the oldest in the group. He was approaching retirement age but he'd told Harry he wanted to keep working.

'What would I retire for?' he said. 'I don't want to sit at home and do nothing. I'd rather keep doing this. I've been driving a lorry for thirty years now so I might as well keep going till I die.'

The team had a set routine, Bert would always park in the same places at the roadside each day, unless there was a car in the way, and Rav, Hitesh and Harry would jump off the lorry and load the bins onto the tipping mechanism on the back of the lorry. After it had done its job, the men would replace the bins roughly back in the same place where they had picked them up. That was the normal process, but of course there were always exceptions to the norm and Harry was facing one of those now.

He was standing by a street bin, outside a row of shops. It was a metal bin, painted green, and attached to the pavement below, via two rusty metal feet. Since the terrorist bombs many years ago, there were fewer and fewer of these bins around now, the council had been told to remove them, but this one had survived. As usual, the black bag inside the bin was overflowing and when Harry lifted it upwards half of the contents spilled out onto the wet pavement at his feet. He did his best to scoop the rubbish back into the bag and that was when he spotted the book. He picked it up and had a closer look. It was a slim, black pocket diary with the year printed on the front cover. It was this year's diary and it hadn't got too wet. Harry wiped it on his overalls and slipped it into his pocket, intending to

17

have a proper look at it later. You never know, it might be worth something to someone. Maybe this was his ten thousand pound find. It had to be one of these days, didn't it?

<u>Chapter 3</u>

DI Strong and DC Knight were sitting in Strong's office, at the long table with four half empty coffee cups in front of them. They'd just spent the last hour and a half discussing the current situation. Knight was sitting forward, elbows on the table, turning a pen over and over in her hand. Strong was sitting at the table end with his long legs stretched out underneath, his feet interlocked a few inches away from DC Knight's chair.

'So, in summary Guv,' DC Knight said. 'We have two gangs, two OCGs if you want to give them their formal title, fighting over the main parts of what's left of Tony Fleming's businesses. Mainly drugs, some extortion and prostitution although at the moment those latter two seem to have largely broken off into several smaller groups based on their location. From our point of view, they're pretty easy to manage, we know where they are and the people who are running them. They're not causing us any bother. It's the core stuff, the drugs and the clubs that are up for grabs. On the one side we have what's left of Fleming's mob, now apparently headed up by the Bolton family, with Ally Bolton being the one in charge along with his brother and

19

cousin, aided by the lawyer Max Murray. The Boltons all worked under Fleming for years and we can assume they'll try and carry on with a business as usual approach. And on the other side, we have the East European mob, mainly Romanians, and their top man seems to be a Bogdan Popescu, known simply as Bog. He's a hard man with a long criminal record back in Bucharest, although most of it he seemed to get away with.'

Knight took a sip of her, now lukewarm, coffee before continuing.

'The Boltons are still in control of all the main clubs but Bog's team are gradually taking over some of the smaller bars and clubs and cutting off some of the Boltons' supply line. They're also disrupting some of the more major lines of activity by initiating fights and the like on a regular basis at the main Bolton run places, usually in their larger clubs.'

Knight took another sip of her coffee and stood up to stretch her legs, smoothing down her skirt, as she continued with her summary of the current situation.

'The Romanian strategy seems to be to take a gradual approach, slowly building up their business, rather than an all-out war. But we're starting to hear, from our guys on the street, that the Boltons are getting extremely pissed off by all of this, as you might imagine. It looks like they have had enough hassle and are now gearing up to do something big to teach the Romanians a lesson. Maybe try and take out Bog or one of his main men.'

'Mmm…maybe that wouldn't be the worst thing though?' DI Strong replied, thinking it would be good to get the Romanian off the streets.

'Yeah, I guessed you'd say that,' DC Knight replied smiling as she sat back down at the table. She'd worked closely with her boss on a number of cases over the last year and knew how he liked to work. She was learning a lot from him and she found him inspiring. Strong seemed to have one simple objective and that was to stop serious crime. And he didn't really give too much thought as to how that was achieved. If it was possible to convict them through the criminal justice system, then great. But if it wasn't, and you still got the same end result, then that was still better than leaving them out there to carry on with their criminal activities.

DC Knight was pretty much of the same opinion as her boss, but she knew it was risky to express that openly as not everyone agreed with such an approach. There were still a lot of her colleagues who believed everything had to be done by the book and Knight didn't know herself how far she would go in bending the rules to get justice. Or how far DI Strong would go. Also, being a woman, she knew that there were a number of her male colleagues who would like to see her take a fall. They didn't like to see a woman do the job better than them. Poor blokes.

'The trouble is if we let them do that,' DC Knight continued, 'then it's very likely that the violence will escalate. From what we know of the Romanians they wouldn't take that lying down. They have a more structured gang, and so even if

21

Bog was taken out we think they'd quickly regroup with a new leader and look to hit back at the Boltons' gang. It's like *Whack a Mole*. You knock one down and another one immediately pops up.'

'Yes, I think you're probably right, that's what I've heard too' Strong replied. 'I think what we need to do is get someone in with Bolton mob and find out exactly what they are planning. Then we can put a plan together ourselves to take the initiative from both of them and get everything back into a manageable position.'

'What are you thinking Guv?' DC Knight asked. 'An undercover cop?'

'Sort of, but not exactly. I'm thinking of using a guy I've used in the past,' Strong replied. 'If we can get him in close with Ally Bolton and his crew then we might be able to find out what they are planning. Let me have a think about it. Would you be okay with that?' Strong asked, keen to see what Knight's reaction might be, hoping that she would agree to his suggestion.

'Sure, sounds good,' Knight replied without a moment's hesitation. 'Anything that helps us get a lid on this and bring things back under control is fine by me.'

'Good, good,' Strong replied. 'But remember Laura, this must only be between you and me. No-one else can know. I need to protect this guy. You understand?'

Strong looked directly at DC Knight and moved his hand in her direction. For a moment she thought he was going to touch her arm and she could feel herself beginning to blush, but he stopped short leaving his hand on the table midway between them.

'Yes, I…, I understand,' Knight replied, hurriedly, wondering why she was feeling this way with her boss calling her by her first name, but she quickly regained her composure and understood the significance of the conversation. The current turf war had been going on for too long now, with regular outbreaks of violence and DC Knight knew that others in the police force would be using that to question Knight's abilities as a detective. Not that they would be able to do any better, but she had no doubt they would stir up anything they could to bring her down. But she wasn't going to let that happen. She wasn't going to fail, she'd invested too much in her career for it to go wrong now.

DC Knight knew she had taken an irreversible step forward with DI Strong and whatever he was planning to do. She was now committed. It was exciting and she quite liked that.

Chapter 4

'What's that you've got there then?' Rav asked Harry as they both took a bite out of their sandwiches, Rav's teeth chomping down on his as he spoke with an explosion of crumbs falling down on to his overalls.

Rav was eating a cheese and ham sandwich and Harry's was filled with strawberry jam. Harry liked something sweet at this time of the day. A morning on the bins could often leave a bitter taste in your mouth and the jam helped to counter that. Strawberry was his favourite with raspberry a close second. Anything else he found a bit disappointing and so he tended to stick to either of those two.

Both men were sitting in the grey council portakabin, enjoying their mid-morning break. It was their little bit of sanctuary. Inside, there was a plastic, fold-up table and four white plastic, patio-style chairs. All of the furniture had been rescued from the waste recycling centre and been given a second chance in the worker's cabin.

It had finally stopped raining and the sun was out for the first time in what seemed like a long time. Bert and Hitesh were taking advantage of the better weather and were standing outside. Bert was leaning against the cabin wall having a cigarette, while Hitesh was on the phone with his wife. They were expecting their first child and as the date got nearer the frequency of the phone calls seemed to be increasing exponentially. Inside the portacabin, Harry looked down at the diary in his hands and responded to Rav's question.

'It's a diary I found earlier in one of the street bins. It looks quite new, in fact it's this year's. I thought I'd have a look at it. Might be worth something to someone, you never know,' Harry replied. 'It might belong to someone famous.'

'Ach, you and your rubbish,' Rav replied.' I don't know why you bother. You'll never find anything worth anything, will you? It's all just rubbish. That's our job, to clear up other people's trash. Stuff that nobody wants.'

'Well, you never know,' Harry replied, still feeling optimistic despite Rav's declaration.

He'd worked with Rav long enough to know that he was a glass half empty type of guy. He was always moaning about something. If it wasn't his job, it was the government, or the weather, or his family. There was always something. Nothing was ever Rav's fault, it was always somebody else's and Harry had learned just to nod along with him and let him have his rant. But despite his often negative attitude, Harry liked Rav. Underneath that bluff exterior he was really just a big softie and he was the one who had helped Harry most, in the early days, as he learned how to become a bin-man.

Harry started to casually flick through the diary to see if there was anything of interest. Even if it didn't belong to someone famous maybe there was still a story in there. Perhaps details of an illicit affair or a secret code that would lead Harry to buried treasure! Harry didn't expect that but it was fun imagining it. Looking closely at the diary, it appeared to have been used up until sometime in April. The last entry was on Tuesday the twentieth of April and then after that there was nothing. They must have lost it then, or just got bored with filling it in every day, Harry guessed. That was probably why he had found it in the bin. He turned back to the first few pages and saw that the diary owner had filled in their personal details. Name, address and telephone number.

'It's got an address and phone number,' Harry said and he looked at his watch. Rav made a sound, which wasn't particularly positive and carried on eating his sandwich, stuffing the last bit of crust into his already full mouth.

Harry still had another ten minutes before they were due back out for the next bin run and so he stood up and walked outside. He nodded to Bert and turned to the left to be on the opposite side of the cabin to Hitesh, who was still on the phone with his wife. He was talking quickly in that other language that Harry didn't understand, engaged in what appeared to be an animated conversation, his free arm moving wildly as he spoke.

It was still sunny and Harry glanced up at the yellow ball in the sky, feeling more optimistic again. All the really dark clouds, the rainy ones, seemed to have passed over. He opened the diary and looked at the phone number, reading it out as he punched it into his own mobile. He waited a few seconds and then there was a click.

'*This number is no longer in use,*' a female sounding voice unemotionally announced, before the line went dead.

Harry tried again, carefully, making sure he dialled the correct number, but the result was just the same. He put his phone and the diary in his pocket and walked back into the cabin. Bert and Rav were putting their black and yellow fluorescent jackets on, getting ready to go out on the next run.

'What happened then?' Rav asked, smiling mischievously and Harry could see pieces of ham caught between his teeth. 'Are they going to pay you a million pounds reward to give them their diary back then?' he said laughing at his own joke.

'Yeh, but I'm holding out for a couple of million,' Harry replied, smiling back. 'There's some dynamite in here mate. He wouldn't want the press getting hold of this, I can tell you,' he said, still smiling as he patted the diary, hidden in his pocket. He wasn't going to let Rav get one up on him today.

Later that day, having finished his shift, Harry was in his bedroom at home. He'd had a shower and changed out of his dirty overalls, handing them to his mum to put in the washing machine to be ready for the next shift. Harry could easily wash his own overalls but his mum seemed to want to do it. She liked looking after Harry and his two brothers even though they were all now adult men who could easily fend for themselves.

Harry Kane and his two brothers, Sam and Phil all lived at home with their mum and dad. Sam was the oldest, then Harry, with Phil bringing up the rear. They were all in their mid to late twenties with there being only four years between all of them. They all worked, and made reasonable money, but their wages were still not nearly enough for any of them to be able to afford a place of their own in the area where they lived and had grown up in. The property prices were way out of their league, unless they all combined their funds, and even then they would only be able to afford a small flat where they would have to share rooms, or have one of them sleeping in the living room. The only other alternative was to move up North where property prices were cheaper, but all of their friends lived locally and none of them wanted to move away from the place where they'd always lived.

Besides, there were advantages to living at home. They all had their own rooms and they got their meals cooked for them most nights, as well as having their laundry done. It was much better than being crammed into a one bedroom flat which took up most of your wages and where you had to do everything for yourself, or living in an area where you didn't know anyone. Of course there were disadvantages too, especially when it came to relationships. Thankfully, Harry had a girlfriend, Kerry, who understood his situation. Even better, Kerry shared a flat with another girl who went to her own boyfriend's place most weekends, leaving the flat free for Harry and Kerry to enjoy.

Right now though, Harry was in his own bedroom, sitting on his bed, the large wall mounted television playing in the background, although he wasn't really watching it. It was just comfort TV. Something to fill the void. He was looking through this morning's find again, the diary. He had read a number of the entries but they were all pretty boring, just a brief record of what this guy, this Dylan Hughes, had done that day. *Went to work....went to the pub...watched something on TV....blah, blah, blah...*

Harry began to wonder about why someone would write stuff like that. What was the point? Who was it for? Did the guy who wrote it go back and read it? If not who would he show it to? It wasn't the least bit interesting, at least not to Harry, and he couldn't imagine to anyone else either. He soon got bored with reading every individual entry and flicked forward to the last date that had anything written. It was on the twentieth of April. It said something about someone called Fleming and the Strongs, but it didn't make any sense to Harry. "Fleming and the Strongs." It sounded like an old rock band. He wondered why that was the last entry. Why had he stopped writing in his diary that day? Presumably he must have lost it then. Maybe it had fallen out his pocket or something and someone had picked it up and put it in the bin where Harry had come across it. Harry got bored trying to work it all out and he put it his bedside drawer just as he heard a call from downstairs.

'Harry, dinner's ready,' he heard his mum's voice calling him and he left his room, following the alluring aroma of his mum's cooking coming from downstairs.

Two Wrongs

The next day was Saturday and Harry didn't have anything planned for the day, other than a long lie in. That was mandatory for a Saturday, especially if he'd been out the night before, or he was staying over at Kerry's place. But that wasn't the case this weekend, Kerry had gone to Bristol to see her mum and wouldn't be back until Sunday evening so Harry had the whole weekend to himself.

He was lying in bed. He was fully awake, but it was still too early to get up on a Saturday. It wasn't even nine o clock yet! He reached across to his bedside cabinet and took out the diary. He pushed himself up so that his head rested halfway up the headboard and opened it up. He started with the opening pages of the diary again and read Dylan Hughes' address. It was 5 Dartnell House, Holmesly. That wasn't far from here, Harry thought, and an idea started to form in his head. He could take the diary round to Dylan's house and maybe he would give him a reward for returning it. Or, if not, at least he might find out what had happened. Why it had been in the rubbish bin outside the grocery shop. Had he put it there or had it just been lost? A reward would be better though.

Harry slid down the bed again, throwing the diary to the bottom of his bed, and tried to get back to sleep. But it was no good, he was too awake and reluctantly he decided he would have to get up. He could hear his mum moving around in the kitchen below and there was a definite smell of breakfast being prepared. His mum always did what she called a "proper breakfast" at weekends. Sausage, bacon, eggs and plenty of toast to go with it. She firmly believed, and often repeated it, that breakfast was the most important meal of the day. No way was she going to let her three boys leave the house without a "proper breakfast" inside them. Although that didn't seem to matter so much during the week when everyone was in a rush and it was a case of just grabbing what you could. A quick piece of toast and then out the door.

Harry made his way downstairs and sat at the kitchen table. His mum was standing at the cooker, with her back to him, wearing a blue and white striped apron tied around her waist. She turned around towards Harry and walked across the kitchen with a plate of scrambled egg on toast. She knew that was his favourite and Harry eagerly set about eating it.

'You sure you don't want some sausage and bacon with that son?' she asked him. She always asked him.

'No thanks,' Harry replied, shaking his head as he continued eating his food. He never said yes.

'You're up early today,' his mum said. 'Your dad's gone to get a paper but there's no sign of Sam or Phil yet, as usual,' she said, laughing.

'Yeh, I've got to go and see a man about a dog this morning,' Harry replied, while chewing on another piece of toast. 'Just a little errand over in Holmesly, so I thought I might as well get up and go.'

Ten minutes later, breakfast done, plate wiped clean with a final piece of toast before being passed back to his mum, Harry set off in the direction of Dylan Hughes' residence, with the missing diary firmly stuffed in the back pocket of his jeans.

Another twenty minutes after that and he was at the door of flat five in a block of flats which looked like they could do with a bit of tidying up. The flats had been built around twenty years ago and were beginning to show their age. The entrance didn't look too bad, but after that, as you got further in to the building, the corridors became shabby and the walls marked with various blemishes. They were crying out for a good clean and a fresh coat of paint.

Harry knocked on the door of flat number five and waited. It was a dark green door but some of the paint had flaked off to reveal a few patches of blue underneath. There was no obvious sound from inside the flat and so he knocked again, this time harder. Another few minutes passed and still no-one came to the door. Harry bent down and peered through the letterbox but it was dark inside and he couldn't see much, just the outline of a hallway and what looked like a door on the right hand side. The door looked like it could be open, there was some daylight, but he couldn't see inside it, even when he tried shifting his head to the left. There definitely weren't any lights on inside the flat and Harry guessed that Dylan Hughes must be out and that there was no-one else at home.

He opened the diary and tore out a blank "notes" page from the rear. Leaning against the door, he took a pen from his jacket pocket and wrote his name and contact number on the paper, along with a short paragraph detailing where he'd found the diary. He inserted the page into the front of the diary, leaving the top sticking out so that it would be easily noticeable and then carefully pushed it through the letterbox, hearing it drop onto the hallway carpet inside the flat. He stood there for a moment thinking, tried knocking one more time, and then decided there wasn't anything else he could do. Hopefully Dylan Hughes would give him a call to at least thank him for returning his diary, although he guessed a monetary reward was now looking less likely. Harry set off for home feeling a little disappointed and wondering if his mum had started making lunch. All this walking was making him feel a bit peckish.

Chapter 5

After his meeting with DC Knight reviewing the current problems they were having in the clubs, DI Strong had started to put some more thought and substance to his plan. If it worked then he hoped it would result in significantly less violence and that things would soon return to normality, whatever that was. But whatever happened, it should certainly be better than it was now, with regular disturbances in the clubs. He hadn't told DC Knight exactly what he was planning to do yet. He might do in the future but the jury was still out on that one. It was risky telling someone else, he had to be completely sure that Knight was absolutely trustworthy. Fully on board. She was certainly showing good signs. So far she had agreed with Strong's general approach to getting criminals off the street and more specifically she'd gone along with his conclusion on the Tony Fleming and Dylan Hughes killings, which they both knew wasn't completely correct. But she didn't know how deeply involved Strong had been in those killings and Strong wasn't sure whether she would still have been on his side if she had known the two deaths had all been part of his plan. In effect he'd directed the whole episode. DC Knight didn't know how far her boss would go to get justice, or the extent of what he had done in the past. Would she still be on his side if she knew that? How far would she go, Strong wondered. He, himself, had gone further than he'd envisaged when he'd first helped Andy Austin get revenge. It was Austin that had first gone off piste, killing two innocent people, but that in itself had helped Strong use Austin to carry out his plans. And it had worked. It had resulted in serious, violent, career criminals getting what they deserved. Yes, Strong had gone further than he'd originally intended to, but overall he still believed he was doing the right thing.

The first part of his plan to sort out the Romanians versus the old Fleming mob, or the Bog versus Bolton mob, to be more specific, was as he'd briefly discussed with Knight. He hadn't gone into any detail with DC Knight but had told her that he would get someone into the Bolton group, on the inside, to see what information they could get.

That someone was Jack Wilson. Strong had used Jack Wilson in the past in a number of 'cleaning up' activities, including the killings of Tony Fleming and Dylan Hughes. Strong knew that Jack had run down Andy Austin and his family in the past and he'd used that information to 'persuade' Jack to carry out a few jobs for him. Jobs that would result in disrupting criminal activities, or targeting serious criminals, and stopping them, by whatever means necessary.

Strong had arranged to meet Jack again in a quiet country pub, one that they'd used on a number of occasions in the past. He'd explained the situation to Jack and what he wanted him to do. Strong had been pleasantly surprised by Jack's attitude. He seemed really keen on helping the detective again, almost like it was an exciting pasttime. Strong had been worried that, after the Fleming and Hughes killings, Jack might have lost his nerve. He had panicked a bit on the night and it was only with Strong's persuasion that he went back in to finish the job. Strong questioned him about that.

'What if we had to do something like that night in the deserted farmhouse again? Do you think you'd be able to handle that this time?' he asked Jack.

'Yes, I think I would,' Jack replied, confidently, pushing himself up in his seat. 'I know I bottled it a bit that night but now, having had time to think about it, I'm sure I'd be okay next time. That night was my first time really, you know, and that guy pointing a gun at me, well that had never happened to me before. But I'd be ready for it now. In fact I think I'd quite enjoy the excitement of it all. And if it means getting rid of violent criminals, as you say, then I'd do it again, definitely.'

That might be required again, but not just yet, Strong thought. That could be part of a future plan, but all he wanted Jack to do at the moment was gather some information that would allow the police to make some arrests and generally disrupt the Bolton organisation.

He wasn't sure how he could do the same with the Romanian mob though. Strong knew he'd have to find out what their plans were as well, otherwise if the police messed up the Boltons' business, the Romanians might just march in and take over and the situation wouldn't be any better. It was a fine balance to keep the peace. Strong knew he could never stop all the criminal activity, his goal was just to keep it at a manageable level, with no one person, or gang controlling too much. In the current situation, whatever he did next needed to cover both gangs, but he'd have to start off with Jack infiltrating the Bolton premises and seeing where that took them. If, as DC Knight had heard, the Boltons were planning some sort of major hit on Bog and his Romanian mob then that might be the ideal time for Strong to manipulate things to ensure that both gangs were equally badly impacted. But firstly he needed that inside information.

Chapter 6

Marsha knew she'd been putting it off for too long now. She was staring at it again. Standing by the bedside wearing a blue sweatshirt and a pair of black jeans, her brown hair held back from her face by a white headband. It was just a box, one single, cardboard box. Not much to sort out really. It should only take a few minutes, half an hour at the most. But of course it was more than just a simple box. It was all she had of her son now. The box contained everything that she had taken from Dylan's flat, all the personal stuff. His laptop, some books and magazines. The silver pendant chain he'd got from his grandfather and had worn all the way through to his late teens. It was all in there. What was left of his life, neatly packed into a small cardboard box.

But Marsha felt determined today. It was now or never, that sort of approach. She picked the cardboard box up, expecting it to be heavier than it actually was, and carried it through into her living room, placing it carefully on the wooden coffee table. She sat down on the sofa and just looked at it for a few minutes as if she was expecting it to do something, maybe open up and a puppet jump out. A Jack in the box. But she knew that wasn't going to happen and she leaned forward and carefully opened it up. She pulled out a few of the magazines. They were all to do with cars, with shiny, colourful vehicles on the front covers. Cars that most people, including Dylan, would never be able to afford to buy. They could only dream.

Some days Marsha still couldn't believe Dylan was no longer around. That he never would be again. She kept expecting him to call her, or just pop round for tea. She still had a packet of his favourite biscuits in the cupboard. Custard Creams. It was another reminder of him everytime she opened the cupboard door. They just sat there and looked at her. Remember me? they seemed to say. She couldn't bring herself to eat them. It would be like getting rid of another part of Dylan.

And the manner of his death, she also found inconceivable. Dylan was never a drug dealer. Marsha knew he liked to smoke a joint, but it was never anything more. Marsha was sure of that. And Dylan was a gentle soul, he'd never harmed anyone in his life, and she was certain he didn't have a gun. Why would he?

But that was what they'd found. Dylan and Tony Fleming had killed each other in a drugs dispute in a deserted farmhouse. The evidence was there. DI Strong had seen it for himself and told her what had happened. It still didn't make sense to Marsha, but that was the conclusion. One of life's paradoxes.

Marsha put the magazines on the settee beside her and reached back into the box, extracting a couple of books. His favourite books. *One Shot* and *Killing Floor*. Both *Jack Reacher* novels by *Lee Child*. Ironic titles really when you consider how Dylan died. She put them on top of the magazines. She might have a go at reading them in the future, but they weren't really her genre, she preferred romantic novels. Maybe she would take them to a charity shop instead, but not yet. They still felt part of Dylan. She reached back into the box and felt the cool, tactile touch of the silver chain. She pulled it out and let it fall into the palm of her hand. It was a plain silver chain, nothing special, but it had been special to Dylan. Marsha's dad, Old Bob, had given it to Dylan as a Christmas present when he was around ten years old and Dylan had loved it. It was different to anything else he'd ever been given before and he put it on and wore it constantly for the next few years. Dylan had loved his grandad, he was the only male role model Dylan had known in his life since his father had passed away when he was just a baby. After Old Bob suddenly died of a heart attack, Dylan stopped wearing the chain and it was around that time that Dylan had also started to go off the rails. He began to get involved with the wrong people and that's when he began smoking pot. If only his grandad had still been around, Dylan would never have done drugs then. Old Bob would have made sure of it. That had been a hard time for Marsha, Dylan's whole personality changed. He had constant mood swings and Marsha was finding him almost impossible to live with. If he hadn't been her son, she would definitely have kicked him out.

But over time he did change, somehow he got out of it, the downward spiral. He got himself a job and a few months later moved out of Marsha's house into his own flat, with a little financial help from Marsha. But it was the best thing for both of them and for the following few years they enjoyed a pretty much normal mother and son relationship.

That was why Marsha found it difficult to understand how he had died in the way that he did. As far as she knew, he wasn't into drugs anymore, at least not as much as he had been. She guessed he still had the occasional puff but if it had been more than that she was confident she would have seen the signs. The mood swings, lack of interest, no appetite…she'd gone through it all with him before, but there was nothing like that this time. But what was he doing in a deserted farmhouse with a well-known drug dealer and violent criminal? It didn't make sense, but there was no denying that's where he had been found.

Marsha put the silver chain down beside the books and magazines and pulled out Dylan's laptop. She ran her hand across the smooth silver metallic surface before opening it up and turning it on. She sat waiting for a few seconds but nothing happened. Presuming the battery was dead, Marsha rummaged in the box but she couldn't find the power cable. She walked through to the bedroom she used as a study and disconnected the power cable from her own laptop. On returning to the sitting room she plugged it into Dylan's device. Sitting on the sofa with the laptop appropriately positioned on her knees, she heard a few clicks and a whirring noise as the machine fired up and came to life. A screensaver appeared, a photo of a picturesque range of mountains and a lake, set against a bright blue sky. It looked beautiful, but Marsha wasn't particularly interested in it and she quickly hit the enter key. A dialogue box appeared in the middle of the lake asking for a password. Marsha stopped for a few seconds to think. What would Dylan's password be? She thought of her own, usually Dylan followed by a number, a birthdate or year. But she doubted Dylan would do the same. You wouldn't use your own name in the password, would you?

Marsha couldn't think what Dylan would use as a password. He didn't have a girlfriend as far as she knew, and definitely no pets. They were both allergic to animal hairs, so cats and dogs had both been out of the question. Marsha tried a few combinations involving where he lived, where he worked, his favourite football team, but none of them worked. She was keen to see what was on it to see if it gave her any clues into why this had all happened. Maybe there would be some emails linking him to Tony Fleming, or a photo or something. She just didn't know. But having no luck with the password, she decided to leave it for now. She could charge it up and then take it into work sometime to see if young Jason in I.T. could work his way around it and get access to the contents. He was a bit of a technical genius so if anyone could access the laptop, she was sure Jason would be able to.

Chapter 7

'Ah, come on in Mo,' the Chief Constable said to DI Strong. 'Take a seat and I'll be with you in a minute or two.'

DI Strong sat down at the Chief Constable's long office table, same seat as always, and waited. He watched the Chief out of the corner of his eye. He was a big man, big chest and as he got older, his stomach was catching up. He was wearing a white shirt and Strong could see a few straining buttons. His hair was going the other way though – it was getting thinner. Strong had noticed that the Chief tried to cover it up by brushing what hair he had across the top of his head, but it was a losing battle. But even though he was approaching sixty, the Chief still prided himself on being a fit man. Some of the guys in the Serious Crime Team played five a side football on a Wednesday evening at a local school and if the Chief was available he'd try and join in.

When Strong had got the call that the Chief wanted to see him he wasn't sure what it was about. It wasn't one of their regular meetings and Strong couldn't think of anything that had happened in the last few days that would warrant the Chief

Constable's attention. There hadn't been any particularly serious crimes, no murders, just the ongoing club issues along with a smattering of domestic disturbances and some drug or alcohol induced violence. Strong guessed that the Chief Constable probably wanted Strong to fill in for him at some public event. Something that he couldn't make, or didn't want to. The Chief had asked Strong to do that a few times before and, although he didn't particularly enjoy it, he knew it was all part of the role. The public face of the police. Strong knew all the right things to say. He'd been in the police force long enough, done all the PR courses and knew the politics. On the positive side he normally got a free dinner out of it.

DI Strong was the most senior policeman in the region, apart from the Chief Constable, and he knew many people regarded him as the natural successor to the Chief. However Strong hoped that would be some time off yet. He knew the Chief was approaching sixty but Strong was still only a relatively young forty eight. Hopefully the Chief would carry on for a few more years yet. He hadn't said anything about retiring as far as Strong was aware. Strong enjoyed his work and the relative freedom the Chief gave him to just get on with it and run the Serious Crime Team in the way he wanted. He wanted to do that for a few more years yet before he made any move upstairs. In his experience the further you moved away from the coal face, the less interesting the job became. The pay and benefits were undoubtedly good, but Strong could see that the Chief Constable role involved very little police work as such. It was more politics and public relations. Strong still enjoyed the thrill of the chase, catching and convicting criminals or even bringing them to justice in alternative ways as he had sometimes had to do in the last few years. He was very much aware that he was in a unique position to enable him to do that.

The Chief Constable rose from his seat and moved across the room to join Strong at the table. He positioned himself in the same seat he always sat in, stretching his legs out in front of him. He folded his hands behind his head and leaned back in his chair, looking directly at Strong. Three of the buttons on his shirt looked almost at breaking point.

'So Mo, how's it all going? Are we making any progress with Fleming's gang and the Romanians?' he asked Strong.

'Yes I think so,' Strong replied. 'We know who the main guys are on both sides now and we are focusing on them, just waiting for them to make a mistake so we can nab them. I'm sure they will soon. They always do.'

'Yes, I'm sure they will, then it'll be down to the lawyers and judges to sort it out,' the Chief replied. 'The trouble is, as I'm sure you know, we have a new PCC, Police and Crime Commissioner, Diana Gordon, and she is keen to make her mark. She wants to show her public, the people who voted for her, that they did the right thing. Although in fact there was such a low turnout for the election that she'd probably have got in just by her family voting for her. However, be that as it may, she was elected and, like all politicians, she wants an early

45

result. Something to brag about and she's keen to demonstrate that we're doing something to stop all this club violence. She's only twenty eight for goodness sake. What could she possibly know about running a police operation?'

The Chief let out a sigh and Strong could sense that the new PCC had said more to the Chief, but he wasn't going to go into that detail.

'You know, and I know,' he continued, 'that it's not that easy. These things take time and sometimes you have to be creative, wait for that mistake, as you say. But she doesn't get that, or doesn't want to get that. She thinks we can just amble in there and arrest them. The trouble is Ms Gordon wants to satisfy her public and at the same time I need to get her off our backs.'

DI Strong was listening carefully. This wasn't how he'd expected the meeting to go and he was feeling a bit concerned. Although he was beginning to form a plan for dealing with the two mobs, he didn't want to rush it. It could easily go wrong if he wasn't careful and he still needed more time to get everything in place. He didn't want things to get worse and the last thing he wanted was for the Chief Constable to stick his oar in.

'Yes, I understand,' Strong replied. 'I'm sure Ms Gordon is doing a good job. Would it help if I gave her a brief on what we are doing, give her a bit of an insight into the investigation. Maybe reassure her that we are making progress, while at the same time giving her a dose of realism? Do you think that would satisfy her for a bit? Maybe buy us enough time to end this whole thing? I think we're getting closer, maybe a few weeks.'

'No, I don't think it would,' the Chief Constable replied, shaking his head. 'I've tried that, giving her a few hints, but to be honest she just isn't interested. She's one of those politicians who simply doesn't want to get involved in the detail, presumably so that she can't be blamed for anything that goes wrong. You know the kind, they just say it's your job, do it and tell me when it's done. But make it quick.'

'I see. Well I'll certainly make the team aware of the urgency,' Strong replied. 'Not that they don't already know. Other than that I'm not sure there's much more we can do at the moment. DC Knight is leading the case and I am putting as much time into it as I can,' DI Strong replied.

'Mmm, how is Knight doing? As you and I have discussed before, I'm keen to give women a fair chance in my team. There are a lot of people, politicians, who would like to see more women at senior levels, but they still need to prove they can do the job. You and I know it's not easy and the fact is it's still largely a man's world in the police force. Do the men here accept her as a leader do you think?

'Yes, I believe so,' Strong replied, nodding as he spoke. 'She's a hard worker, but also clever too. I think the rest of the team can see that. I'm sure there are always going to be one or two comments behind her back but that's just the way it is. As far as I'm concerned she's doing a good job now. She's learning and I think once we're over this hurdle with the turf war, she'll be ready to step up to the DS role soon.'

'Good, I'm glad to hear it,' the Chief replied. 'Good detectives are what we want, male or female. Okay,' he said sitting forward and apparently ready to change the subject, 'I've been putting some thought into this. What can we do. There aren't too many other major cases on the go at the moment are there? Apart from the gang turf war, I mean,' the Chief asked, then continued without waiting for a reply. 'I think we should put all our resources on this, just keep a skeleton staff on any of the other stuff, maybe with DC Harris in charge of that. He's quite solid isn't he? I'm going to draft in another detective to work with Knight and yourself on this. Hopefully that will help push things along, get us to a speedier resolution. I've spoken with my counterpart in Leeds and they are having a fairly quiet time at the moment so he has agreed to us having Joe Campbell back for a few months to work on this with you. Of course Joe knows how we work and so he'll be able to step straight into it and work with you. I'm sure his methodical approach will be a great help to you and DC Knight.'

The Chief sat back in his chair and looked across at Strong. The detective was slightly taken aback by the Chief's proclamation. Normally he would discuss these sort of operational changes with Strong before he acted. In fact Strong would usually be the one to make such decisions. The two men had always had a good working relationship, but it appeared this was already a done deal and there would be no benefit in Strong raising any objections. It wasn't that he didn't agree with what the Chief had done. He was right, Joe Campbell would be a good asset to the team. He was a good detective and had worked for Strong as his detective sergeant, essentially as his right hand man, for a few years, before transferring North to take up the lead position of detective inspector in the Leeds team.

Strong and Campbell had worked well together, Strong would often use him to bounce ideas off, much as he was now doing with DC Knight. However Campbell was a different character to both Strong and Knight. Campbell believed in playing by the rules, however difficult that was. He'd challenged Strong a couple of times on some of the things he suspected Strong might have done which weren't completely by the book. But he hadn't had enough evidence to prove anything definitively and Strong had always had a good enough explanation for his actions. However Strong knew that, despite Campbell's undoubted loyalty to him, he wouldn't hesitate in calling his boss out if he found out he was definitely doing something outside of the rules. And he'd come close a couple of times. Especially in a previous case where Strong had used a wanted murderer, Andy Austin, to carry out "acts of justice" on serious criminals who had managed to avoid being caught and convicted, often through intimidation of witnesses. Strong knew he'd made a couple of mistakes which Campbell had picked up on, but there wasn't quite enough to make any more of it. But there was a lot Campbell didn't know and if he found out any more, even a small part of that, then he could make serious trouble for DI Strong.

That was one of the main reasons Strong had helped Campbell get the DI role in Leeds. In fact it was more than just help if Strong was being completely honest. Strong had made sure Campbell would get the job by calling in a couple of favours with some of his senior colleagues. Locating Campbell two hundred miles away in a difficult, time consuming role meant that Strong could carry on with his successful approach of decriminalising his area, without the worry of Campbell looking over his shoulder at how he was actually doing that.

But now it appeared that Campbell was coming back, just when he was looking at putting a new plan in place to sort out the trouble between the Boltons and the Romanians. Strong knew he would need to be extra careful now. He couldn't do anything that would make Campbell suspicious. Strong was confident that he had DC Knight on his side with the plan, but he was equally confident that Campbell wouldn't be, should he find out what was going on.

Chapter 8

Marsha picked up her desk phone and punched in the four numbers for the I.T. help desk. Four fives, easily remembered, often required. Despite the police having some state of the art, sophisticated technology, most of that tended to be in specialist technical areas of the force. The rest of the staff had to put up with some fairly old office and administration software. Much of it had been developed in-house many years before and the rumour was that no-one actually knew how it worked now, but they were frightened to replace it in case they lost all of the existing data it held. So the police staff just had to work with it as best they could and four fives was the most commonly used internal phone number.

Although it was known as the I.T. help desk, which sounded grand, like a proper department, due to cutbacks and budget freezes, it was actually just young Jason sitting at his desk. On his own. At some points of the year a graduate trainee was also assigned to work with Jason on the I.T. help desk for a few weeks. These temporary helpers were generally skilled at downloading apps to a mobile phone and at explaining what the various emojis actually meant, but the aged intricacies of the day to day police systems were too confusing for their modern technology brains.

'Can't you just click on the screen and swipe it to the right to get the next one?' they would ask innocently.

'No,' was the simple and constant answer. So the problem wasn't that Jason wasn't good at his job, he was very good in fact. The issue was it was just him. Jason *was* the I.T. help desk and he was often in great demand.

'Hello I.T. help desk, how can I help you?' Jason answered after a few rings.

'Hi Jason, it's Marsha here. Are you okay?' Marsha replied, visualising Jason working on a laptop while he spoke to her. She'd visited him many times at his desk in the I.T. department and he always looked the same. A head of messed up brown hair, usually a white shirt, sleeves rolled up, and a pair of dark coloured chinos finished off with either blue or brown deck shoes. His desk was usually cluttered with bits of electronic equipment, cables and plugs that only he knew what they were for or where they had come from.

'Yes fine Marsha, what can I do for you?' Jason replied as he typed a command into a device to his left and watched as a scroll of white lines of text and numbers appeared against the dark background of the screen. He hit another key and it stopped at a line of code Jason wanted to see.

'Well, it's a bit of a personal ask, but I wondered if you could help me,' Marsha started, trying to use her friendliest tone of voice.

'Sure, what is it?' Jason replied, thinking not another personal request. He had enough office stuff to do without getting bogged down with outdated personal laptops. But he liked Marsha, she'd always been very pleasant to him, even when he could see she was stressed by her latest I.T. problem. And he'd heard about her son. Some of the others in the police office weren't quite as nice as Marsha and would take their frustrations out on him, which was the worst part of the job. It wasn't Jason's fault that the police software was so old and he was trying to help them.

'Well, I guess you heard about my son, you know, passing away?' Marsha said hesitantly. 'Well I've got his laptop now but I don't know his password and so I can't get into it. I'd like to see it as I'm sure there'll be photos and the like in there. Do you think you'd be able to get access in some way? I don't know, as the administrator or something?' Marsha asked, hopefully.

'Possibly, but there are some rules about us using, or even working on, any personal devices on police premises. We'd need to get the proper approval first,' Jason replied, brushing his hair back from his forehead and typing a command into the device he was working on. The screen started scrolling again with hundreds of lines of white code running down the page.

'I'm afraid it would need the top man, DI Strong, to authorise me to work on it,' Jason continued while pressing another key to make the scrolling screen stop again. 'Do you think you can get him to send me an email saying it's okay to have a look at your one? He's usually okay with it, but he sometimes takes a couple of days to reply and he doesn't like it if there's more than one on the go at the same time. He knows I have enough police work to do.'

'Oh, okay, well yes I can ask him I guess. Hopefully he'll be okay with that, just an email is that right?' Marsha asked.

'Yes that will do it,' Jason replied. 'Just a brief description of what you need. It's just something for my records in case anyone asks what I'm doing with a non-police laptop. The Computer Audit guys sometimes turn up at random and ask. Stupid I know but that's how it is. Ah there it is,' he said out loud as he spotted a line of rogue code on the device he was working on.

'Sorry?' Marsha asked and Jason apologised explaining he'd just found something on another device.

They ended the call and Marsha sat for a few seconds looking at the laptop sitting in front of her on the desk. That shouldn't be too difficult, she thought. DI Strong had always been very helpful to her and they had worked well together on bits and pieces over the years. He'd been even more compassionate and helpful since the death of her son. He would understand why she wanted to access the laptop, Marsha was sure of that. She had little doubt that he would send the necessary email to Jason in I.T. and then, hopefully, Jason would be able to help Marsha get access to Dylan's device. She really wanted to see what it contained. She knew it might be nothing but she just had a feeling there would be something there. Something that would help her understand why Dylan died the way he did.

Determined to find out, Marsha stood up from her desk, picked up Dylan's laptop and quickly made her way to DI Strong's office. She knocked lightly on his door and slowly eased it open.

'Do you have a minute Guv?' she asked as she poked her head around the door. DI Strong was sitting at his desk and looked up at the sound of her voice.

'Sure, come in Marsha,' he replied, waving her in with his hand and indicating a chair at the front of his desk. 'How can I help you?' he asked, sitting upright in his chair.

Marsha sat down on the chair, placing the laptop on the desk in front of her. She sat up straight, her legs pressed together with her hands interlocked and resting on her legs, just above her knees. She explained it was Dylan's laptop and how she now needed DI Strong's authorisation to allow Jason to try and access it.

'Of course, I'll do that,' Di Strong replied smiling. 'Can you just leave it with me? I'm in the middle of something here. I'll do the email as soon as I've finished and I'll tell Jason the PC is here. He can come and get it then.'

'Thank you Guv,' Marsha replied and she quickly got up, smoothing down her skirt as she rose, and left DI Strong's office, pleased at how helpful he had been, as he always was. She was both nervous and excited at what the device might contain but she was sure it would help her get some closure on the death of her son.

Back in the detective inspector's office, DI Strong got up from his desk, picked up Dylan's laptop, and walked across the office to the long conference table. He sat down on one of the seats and opened up the laptop. He switched the device on and a dialogue box appeared on screen, asking for a password. He typed in the obvious 'Dylan' and wasn't surprised when that didn't work. He guessed Marsha would have already tried a number of possibilities, but obviously with no luck. He shut the laptop down again and returned to his desk where he picked up his phone and dialled four fives.

'Hello, I.T. help desk, how can I help you,' Jason's voice sounded at the other end of the phone.

'Jason, it's DI Strong here. Can you just pop along to my office please?'

'Of course, I'll be there in a minute,' Jason replied, standing up as he spoke. All the other stuff would have to wait, he thought, glancing at the various devices on his desk. When the boss called, that became the number one priority.

Jason quickly walked the short distance to DI Strong's office. Despite having worked there for three years, he had only been in Strong's office once or twice before, but he liked Strong. Everyone liked him. He always spoke to Jason if the two of them passed each other in the corridor. It might just be a 'hello' or 'how are you Jason' but Jason appreciated it. A lot of the policemen just ignored him, he wasn't important enough, except when they wanted him to fix their PCs or phones, but even then they could be quite rude, looking down on him because he wasn't one of them. Not a detective, solving crimes. But DI Strong wasn't like that at all. He seemed to know everyone and have time for them too, no matter what their role was.

Jason knocked on Strong's office door, pushed it open and stepped inside.

'Ah, Jason, just give me a minute, I just need to finish this,' Strong said as he tapped away at his computer. 'Take a seat,' he said motioning towards the table where Jason saw there was a closed laptop.

Jason sat down and waited. After a few minutes Strong stopped typing and then, seemingly satisfied with what he had done, he hit the enter key and stood up. He walked across to the table to join Jason. The detective shook his hand and thanked him for coming. Strong then spent the next few minutes explaining the situation to Jason. Marsha had found her son Dylan's computer but couldn't get access to it. Jason knew that. Strong went on to explain that Dylan had been involved with drugs and had died in a shooting along with another drugs dealer. Jason had heard some of that before, but not all of it and not direct from the horse's mouth, so to speak. It made it more interesting, like he was actually involved in the case. Strong carried on, telling Jason that Marsha didn't know how deeply Dylan had been involved in criminal activity. Strong had known but he hadn't told Marsha and he didn't want her to find out.

'It was bad enough her losing her son like that. She was devastated, completely devastated,'

Strong told Jason. 'If she found out more about him, what he had been up to....well I don't know how she would take it. It could be too much for her, do you see what I'm saying?'

Jason nodded and brushed his hair to the side with his hand. He'd never been in an encounter like this with DI Strong before. Strong was talking really seriously to him and he was getting it. He realised how important this must be and understood where Strong was going with it.

'So I'm concerned that there may be things on Dylan's laptop that Marsha shouldn't have to see,' Strong said, looking intensely at Jason. 'It's a delicate situation and it wouldn't help Marsha in any way whatsoever. Her son Dylan is dead now and I think it would just bring it all back to her, but also, from what she might find on the laptop, it could make it all much, much worse.'

Jason was nodding as Strong spoke. He got it. There was no point in upsetting Marsha for no reason. Best to leave things as they are. From what Strong had said, it all made sense. Strong had stopped speaking and Jason looked at him.

'What, emm, what do you want me to do then?' Jason asked the detective. 'Just tell her I couldn't access the laptop and give it back to her? I could say it had built in security which wouldn't allow me to access it, or something like that?'

'No, my worry would be that if we did that, she might take it somewhere else, you know one of those PC places and they'd unlock it for her,' Strong said. 'We're lucky she brought it here first. I think what we need to do is wipe it, do a factory reset or whatever it's called, so that we get rid of all the data on it. Then you can give it back to her and tell her you tried a few things but you couldn't access it, whatever reason you want to give. But don't mention wiping it of course. And don't tell anyone else either, otherwise it might get back to Marsha. We're doing this to protect her. Do you understand?' Strong said, looking intently at Jason.

'Yes, of course I get it,' Jason replied, nodding. 'But if I wipe it, she'll see that it looks different on the home screen when she switches it on….but, wait, I guess I can just say that was because I had to change a few things in my failed attempts to get access.'

'Yes, that sounds good. I don't think she's especially technical and I'm sure she'll accept whatever you say. Remember we're doing this for Marsha. She doesn't deserve any further upset and I'm worried what she might find. We need to protect her from that,' Strong said. 'Can you do it now, here, I mean? I'd like to see how you do it.'

'Emm, yes, okay, I guess so. It's pretty straightforward actually,' Jason replied and he reached across and opened the laptop.

Jason typed in a few commands and ten minutes later it was all done. The laptop was clear. None of Dylan's data remained. It was gone, just like him.

Chapter 9

Ally Bolton was furious. 'Who do these Romanian fuckers think they are, coming to our country and thinking they can just take over our business?' he said with anger in his voice, his face bright red. 'Have they got no respect? This is our patch, we spent years building this up with Tony. They need teaching a lesson and that's what's gonna happen. They'll wish they hadn't messed with us.'

Ally Bolton had just turned forty and he had lived in the area all his life. His area. He was a tough man, having boxed quite a bit when he was younger. Not bad at it either, he'd reached a good level and he was proud of his record of twenty seven wins and two losses. He didn't talk about the two losses much. They had been his last two bouts and that was when he'd realised he was getting too old to compete seriously. His opponents had been ten years his junior and their reaction times were just that bit quicker than his. How his used to be. He didn't want to end up with his face a mess, or worse, so he'd stopped boxing after that second defeat. One tiny scar under his left eye was the only sign that he'd ever been a boxer.

That was when he started working for Tony Fleming. Initially, he was a doorman at one of Tony's clubs, The Lighthouse, and then over the next few years he gradually worked his way up until he became part of Tony's inner circle. One of his trusted men. The team that ran the businesses. The clubs, the protection business, the girls and of course the drugs. That was by far where most of the money came from, the drugs. As he moved up the ladder, Ally started to make good money himself and although he knew most of it came from the proceeds of criminal activities he didn't care. There would always be addicts needing a fix and they were just providing a service. If the Boltons weren't doing it someone else would be. Right now, it would be the Romanians. Anyway, who was to say what was right and what was wrong. It was just a set of rules someone had set to suit themselves. As far as Ally was concerned, everyone was on the take somehow. Look at the MPs and their expenses. In Ally's eyes that was just as bad as some of the activities he was involved in. And no-one had voted for him!

When Tony Fleming had disappeared everyone was shocked but most people expected him to reappear at some point. But not Ally. He was sure something bad had happened to Tony. It was true he had gone missing before, but only for a day or two and that was when he was in secret meetings building up the business. Doing deals with other people just like him. Men happy to make money from other people's misfortunes. This time it was different though. It had been too long. It could only be bad news. Ally had suspected the Romanians, but the word on the street was that they were as surprised by his disappearance as anyone else. The most baffling thing was that there were no whispers about what had happened or where he had gone, nothing at all.

The businesses kept running as normal but as time dragged on, with no-one in overall control, people began to see opportunities for themselves to make more money and so started taking advantage of the lack of overall leadership. Tony Fleming had ruled with a rod of iron. Sometimes quite literally, but more often with a knife or a gun. He was a hard bastard and he made sure everyone knew that by punishing anyone that dared to cross him, or even looked at him in the wrong way. By doing that, he made sure all the money flowed through to bank accounts that he controlled. Fleming was also very clever though and he made sure he was never connected with any of the illegal activities. No paper trail, no digital records. As well as intimidating potential witnesses, he made good use of his lawyer, Max Murray, and he would regularly laugh at the police trying to pin something on him.

Then when Fleming was found dead at the deserted farmhouse, everything began to get chaotic. Everyone wanted to get a slice of the pie and on top of that the Eastern Europeans started to try and take over some of the businesses too. It was at that point, with the Romanians getting stronger, that Ally Bolton had called a meeting with a few of the senior members of Tony Fleming's gang. They agreed that a new leader was required to bring it all together again and ward off the Romanians. Ally was elected as that man, largely helped by the fact that two of the other men present at the meeting were his brother Charlie and his cousin Eddie. But Ally had been the natural replacement. It needed a tough man in control to bring it all back together and Ally fitted the bill.

Within a few weeks they'd managed to establish some order, largely through threats and punishment beatings where necessary, so that most of the old business lines were now back under their control. But in the time it had taken to do that, the Romanians had managed to get themselves a foothold. And they were now trying to expand that, causing trouble for Ally Bolton's supply lines and in the clubs.

They had to be stopped and Ally had called a meeting of some of his top men. There were six of them in the room. Ally, Charlie and Eddie and they had been joined by three others, three seasoned criminals, Smithy, Chopper and Scotty. Ally had known them all for many years and he knew he could trust them as much as he could trust anyone. Heading up a criminal business empire was not easy and you had to be constantly watching your back. You just had to look at what had happened with Tony Fleming. Some druggie had apparently lured him to a remote farmhouse and killed him.

But this group of six had history. They all knew things about each other. They'd seen things. Things that could land any of them a long stretch in prison and that knowledge bound them together as much as anything else.

'What are you thinking we should do? We know where they hang out, mostly over at the snooker club. Should we do a raid on it, smash it up a bit?' Charlie asked, keen to hear what Ally was considering.

Charlie was two years younger than Ally and he'd always looked up to his big brother for advice and guidance. He was much smaller than Ally and Ally had always looked out for him, making sure he didn't get picked on. Apart from the difference in build, Ally and Charlie looked similar and when you saw them together you would guess they were brothers. When they were younger, occasionally people with a grievance would try and take it out on Charlie, seeing him as the easier option. But that never worked. Ally would always be there to stop them or, on the few occasions he wasn't, his revenge was much, much worse.

'Well, we do need to strike hard,' Ally replied determinedly. 'Show them that we're in charge here. We don't want them on our patch. It's like there's more of them appearing every day. Soon they'll be a big mob with a lot of resources. As much as us. We need to stop them before that happens. Get them to move on, go somewhere else. Back home maybe but I don't care where, just not here.'

'Aye so do we smash up the snooker club, like Charlie said? I'd be up fir that,' Scotty said, leaning forward in his seat.

Scotty enjoyed a fight. He wasn't the biggest man ever. He was around five foot nine and quite slim, wiry you might say. But he was deceptively strong. Whatever muscle he had was toned, and he was quick. He didn't lose many fights and he'd been in plenty.

Scotty was originally from Glasgow but had moved South many years before and, after drifting around, in and out of prison, he'd ended up working for Tony Fleming. He was an unpredictable character but someone you'd always want on your side when it came to a fight. The men in the room had all witnessed Scotty enjoying handing out beatings and he'd had to be pulled off his victims a few times when it had got too much. He just didn't know when to stop. Or he didn't want to stop.

'We could do the snooker hall,' Ally replied nodding, 'but I think that's too predictable. They might be expecting us and it's their place so they would have the upper hand and probably a lot of muscle on hand. I think we need to do something else. Something that will stop them in their tracks and make them move on.'

'What are you thinking then?' his cousin Eddie asked. Eddie's dad and Ally's mum had been brother and sister but his dad had died when he was young. Eddie couldn't remember much about him but from what he had heard, he'd had a drinking problem which had brought about his early death. Eddie had spent a lot of his youth with Ally and Charlie, almost like a younger third brother. Physically, he was in between the two brothers but his main talent was his brain. He was clever and, often came up with solutions to whatever problems they were having. Ally knew that Eddie would never be the first to speak though, he didn't seem to

65

think of himself as being at the same level as Ally and Charlie, and so it sometimes took a bit of time and coaxing to get Eddie to say what he was actually thinking. Either that or it just took him a bit of time to come up with ideas. Whatever the reason though, his ideas were usually pretty good.

'I'm thinking that maybe we should do a hit on Bog, take out their top man. Show them we're the only game in town,' Ally replied and he looked around the room to see what the reaction was, wondering if Eddie was ready to contribute yet.

No-one said anything for a few seconds then it was his brother Charlie who spoke up.

'We could do that. It would definitely knock them back a bit. Maybe it would move them on,' he said nodding. 'But it could have the opposite effect too. They might come looking for us, for you, in revenge. We don't really know them well enough to know what they'd do.'

'Yeh, that's true,' Ally replied, 'but if they did come for us, we'd be ready for them. And I think that, without Bog, they wouldn't be as well organised as us and they'd come off worse. Remember they still don't have half the men we have. I think when they thought about it, they'd realise that, or if they didn't then they'd find out when they tried.'

'Aye, let them come for us,' Scotty pitched in. 'I've no had a guid scrap fir ages.'

The others all laughed at Scotty's obvious enthusiasm for a fight and Smithy gave him a friendly slap on the back.

'How would we get to Bog though?' Smithy asked. Smithy had grown up and gone to school with Ally and Ally regarded him almost as one of the family too. 'Bog always seems to have his heavies with him and they're always carrying. It wouldn't be easy to hit Bog and just get away like that. It could get messy.'

'That's true,' Ally replied. 'That's why I called the meeting here today. We need to discuss it, talk it through and come up with a plan. Something clever. But we need to do it quickly because we're all getting pretty damn fed up at having to deal with this crap that's going on at the clubs every weekend. It needs to stop. We need to put a marker down and show them we're the ones in charge here. Always have been and always will be.'

The other five men all nodded in agreement. Something had to be done and taking out Bog was as good as anything. It would send out a message. Ally and his gang spent the next hour talking through what they needed to do and how they would do it. They traded ideas back and forth and agreed it would be easier if they could somehow isolate Bog, get him on his own and then just take him out. No mess, no retaliatory gunfire, no other casualties. The problem was they knew Bog's regular movements, and he was never on his own.

'I dinnae mind having a go at him,' said Scotty. 'I could take on twa or three o' them at the same time, nae problem.'

'I know Scotty,' Eddie replied. 'But it's too risky. Remember they're all tooled up. You'd maybe get a couple of them first, but not three or four,' he said shaking his head. 'We need to be clever about how we do this. We need to manufacture a situation where we get him on his own, reduce the odds a bit, give us a better chance.'

'Yeh, how do we do that though?' Ally asked his cousin, eager to see what he was thinking.

'Well I think it could be done,' Eddie replied. 'But we need to find something that would be like an emergency for him. Something that would get him out on his own, maybe in a panic. At least something where he doesn't have time to organise and get his heavies together.'

'Yeh, that's good thinking,' Ally replied. 'What else?'

'So maybe it's the middle of the night,' Eddie continued, 'he's asleep at home and he gets a call from someone close, maybe a family member, saying they need him right away. Something that doesn't give him time to get his heavies out of bed. He can do it on his own and so he just does without thinking because time is crucial.'

'Yeh, or maybe it's just something that he doesn't feel he needs his heavies for,' Smithy chipped in. 'Maybe one of his kids has missed the last train and needs picking up from the local station? Something like that.'

'Yeh that's good,' Eddie replied nodding his head. 'I like that. He's got a couple of teenage kids hasn't he, a boy and a girl. But they don't live with him, they're with his ex-wife over in Stockton. From what I heard she caught him shagging around a few months ago with some young tart and she moved out. What if one of the kids calls him and says they're stuck somewhere and the mum's not picking up the phone? Could he come and get them? He couldn't resist that could he? Apart from it being his kid, he'd also be scoring one up on his ex-wife. From what I hear he still sees the kids regularly so he obviously still cares for them. Surely he'd just get up and go, wouldn't you?'

'Well I wouldn't because my son don't speak to me no more,' Smithy replied, laughing. 'So he wouldn't call me, and if he did I'd just stay in bed. But I get what you're saying. How would we get the kid to make the call though?'

'Do you know, I don't think kids make calls nowadays. It's all texts and WhatsApps isn't it?' Eddie said. 'But maybe that actually makes it easier. I reckon we could do it. I've done a bit of stuff with mobiles before and I know how to set it up so that we can send a text that would look like it had come from his kid's phone. He would be none the wiser. I think it could work,' Eddie said, nodding his head.

'What if he's asleep though or he's switched his phone off?' Charlie asked.

'Yeh that's possible,' Ally replied. 'But I think, with who he is, running his mob, with all sorts going on at all hours of the day, I think he'll always want to be contactable. So I'd bet he keeps his phone by his bedside and if it goes off he's awake straight away. That's what I do. I've had a few late calls when there's been trouble at one of the clubs and I wasn't there.'

'Okay so he gets a message that looks like it's from his daughter, she needs picking up from somewhere, maybe a train station or somewhere,'

Eddie went on, the ideas flowing now. 'Actually we could set up the place to make it easier for us, maybe a park or something. She's been there meeting friends and didn't realise the time. She can't find a cab.

'But what if he phones or messages her back,' Smithy asked. 'Wouldn't that muck it up for us?'

'Well yeh, that's a bit trickier,' Eddie replied. 'But with a bit of work, I can set it up so that there is a temporary diversion from her phone to ours without anyone knowing. That way we'd get any calls or messages from Bog and so we can manipulate any replies to make sure he comes quickly.'

Eddie was smiling now, conscious that everyone was watching him, listening to his every word.

'Bloody hell, can you do that?' Charlie exclaimed. 'That's genius.'

The six men discussed the plan for another half hour making sure it was solid and that there was little room for error. Finally when they were all happy that it would work there was just one thing left to sort out.

'When are we gonna do it then?' Smithy asked.

'The sooner the better,' Ally replied. 'I'd suggest we put everything in place and if everything looks right, we aim do it next Saturday night. All agreed?'

The other five men nodded their heads in agreement.

'Okay, let's go and have a pint then,' Ally said and the six men got up and left the room, none of them aware of the listening device planted neatly at the join of a table leg and the underside of the table top.

Chapter 10

Kyle Smith unlocked the door to the Wintergreen Estate Agents office and flicked the light switch on as he walked towards the back of the office, and his desk. As usual, he was the first one in. He liked to get in early and get started so that he was always ahead of the game. He slipped his suit jacket off and carefully hung it on the back of his chair. Under his jacket, he was wearing a white shirt and red-striped tie, corporate colours, finished off with a pair of shiny black brogue shoes. He smoothed back his newly cut hair and picked up a red, Wintergreen branded mug from his desk.

Kyle had been working at this particular office for the last two years and, although he wasn't the manager yet, his business card did say "Senior Estate Agent" which was only one step away. The current manager, Jim Ashfield, had worked at Wintergreen all his life and, although he had been good to Kyle, it was time he moved aside and let a younger man take over. It was only a matter of time. Then, after he'd managed a branch for a year or so, Kyle could look at starting up his own agency. That had always been his plan, to be his own boss. To run the estate agency in the way he wanted, a modern, efficient operation. He'd handpick the staff and he knew a number of his most loyal customers would come with him. Over time he'd focus on the more expensive properties and become a specialist in that sector. That was where you made the most money and, frankly, he'd shown people round enough two-bedroomed maisonettes to last a lifetime. You could only pretend it was someone's dream home so many times, with a smile on your face and a damp patch on the wall.

However, things had changed a bit recently and so his grand plan might not work out like that any more. At least the location might be different. But that was fine.

He'd started living with his girlfriend Karen, and she had ambitions too, which, if push came to shove, he would probably be happy to go along with. Karen was the first girl Kyle had ever met who he thought was smarter than him. And she was beautiful too. He definitely felt like he was punching above his weight and he had to keep reassuring himself that she actually was his girlfriend.

Karen worked as an assistant executive for an advertising company, specialising in film and TV adverts. Her job involved helping organise the production shoots and that meant a fair bit of travelling in the UK, and occasionally abroad. She also got to meet quite a few of the celebrities they used on the shoots, mostly fairly minor, but occasionally a bigger star and she had been able to take Kyle along to a couple of red carpet, film premieres.

All of this mingling with the rich and famous had given Karen a taste for the high life and she had ideas of travelling and perhaps living and working somewhere more exotic than Leeds. Somewhere like New York or Los Angeles. Kyle was content with that and he had already looked on-line at Estate Agents roles in the USA. They seemed to be pretty similar to what he did in the UK, except over there, they called themselves "Realtors" or "Real Estate Agents." Like everyone else was somehow fake. Looking at some of the prices though, there was definitely a market for expensive properties and he was sure he'd be able to get a job and then look at setting up on his own. The same grand plan, just a different country.

Back in Leeds, Kyle started up his computer and, after making himself an instant coffee in the back kitchen area, he returned to his desk and sat down to look at his schedule for the day. He had two visits to do, one in the morning and the other planned for later in the afternoon. Both visits were to two-bedroomed flats they'd been trying to sell for a while, and he knew he'd have to really talk them up to try and get them sold. Between those visit times he would be mostly on the phone or doing emails to try and generate more new business. Encouraging people to sell their houses so that he could match them up with one of the buyers on his books. It sounded simple when you said it like that.

The Wintergreen agency also knew the benefit of customer satisfaction. If you treated your customers well then there was a higher chance that they'd engage you again for their next move. It was a well-known fact, and so Wintergreen had a process where every past customer would be contacted a minimum of twice a year as part of their customer service. Of course the real reason was to find out if they were thinking of moving again or, if not, to put the idea in their heads.

'Have you seen the new development out at Brumin? I think it's the next step up from where you are now. They've just opened the show house and it looks fantastic. We're not supposed to have access to it yet, but I know the site manager and so I can get you a private look around it. Shall we say Thursday at 2pm?'

That was how the script went at least, get them moving, that was how you made money. Kyle had a number of those calls to do today. Regional management had set each of the offices a daily target of calls to make and they were then allocated out amongst the various staff, depending on their level of experience. Jim Ashfield, the office manager, took the most and Kyle had a daily target of ten calls to do which he would always try and exceed to ensure he would get his full bonus at the end of the year. He would only beat his target by one or two though as he knew, from experience, that whatever level he hit would likely become his new target for the following year. He'd made that mistake once before, when he was new into the job and his target for the following year had gone up by fifty percent. He wouldn't make that mistake again.

Kyle flicked down his call list to see if any of the names stood out, and he was immediately drawn to that of Joe Campbell. Of course, Joe

Campbell, TV star, Kyle smiled to himself. At least that would be something interesting to talk about if he got past the usual initial rejection. Despite the script having been developed by a team of specialist, highly paid consultants, the conversation was usually pretty brief and one-sided.

'Just checking to see how things are with you. Are you thinking of moving again? No? 'Have you seen the new development out at...No? You're not looking...Well if you do change your mind, you know where I am. Just give me a call.' And the line was dead.

That was generally how these customer service calls went. They were difficult to do and difficult to generate enthusiasm for. It was obvious the customer didn't really want to speak and they usually had no intention of moving. Otherwise they would have been in touch, something they often reminded him. All in all it was a bit of a waste of time for both parties, but unfortunately something that Kyle had to do. It was a management edict and if it generated even just one sale then it was deemed worth it.

When Kyle had his own agency he was determined that there would be no cold calling. He wouldn't need to chase business, his reputation would mean that the customers would come to him. And they'd recommend him to all of their friends too! However he wasn't there yet and so he decided to make a couple of the calls now, just to get them out of the way, get ahead of the game.

Just a few minutes later they were done. The same outcome as usual. No interest. Kyle took a sip of his coffee before moving on. He was about to give up for now and do something else when he saw that Joe Campbell was the next name on the list. At least this one might be more interesting, Kyle hoped. He might be able to have some sort of conversation with him about his appearance on the television. He dialled the number and after a few rings it was answered.

'Hello, Joe Campbell here,' a man's voice said. It was a deep growl. One that sounded like he didn't want to be interrupted from whatever he had been doing.

'Hi, it's Kyle Smith from Wintergreens, the estate agents,' Kyle replied. 'How are you?'

'Oh, right, yes good,' Campbell replied. 'And you?'

'Yes, all good here in the land of property,' Kyle replied, laughing. 'I'm just phoning as a catch up to check everything is okay or to see if there's anything I can do for you.'

'Oh, okay,' Campbell replied, thinking about how he could end the call as politely as possible. He had no need of an estate agent at this point in time and there were lots of other, more useful things, he could be getting on with.

Campbell was due back in his old office with the Serious Crime Team down South the following day and he wanted to get a few things sorted out in Leeds before he left. He was feeling good though, excited to be moving back home.

'Everything's okay with the flat,' Campbell said. 'I don't think there's anything I need. In fact I'm locking it up tonight as I'm working back down

South for a bit so I won't be using it much during that period.'

'Oh, okay,' Kyle replied, immediately seeing a potential opportunity. 'Have you thought about letting it out. You could make a bit of money from it while you're away. How long are you going for? I could look at a short term renter for you. I've got a few on my books who would jump at it. All professional people like yourself, working in Leeds for a short period and looking for something better than just a hotel bedroom while they're here. It's in a good area, well sought after.'

'Ah, no it's okay,' Campbell replied. 'I don't know how long I'm going to be away for. It may only be a few weeks depending on how things go, and I may need to pop back every now and then, so I couldn't really commit to letting it out. But thanks for asking anyway.'

'Okay, no worries,' Kyle replied, slightly disappointed that he couldn't get a lease deal out of his customer. But at least he'd tried.

'Well thanks for the call, is that all you wanted?' Campbell asked.

'Well actually there was one other thing,' Kyle started, not sure whether he should bring this up, but now that he'd started he carried on. He might as well, otherwise he would have to start on his emails or another waste of time call. 'I, emm, I saw you on the TV the other week. Some crime drama thing. Real life crime, I think it was called. The wedding killer or something wasn't it?'

'Ah, I think you mean The Anniversary Killer,' Campbell replied. 'Yes that was a case I worked on a couple of years ago. Some TV company decided it would make a good programme, but the police weren't very keen to publicise it so you might have seen we didn't get involved. They just used actors and a couple of still photos they had. I don't know where they got them from but they seem to have access to a huge library of photos. I suppose that's a key part of their job.'

'Yeh, that's it. The Anniversary Killer. My girlfriend loves watching these kind of things and I just caught a bit of it,' Kyle replied. 'There was one thing I noticed though, which was a bit weird, and I'm not sure if I should tell you or not.'

'What was that?' Campbell asked, partly interested, his detective brain picking up on something, but still keen to end the call with this estate agent so that he could get things done.

'Well, the guy in the programme, the emm, Anniversary Killer bloke, you know the one who did it,… well, emm, he emm. Well I got mugged one night on my way home from work in Leeds and, well, ….this bloke he was the spitting image of the guy in the programme,' Kyle replied.

'Wait, who? Andy Austin, the killer?' Campbell asked, feeling a tingling sensation.

'Yeh, …well yes. But I know it couldn't be….and I only saw it for a few seconds, but I have to say it did look like him,' Kyle replied nervously, wondering if he should have just kept quiet about it. It was in the past, maybe it was better off staying there.

'Okay, that's interesting,' Campbell replied, thinking, his mind working furiously. 'If I can get a hold of a tape of the programme would you be willing to go through it with me and see what you think then? See if you can positively identify him as your mugger?'

'Emm, yes…yes, of course. I guess I can do that,' Kyle replied. 'You know he's apparently dead now though,' he added. 'The bloke, Austin.'

'Yes, I know, but it would still be worth looking into. I'll see what I can find and I'll be back in touch,' Campbell said and he ended the call.

Campbell sat for a few minutes thinking. He was feeling excited, but apprehensive at the same time. He'd been down this road before with his suspicions about his old Guvnor, soon to be current boss again, DI Strong. There had been a couple of things which had happened in the past, while they had been on the Anniversary Killer investigation. Things that had worried Campbell. Niggled at him. He had a nagging doubt that somehow Strong wasn't telling him everything, and that he seemed to know more about Andy Austin than he was letting on.

If Kyle Smith positively identified his assailant as having been Andy Austin, what did that mean? It meant that Austin had been in Leeds, that was true. But not just that. He was in Leeds at the same time as Strong had been and the mugging had taken place on the same day that Strong apparently had a friend staying at his house in Leeds. But did that mean anything, or was it just a coincidence? And even if Austin and Strong did have some sort of secret connection what could Campbell prove? And more to the point if he did manage to prove some sort of connection to Strong what would he do with that information? Austin was dead now. Why would anyone be interested in what he had found out?

All of these questions, these doubts, were running amok in Campbell's head but equally he knew he had to take that next step to see what he could find out. It was his job, it was in his DNA, he was a detective. In his mind he didn't have any alternative, he would have to contact the TV production company and arrange a viewing of the programme with Kyle Smith. After that, who knows?

Chapter 11

'Come in,' Strong said as DC Knight opened his office door and poked her head around the corner, her long dark hair falling across her shoulder.

'You wanted to see me Guv?' DC Knight said, a smile on her face, as she walked forward and took a seat across the desk from her boss. Knight had been in Strong's office a lot in the last few months and she now felt very comfortable working closely with him. She noticed he was smartly dressed in his usual outfit, dark suit, white shirt and coloured tie. A blue one today.

'Yes. I've had some intelligence from one of my sources that the Bolton gang are planning to do a hit on Bogdan Popescu, the head of the Romanian mob,' Strong said, getting straight down to business.

That was something Knight had come to recognise and respect with DI Strong. He was always pretty direct. No flaffing around. She liked that, although occasionally, lately, he had become more informal with her at times and she liked that too. To Knight it showed they were developing a good working relationship, and that could only be good for her career. She moved forward in her chair.

'Okay, do you mean they're going to actually murder him or just give him a good kicking?' Knight asked her boss, shifting slightly again in her seat as she spoke.

'I'm not sure,' Strong replied. 'Could be either I think, depending on what happens, my source didn't know.'

'Okay, did your CHIS tell you any more? Did he give you any idea on where, or when, it's going to take place?' DC Knight asked, keen to get as much information as possible from her boss. CHIS was the new, politically correct term for a police informer and stood for "Covert Human Intelligence Source."

DI Strong nodded and eased himself back in his seat while going on to tell his colleague how the Boltons were planning to carry out the hit the following Saturday night by luring Bog out on his own with a false text message. The message would appear to have come from his daughter, asking him to pick her up and when he turned up, it would be a trap and the Boltons would attack him then.

'Apparently Bog doesn't travel much without his heavies being with him,' Strong said, 'so the Boltons are gambling on the fact that he won't be able to resist a cry for help from his daughter in the early hours of the morning. He'll just get up and go on his own.'

'Sounds possible, I guess,' Knight replied. 'Your source certainly seems to have got a lot of detailed information. Is he totally reliable do you think?'

'Yes, I've no doubts about that,' Strong replied. 'In fact I'm hoping we might get some more information before next Saturday, especially regarding the precise time and place. Meantime you should get a team ready. I'll approve whatever you need.'

'Thanks Guv, will do.' Knight replied smiling, and she got up, smoothing down her skirt, and left Strong's office.

Back at her own desk, she started putting her plans together. Preparing for this sort of event was something they'd covered in training but this was the first time she'd had to do it for a real life situation. There were a number of basics. The time and the place were two key elements which she didn't know yet, but she would hopefully get from Strong before the day. He seemed confident of that.

DI Strong, and the information his CHIS was providing them, were invaluable. She knew she couldn't have done this without him and she was happy that he seemed to have confidence in her abilities to do this. Although they didn't have all the information as yet, they could still make some sensible assumptions. It was probably going to be in the early hours of the morning and it would likely be in a quiet place, somewhere where the Boltons could lie in wait. Maybe woodlands. Knight would have to put a team together to cover such a location, but also without being visible. They would probably need quite a lot of resource to cover a fairly wide area and they would need a number of policemen to be carrying firearms. It could get messy.

One of the key decisions she would have to make would be when to move in and start making the arrests. They needed to catch the Boltons in the act of actually committing a crime. If they moved too early then they might only get them for something fairly minor such as possession of offensive weapons and there was every chance their lawyer would manage to get them out of that. This was the police's chance to get them for something more major and so get them locked away for a long time. She needed to be able to prove they were going to assault or even kill the Romanian. That would require some fine timing and it was something she would have to agree with DI Strong up front. When do they actually move in, before any assault, or after it has started? She knew this was something she would have to get right. This could be a career defining opportunity for her. If she got it right she'd be flavour of the month and she could push for the DS role with maybe a good chance of getting it. If it went wrong though it could go the other way and blemish her currently spotless record as a detective. That could be a hard one to come back from. Failures were always difficult to shake off. She'd seen that happen with other detectives and she knew she'd have to make sure her plan was as solid as possible. That was all she could do at this point until Strong got more insight as to what was actually going to happen.

Knight spent the next hour putting together her initial framework plan for the exercise, who and what she might need resource-wise, and then emailed a priority one meeting request to her colleagues in the Serious Crime Team for a nine a.m. meeting the following morning. This would be her most important meeting to date and she had to make sure she had everyone on board with her.

Chapter 12

Marsha's phone started to ring and she picked it up, hitting the answer button.

'Hello, is that Mrs Hughes?' a voice asked from the other end of the line.

'Yes it is, who is this?' Marsha replied, not immediately recognising the voice although it did sound somewhat familiar.

'It's Stuart Johnstone, from Churchman Estate Agents,' the voice replied. 'I'm just calling to let you know everything is going well. I took Mr and Mrs Peebles around the flat this morning, for their second viewing, and they seemed very happy with it. They were measuring things up and stuff and talking about what furniture might go where.'

'Oh right, that sounds good,' Marsha replied. 'Do you think they'll make an offer then?'

'Yes, I think they will,' Stuart replied. 'They asked me about the price, was it fixed or would you take an offer. I told them what we'd agreed, that you'd accept a price a little under but not a huge amount. They seemed okay with that and they would be first time buyers so that means things should move quite quickly if their offer is acceptable.'

'Oh that would be nice,' Marsha said. 'It would certainly be good to get it sold.'

The sale of Dylan's flat had dragged on longer than Marsha had hoped it would. It had been her own fault initially. It had taken her some time to get around to putting it on the market. It felt like a betrayal of Dylan, firstly getting rid of all his stuff and then finally selling his flat. The place where he had lived. She couldn't do it for a while but then, one day when she was cleaning it again, she realised there was no point in hanging on to it. Dylan wasn't here any more and it was just a building. She realised she needed to let it go and move on.

She'd contacted Churchman, her local estate agents, they seemed a friendly bunch, and at first it looked like it would be sold really quickly. There were a lot of viewings, according to Stuart, the smart young estate agent who was handling it. But there had been no offers, or at least no sensible ones. A couple of people had made offers at around half of the listed price and she had turned them down. She wasn't a charity and she wasn't going to just give the place away. It would seem like she was letting Dylan down. The process had dragged on and Marsha had changed from a 'reluctant to sell' owner to one who was now really keen to get shot of the place and move on. It was becoming like a millstone around her neck.

'What happens next then? Do you think they'll make an offer on it?' Marsha asked.

'Well the Peebles said they'd phone me back in the morning,' the estate agent replied, 'so let's see what they say. Hopefully I can persuade them to put in an offer in the range you're looking for. Are you around if I need to speak with you in the morning, on this number?'

'Yes, that's fine,' Marsha replied. 'I'll be at work, but this is my mobile number so I should be able to talk or at least phone you back.'

'Okay, hopefully we'll speak tomorrow with some good news then,' Stuart replied and ended the call.

Without moving from his position at the desk, he immediately dialled another number.

'Hello, Mr Peebles? It's Stuart here from Churchman, the estate agents. I've just spoken with Mrs Hughes about her flat and she's very keen to sell it. I think she would be absolutely open to an offer at around the price we discussed earlier. I know it's way lower than what it's currently valued at, but the flat has been on the market for a while now and I'm pretty sure I'll get her to accept your offer. I said I'd call her again in the morning to discuss it. Is that okay with you?'

After Mr Peebles confirmed that he was happy with Stuart's plan, Stuart leaned back in his seat, hands crossed behind his head, and smiled to himself. Selling houses was a bit like dating. All you had to do was find two people, a buyer and a seller, and match them up. Not with looks or hobbies but with a number. A number that was acceptable to both of them. Sometimes it could take a bit of persuasion, a bit of charm on Stuart's part, but once you'd worked out what that number was, that was it. Job done.

Getting the flat sold would earn Stuart a nice bit of commission, and at a good rate too. Mrs Hughes hadn't tried to talk him down on that, even though he would have reduced it by a further percentage to get her business. Sometimes things just worked out nicely. He opened his desk drawer to take out a piece of chewing gum and saw the diary sitting there, looking up at him.

'Shit,' he said under his breath, quietly enough so that no-one else heard him swear.

He picked the diary up and flicked through the pages. It seemed it belonged to Dylan Hughes, Mrs Hughes' son, the guy who had owned the flat before he was murdered. Mrs Hughes hadn't said much about him, just that it had been some sort of tragic accident. Stuart thought he'd seen something about it on the news a while back, but he didn't really care. He'd heard all sorts of sob stories over the years and all he really wanted to do was to get her business and sell the flat. It was a reasonable size and would give him a nice pay packet.

The diary had been lying on the hallway mat, just inside the front door. It was one of those brown, fibrous "welcome" mats that often seemed to be built into the carpet in people's hallways. The diary had been lying there on top of a bunch of junk mail. Stuart had found it that morning when he'd gone to the flat to show the Peebles around. It wasn't in an envelope or anything and Stuart assumed someone must have just pushed it through the letterbox. He had picked it up and put it in his pocket, transferring it to his desk drawer when he'd got back to the office. He had meant to tell Mrs

Hughes about it on the call, but it had completely slipped his mind. He had been too focused on getting her lined up for the sale. He'd have to try and remember to tell her the next day when they spoke, or if he forgot, he might just throw it out. There was probably nothing important in it anyway and he doubted Mrs Hughes would want it. She probably didn't even know it existed. Stuart had read a couple of the entries as he flicked through it and they seemed pretty banal. There was also a note with it apparently from whoever had pushed it through the letterbox, someone calling himself Harry Kane. That couldn't be right, Stuart thought, it must be some sort of in-joke. Why would the captain of the England football team have done that?

Chapter 13

The Bolton crew had assembled back in their usual meeting room in the back of the nightclub. There were five of the normal team of six present, only Scotty was missing. It was his night off at the club and, rather than call him in, they had decided that one of the others would just update him on anything he needed to know the following day. Besides Scotty wasn't really a detail man, he would be there to take care of any situation which might arise, where simple violence was required. There wasn't much else that Scotty really needed to know. Just point him at a fight and he's your man.

Ally and Charlie were sitting at the far end of the table, with Eddie and Smithy on one side and Chopper sitting across from them. Ally had called them all together to review where they were on the plan for their attack on Bog.

'So Eddie, do you want to go first?' Ally started. 'It all kind of depends on you. How have you got on with the phone stuff?'

Eddie nodded, 'Yeh, all good. Just one or two techy bits to complete but I'm pretty sure I'll be able to do it. I've been testing it out on a couple of burner phones and it seems to work okay. The diverted number and false texts, that is. Trouble is I can't do it too often, testing it I mean, because the mobile phone company might pick up on the temporary diversion part and start asking questions. That is unlikely though. It's not something that would usually happen, the temporary diversion I mean, but they normally need someone to complain that something funny is going on before they look into it. But I don't want to take any chances so I'm not going to do it too much more. But I am happy with the tests I've done so far. It's all worked. So I think we're okay.'

'Good, well keep us posted,' Ally replied. 'If anything goes wrong, let us know in case we have to change our plans or call it off.'

'Have you got Bog's daughter's number?' Charlie asked.

'Yep, my contact at the phone company let me have it,' Eddie replied, 'and we've confirmed it's hers. We rang the number once when we were watching her in a bar and we saw her answer it before we cut the call.'

'Good man,' Ally replied. 'Do we know her routine? More specifically do we know where she is likely to be on Saturday night and what time she normally gets home? Did you find anything out Smithy?'

Smithy leaned forward and rested his forearms on the table, before replying.

'Yep I think so. She's sixteen but can easily pass for eighteen or nineteen, I guess. From what we've picked up she's usually out with her mates on a Saturday night. Pubs and clubs mainly. Some ours, some not. We've picked her up on CCTV a couple of times. We haven't seen her with any boys. Her and her girlfriends just seem to stick together and do their own thing. It looks like they all usually head for home around one in the morning. Last trains and night buses, that sort of thing.'

'Good and that's a pretty regular routine for her is it?' Ally asked him.

'Yep, it seems to be,' Smithy replied. 'As I say we've picked her out a few times on the cameras. Saturday night seems to be their big night out.'

'So let's say we were to text Bog around two a.m. Sunday morning then,' Eddie said. 'That would seem to be about the right timeline. The sort of time Bog would usually expect his daughter to have been home, but this time she's stuck somewhere. Of course she'll really be at home and hopefully fast asleep with her phone switched off but he won't know that.'

'What if she leaves her phone on, will she see anything, any of the messages or anything strange?' Smithy asked.

'No, she shouldn't do,' Eddie replied. 'Her phone might not work for a bit while we're using the number, but I guess she would just leave it until the morning before she did anything and by that time it will all be back to normal.'

'Right, let's aim for next Saturday night then,' Ally replied. 'Chopper, can you let Scotty know, make sure he knows to be ready. We'll do this one ourselves. Just the six of us. No-one else needs to know. I want Bog to know it's us, he needs to see us and know we are in charge, this is our manor, whatever happens.'

The five of them then spent the next forty minutes putting the finer detail to their plan. How they would do it, who would do what and, crucially, what the outcome would be. They needed to be sure they'd give the Romanians a message. A message that would get them to move on and set up somewhere else.

Of course what the Bolton gang didn't know was that their plan to deliver that message to the Romanians was also being recorded, to be listened to by the head of the Serious Crime Team, Detective Inspector Strong.

<u>Chapter 14</u>

Marsha was on her way to the office of Churchman Estate Agents. She was wearing a dark blue jacket and skirt and a white blouse. Her hair was tied back, away from her face, with a black and white patterned scrunchie. She was walking briskly, it was her lunch hour and she wanted to get this whole thing over with as quickly as possible. The Estate Agent had promised her it should only take twenty minutes or so and she hoped he was telling the truth, for once.

The Churchman name was proudly emblazoned in dark blue lettering above the office window with the additional phrase, "A Family Business Founded in 1922". That was true, to an extent. It had originally been set up by Harold Churchman who then passed it on to his son, Albert in the nineteen fifties. Albert had run the business for a further twenty years before it was taken over by a High Street Bank, keen to expand further into the property business. A few years after that, when the Bank had a change of track and decided to pull back from the residential property business, it was sold to a large nationwide chain of estate agents. However throughout all these changes, the

Churchman name and brand had been retained to encourage the public to believe that it was still a family run business with a Mr or Mrs Churchman sitting in a boardroom somewhere as the agency's chairperson. Somehow it made the business seem more friendly rather than it being what it actually was – a large corporate business out to make as much profit as it possibly could.

However, despite the lack of any Churchmans in the business, they'd finally sold Dylan's flat, thank goodness. Although not at the price it had been valued at, in fact it had ended up quite a bit lower. Stuart Johnstone, the agent who had been handling the sale, had persuaded Marsha that it was still a good price. The best she was likely to get in the current market, he'd said. Marsha suspected he was bullshitting her, but in truth she had reached the point where she just wanted to get rid of the flat. She didn't want the responsibility of looking after it any longer. At first, when Dylan had died, she didn't know what to do with it but it had been hanging over her for too long now and it just brought back bad memories. Memories of her son Dylan, and how he was no longer here.

So Marsha had just accepted the lower offer and now she was going in to sign the various pieces of paperwork needed to complete the transaction. It seemed, even in what they called the digital age, the pen and paper still ruled when it came to selling your house. Marsha had lost count of the number of forms she'd had to fill in and sign over the last few months. It was even worse than working for the police and they definitely had their fair share of form-filling.

A few minutes later, she was sitting at the desk of Stuart Johnstone. He was a young man, about the same age as Dylan and Marsha imagined what life would have been like if this man had been her son. He probably did well at school and now he had a proper job, dressed smartly in his dark suit, white shirt and dark blue tie with a nice smile. Well manicured teeth. If he had been a horse, the Vet would have been pleased. He probably had a nice flat and a beautiful, clever girlfriend. Why couldn't her son have been like that? Marsha had loved Dylan more than anything in the world, but why did he go down the road that he did? Why wasn't he a bright, young estate agent now instead of being a man who was killed in a drugs dispute? Who made those decisions? Was it her fault? She'd tried her best to bring him up well, but it wasn't easy being a single parent. Did she get it wrong? If there was a God controlling everything, why would he end Dylan's life the way he did?

'Just this final one and then that should be it,' Stuart said, shaking Marsha out of her thoughts and pushing yet another document across the desk in her direction with that charming smile he had.

Marsha scanned through the pages of this latest document, not understanding what it was and barely taking in any of the text. Some of the wording was very old fashioned and it was all becoming a bit of a blur. It just looked like all the others she'd signed this morning. All legal stuff which she didn't understand and after a while she just gave up trying to pretend she was actually reading them and simply signed where she was told to. It was easier to do that.

She reached the last page of the final document and signed and dated it as instructed, putting the Churchman branded pen down on the desk beside the document with a thankful sigh. She felt there should be some sort of fan-fare to celebrate the moment of document completion. Maybe a couple of trumpeters appearing from the back office but, of course, there wasn't. Stuart reached over and slid the document back across his desk, placing it in a file with all the other documents that Marsha had previously signed that morning. It was a thick file.

'That's it. All done. Not too painful was it I hope?' Stuart said, smiling at Marsha with his nice, even set of white teeth. 'The sale should go through in the next couple of weeks. I don't think there will be any problems. As you know, the Peebles are first time buyers so there's no chain to worry about. Fingers crossed, you should have the money in your account by the end of the month.'

'Okay thank you.' Marsha replied, getting up from her seat, her knees creaking as she pushed the chair back, at the same time thinking maybe she was glad this wasn't her son. He was too smart. Or at least he thought he was.

They shook hands and Marsha made her way to the door, past the other desks where Stuart Johnstone's colleagues were stationed. There were two young women, both very pretty, both with long, straight blonde hair. Marsha wondered if one of them might be Stuart's girlfriend. Maybe an office romance? As she went, Stuart opened his desk drawer to put away the file of documentation and saw the diary sitting there. He looked up just as Marsha was opening the office door.

'Wait,' he called. 'Mrs Hughes.' His two female colleagues looked up from what they were doing at the sound of his raised voice, both simultaneously brushing the hair away from their faces.

Marsha stopped and turned around still holding the open door. Everyone was now looking at Stuart and he took the diary from his drawer and walked towards Marsha. As he passed his colleagues, one of them looked at him and said,

'Everything okay babe?'

His girlfriend. Stuart nodded and smiled at her and both the girls returned to what they were doing, any potential drama now seemingly over. He walked up to where Marsha stood at the door.

'I meant to give you this but I forgot. I found it lying on the hallway carpet in the flat. I guess someone must have pushed it through the letterbox a few weeks ago. There's a note inside it from someone I think,' Stuart said, careful to not tell her that he'd already had a good look at what was really a personal item.

'It looks like a diary,' he concluded as he handed it over to Marsha.

'Oh, wow, thank you so much,' Marsha replied. 'I've been looking for this for ages. It's my son Dylan's, but we couldn't find it anywhere. We thought we'd lost it. Thank you ever so much,'

100

Marsha said and she reached out to shake Stuart's hand again, before leaving the estate agents office feeling unexpectedly excited.

On her way in to see the estate agent, Marsha had noticed, what looked like, a nice little café across the street from the office, and she made her way there now. She went to the counter and quickly ordered a vanilla latte, her favourite drink, before sitting down at one of the tables by the café window. She took a sip of the hot coffee and then reached down and retrieved the diary from her handbag. She handled it carefully as if it was a valuable antique, something she should have worn white gloves for. She looked at it for a few seconds, turning it over in her hands, working up the courage to look inside. As she opened it up, a loose page fell from within the diary and she bent down to retrieve it from its resting place on the tiled café floor. Marsha looked at the loose page and scanned it quickly, then again more slowly this time, taking in each word thoughtfully as she read.

So someone called Harry Kane (wasn't he a famous football player?) had found Dylan's diary in a rubbish bin, or near a rubbish bin, in Greenhill. She didn't know that area very well. It was quite a nice location as far as she knew, with a lot of expensive houses. What would Dylan have been doing over there she wondered? He'd never mentioned knowing anyone that lived in Greenhill before as far as Marsha could remember. And, having gone there, why would he then put his diary in a street bin? That seemed a very strange thing to do. Marsha resolved to call this 'Harry Kane' and thank him for returning the diary and see if there was anything else he knew that might help solve this mystery. Maybe he might add some detail that would twig something in Marsha's brain. She hoped so, because at this moment she had no idea why Dylan's diary might have turned up in Greenhill.

Marsha looked at her watch and realised she should get back to work. Her lunchtime would soon be over and she didn't like to be seen taking longer than she was allowed. She knew in the grand scheme of things it didn't really matter, but she didn't want to take advantage. There were a few of her colleagues in the office who would notice if she was late back and no doubt make some comment about it behind her back. Well, Dorothy would anyway, no doubt adding her usual extra bit of frill to it.

'I saw Marsha Hughes coming back late from lunch again today. She looked a bit dishevelled. I heard someone say she was meeting someone, a man. Have you heard anything?'

But Marsha wasn't going to give Dorothy that opportunity, and she was ready to go back to work anyway. She didn't want to rush into reading the diary here, in the cafe. It wasn't the right place. She wanted to take her time and go through it slowly at home in the evening. It was one of the few things she had left that had some personal connection to Dylan and so it deserved to be given the right amount of time and treated with the right amount of respect.

Chapter 15

DI Campbell was enjoying being back down South. He was back living with his family again, in his own house, and although he was spending long hours at the police station, it meant he got home every night and could usually see his wife and daughter, even if only for a short time. And the same in the morning when he grabbed a quick coffee before heading off to the gym or the police station, depending on the day and his work schedule. Being back home also meant he could do family stuff at weekends again. A walk in the park, or maybe a visit to one of their relatives. There were plenty of them.

Both Campbell and his wife, Femi, had come from big families, many of whom had settled in the same area, along with various aunts, uncles and cousins. When they met, it was all just normal family activities, but Campbell had missed doing that when he'd been working up in Leeds. The first few months of his secondment up North had been incredibly busy and he'd often had to work weekends, which meant that he couldn't get home for a visit. Or, if he did, it would only be for a few hours before he had to head back up to Leeds again.

It was amazing how much he'd missed just doing normal family things.

DI Campbell was also very comfortable back in his old police station where he knew where everything was, how things operated, and indeed who everyone in the Serious Crime Team was. And his colleagues here didn't speak with strange Northern accents! Although he'd been working in Leeds for almost a year, he'd still not got used to their Northern twang and some of the strange phrases they'd come out with.

'Shall we have a proper brew?'

How was he supposed to know that meant a cup of tea? Why didn't they just say that? And the weather was definitely colder and wetter. It seemed to rain for weeks on end till you wondered where all the water went. Sometimes Campbell felt like he was living in a different country, even though it was only a few hundred miles away from his home in the South.

The only thing he missed now was not being the boss. In Leeds he was the number one. Numero uno. He had come in, led the team and got them all working just the way he wanted them to. He was the Guvnor and they would generally do everything he asked of them, without question. His word was final. But now he was back down South, he was no longer the man in charge. No longer the Guvnor. That title, of course, belonged to Detective Inspector Strong.

What Campbell hoped would happen now was that he'd spend a few weeks, or maybe a month or two, on the current investigation into the Boltons and the Romanians. He'd do a good job on that and, along with DC Knight and the team, make some sort of breakthrough on the case. He'd then look to have a bit of time to talk with DI Strong and the Chief Constable about his next role, hoping that they would find something located in the South for him. Somewhere where he could live at home with his wife and daughter, or somewhere that was close enough that he might be able to persuade his wife Femi to move with him.

Now that he was back down South, he knew it would be difficult for him to return to Leeds again. It would be like going backwards, or at least that's how he saw it. Besides, he'd done a good job there and the Leeds operation was running smoothly once more, hitting all its targets. Someone else could easily take the DI role on now and keep it going. Someone from the Leeds office could step up, and he would be happy to make a recommendation.

Hopefully DI Strong and the Chief Constable would understand his position and find him a role. He knew, at the end of the day, he had to go where they sent him, where he was needed, if he wanted to progress, but he hoped that if he continued to work hard and do a good job then that might work in his favour and they'd find him something nearer to home. Although Campbell had always been very career driven, since Rosey had arrived, combined with his posting to Leeds, he'd come to realise that the job wasn't everything. Being able to spend time with his family was just as important, if not more so.

Although Campbell missed being the man in charge, the Guvnor, it wasn't that bad because at least he was working for DI Strong and he was regarded as one of the best. Certainly, in many ways, the best DI that Campbell had ever come across. Campbell had learned a lot from Strong over the years they'd worked together and he'd used a lot of that knowledge when he took on the DI role in Leeds. Although he'd had a couple of doubts about Strong over the last few years, about some of his methods, the good points still far outweighed those minor niggles he had about him.

Campbell was sitting at his desk thinking he should make an effort to get home at a reasonable time for once this week, when someone appeared at his shoulder. He looked up and saw it was Detective Sergeant Harris.

'Hey Tom, how's it going?' Campbell asked his colleague.

'Yeh, not bad,' Harris replied.

DS Harris was wearing a dark grey suit with a cream coloured shirt and a red tie loosened at the collar. He was about the same height as Campbell but much less stocky. He could easily pass for a Geography teacher.

'Have you had any lunch yet, I completely missed mine.' Harris said, 'so I'm going to pop out to the café on the corner for a sandwich and a coffee. Fancy joining me?'

Campbell glanced at the clock on the office wall and calculated how much time he had if he was going to finish up here and get home before Femi would be putting their daughter Rosey to bed. It was late afternoon now and he still had a bit of work to complete before he could switch off. He'd been working late a lot this week and he hadn't seen Rosey the last couple of nights. He didn't want to miss her again. He'd tried asking Femi if she could keep her up a bit later, even phoning from his car on the way home once, but Femi wasn't for budging.

'The baby needs a routine,' she said time and time again. 'You don't realise, you weren't here. You were working in Leeds,' she said emphasising the last sentence as if it was an option he had chosen to take in preference to being at home.

Campbell had tried tentatively asking if the baby's routine couldn't be changed slightly, from time to time. But apparently not. The consequences were unthinkable. So Campbell knew exactly what time he had to be home if he was going to see his baby Rosey. A minute or two late and that was it. He wasn't even allowed to go in and see her then in case he woke her up and disturbed her routine.

Standing by his desk, DS Harris could see his colleague's hesitation and he glanced at his watch.

'Just a quick coffee, you look like you could do with a break and we haven't caught up since you got back,' Harris said, laughing. 'C'mon, you know you want to. I'll even pay.'

Campbell laughed along with his colleague and nodded in agreement, he could do with a break and he still had a bit of time. Harris was right, they hadn't had a catch up since he'd returned and Campbell knew it was important to keep in touch with his colleagues. It was sometimes so easy in this job just to isolate yourself and do things on your own. Campbell knew it was important to keep communicating. Just talking with colleagues was often when you found out something that really helped you with a problem you were trying to solve. He closed up his laptop and stood up from the chair.

A few minutes later the two detectives were walking towards a table in the local café, each with a mug of coffee in their hands. It was a café a lot of the policemen used as it was close to the station and it was a small, independent place where you got a great cup of coffee and were able to have a quiet conversation, off premise, when you needed to.

'So how was Leeds?' Harris asked his colleague as they settled into their seats, Campbell's chair screeching across the tiles as he pulled it in closer to the table and slipped his jacket over the back. 'Was it much different to what we do here?'

'Not hugely, I have to admit,' Campbell replied. 'They speak differently of course, but the criminals are much the same. They have the same types of issues with drugs, prostitution, domestics, you know. All of life's varieties, just like we have here.'

'Yeh, I can imagine. Much the same scum as we have to deal with here then,' Harris replied, taking a sip of his coffee.

'Yep,' Campbell replied. 'The Leeds team were a bit disorganised though. I think the last DI had been coasting towards his retirement so they didn't have much focus. Mistakes were being made. The stats weren't good, all heading the wrong way, which is why they asked me to go in. But from what I found, what I saw there, they were a good team. A good bunch of lads and lasses. They just needed a bit of guidance, a bit of coaching. I just put the same sort of processes in place we work to here, and things started to improve pretty quickly. They just needed a bit of discipline. We've got a proper handle on what's happening now and the stats have started to move back the right way.'

Campbell stopped talking and took a long drink of his coffee, savouring the taste as it flowed down his throat. Leeds hadn't been all bad, but he'd missed this. They really knew how to make a good cup of coffee here. He hadn't found anything like this in Leeds, they all seemed to prefer drinking strong Yorkshire tea which wasn't at all to Campbell's liking.

'So how are things with you then Tom? Is everything okay?' Campbell asked his colleague, sensing that Harris wanted to talk.

'Yeh, you know, a bit up and down really,' Harris replied, frowning.

'Oh, why's that?' Campbell asked, while having another drink of his coffee.

'Ach, nothing really,' DC Harris replied. 'It's just, well, I was doing okay, I thought. After you left, I guess I sort of felt I was the most senior guy left. There wasn't a DS anymore and I was the most senior DC. I'd been around the longest. I felt I'd kind of gravitated into the role, you know, the sort of second in command, and the team and DI Strong seemed to accept that. I was taking on more responsibility and the Guv often seemed to be looking to me to run things for him. He wanted to discuss the open cases with me, you know, things like that. Stuff he used to do with you I guess. It seemed to be going okay but now….I don't know…things seem to be different.'

'Why, what's changed?' Campbell asked his colleague with a quizzical look on his face. He knew Harris wasn't regarded as the most dynamic detective, but in the absence of a detective sergeant in the team Campbell thought he was a perfectly capable second in command. He was pretty thorough, maybe too thorough sometimes, perhaps not as quick as some, but Campbell thought it was better to be that way. Stick to the rules and don't make mistakes and you won't go far wrong.

'Well, it's the Guv I suppose,' Harris replied. 'I'm not sure I have quite the same mind-set as him and I think he sees that. I'd been working a bit more closely with him over the last few months, as I said, and, well, let's just say, some things he does are different to how I would do them. I guess you must know that, you worked with him for a while. You know how he works.'

The detective stopped talking and picked up his cup. He was wary about saying too much as he knew Campbell was close to Strong. He didn't want to dig a hole for himself and make things worse than they currently were. He could easily do some damage to his career here if he wasn't careful. Harris took a long, slow drink of his coffee, watching Campbell over the top of his mug, and waiting for him to respond.

But Campbell wasn't ready to share any of his thoughts, his doubts, of DI Strong's ways of working yet. He didn't have enough evidence of any wrongdoing, nothing solid, and he definitely didn't want to start any rumours or speculation amongst his colleagues. That wasn't his way. Campbell only liked to work with firm facts. He wasn't ready to share yet, but he was keen to see if he could get any more insight from DC Harris.

'What did the Guv do then? Anything specific that you didn't think was right?' Campbell asked his colleague.

Harris took another long drink of his coffee, using the time to think how he should reply. Campbell was his senior officer but his close relationship with Strong was risky for him. If he said anything to Campbell then he might just go straight to DI Strong and that would surely signal the end of any chance of Harris getting the DS role. But, on the other hand, the way things were going at the moment, the chances of him getting promoted were looking pretty bleak anyway. The Guv seemed to be using DC Knight a lot more now. She seemed to be his first port of call when he wanted to discuss any of the cases. She'd also led a few of the major case review meetings recently and there was no doubt she was a very good detective. If Harris had been a betting man, which he wasn't, apart from an annual bet on the Grand National. But if he had been, then he'd have made DC Knight a firm favourite for the vacant DS role. And if that happened, it would then be unlikely that Harris would ever be considered for promotion again. Not at his age. He'd be stuck as a detective constable until he retired. There would always be new, younger detectives coming through and he would be regarded as a "steady Eddie" type detective. Okay in his current position, but not good enough for a step up. Harris knew that this was his time now, his best chance, and if he didn't get the role soon, he could see that it was going to slip away. DC Knight had overtaken him and she was getting further and further ahead. He needed to do something. He needed to take a risk to give himself a chance of progressing up the career ladder.

Harris put his cup back down on the table and leaned in closer to his colleague.

'Well, to be honest,' he said in a hushed tone, glancing around the café to check no-one else could hear him. 'There have been a few things, you know, just the way he does things. How we get convictions. I don't know, I can't explain it really, but he always seems to be involved somehow. He seems to know everyone and, sometimes, he appears to know what's happened, or even going to happen, before anyone else does. I know that sounds crazy. I don't know how, but it's strange. Did you ever find that with him? I know he's a good cop, one of the best, there's no doubt about that, but he just....I don't know.'

Harris stopped talking and looked at Campbell, almost pleadingly, hoping that the detective would somehow help him. But Campbell still wasn't ready to share anything with Harris, although he understood exactly what his colleague was saying. Campbell had experienced the same when he'd been working with DI Strong, but he too didn't have any specific, solid evidence yet to back up his suspicions. He didn't want to involve Harris in any of this unless his colleague had something more definite. Something that he could use. Maybe something that connected the pieces that Campbell had. It was like a jigsaw puzzle, but with a few of the key pieces missing. He needed to prod Harris a bit more, without giving anything away himself.

'Well, everyone has their way of doing things,' Campbell started. 'I always like to stick to the rules, make sure everything's done properly so that it doesn't come back and bite you later.'

'Yeh, me too,' Harris butted in, nodding, glad that he seemed to be on the same page as DI Campbell. 'That's how I like to do it, by the book.'

'I think DI Strong generally does that as well,' Campbell continued. 'But maybe sometimes he, how should I put it, maybe he bends the rules a little to wrap up a case or secure a conviction. Is that what you mean?' Campbell asked. 'Have you seen him do anything like that?'

'Mmm..yeh, I think so. Kind of,' Harris replied, relieved that he and Campbell seemed to be on the same page. Maybe Campbell could help him after all.

'You heard about the killing of Tony Fleming and Marsha's son, Dylan?' Harris asked and Campbell nodded.

'Well I was working on that one, along with the Guv and DC Knight and there were a couple of odd things with it. Things, I guess I would have looked into further if I had been the lead on the case, but the others kind of glossed over them and I was, I suppose, outvoted.' Harris shrugged his shoulders then carried on.

'They just seemed to want to get the thing closed and move on. I couldn't really say anything without looking as if I was just being awkward,' he said.

'What sort of things?' Campbell prodded, looking for more.

'Well there were things in the SOCO report that didn't quite stack up but, as I said, Strong and Knight seemed like they just wanted to wrap it all up. We had a meeting planned to review the case, but I got called out to another incident and when I came back it was all done. They said it was a double killing, both men had somehow shot each other at the same time. Case closed. Move on. But that's not what the SOCO report said when you read the detail.'

'Why? What did it say?' Campbell asked, becoming more interested in what Harris had to say.

'Well there were a couple of things,' Harris replied. 'Firstly the report suggested the two bodies might have been moved after the shootings which would of course imply that there was at least one other person present at the time of the killings, or sometime later, before we found the bodies. Then the report also said that, in their opinion, the most likely answer to what had happened was that Dylan had shot Fleming and then killed himself.'

'What? He committed suicide?' Campbell asked.

'Yes, that's what they thought had happened, what they suggested in the report,' Harris replied.

'But why would he do that? Why kill Fleming and then shoot yourself?' Campbell queried.

'I don't know,' Harris replied, shaking his head. 'That's what DI Strong and DC Knight both said. They implied that the SOCOs must have got it wrong, that the only sensible explanation was that there had been a gunfight, a dispute over drugs, and they'd ended up shooting each other. That's the conclusion they came to and that was it. Case closed. Two more drug related criminals off the street and of course Tony Fleming was a Mr Big. A prize scalp to get for all of us.'

'Seems strange,' Campbell said, shaking his head. 'The SOCOs don't normally get these things wrong. Certainly not something I've seen before. What did the Guv say about the bodies being moved?'

'Well, again he had an answer for it,' Harris replied. 'He said sometimes that can happen, people can move after they've been shot, just before they die. He said that would explain it and of course he was right. That was possible but that's not what the SOCO report said.'

'Mmm….Maybe I'll have a look at the report sometime, just to see what it says,' Campbell replied, non-committedly. This could be useful information but he still wasn't ready to share any of his own thoughts with Harris yet.

'Don't say anything to the Guv please,' Harris said. 'I probably shouldn't have said anything to you. I'm just a bit fed up with everything I guess.'

'Yeh, no worries,' Campbell replied. 'You did the right thing. Got it off your shoulders but let's just keep this between you and me for now. If there's anything else you can think of, or come across, let me know though. I'd like to keep an eye on things. As I say, just between us,' he said giving Harris a knowing smile while reaching across the table and patting him on the shoulder.

As Campbell finished his coffee, he felt a bit anxious. He desperately wanted DI Strong to be the great detective he appeared to be. But, yet again, here was another thing. In some ways, it was a good result, especially with regard to stopping Fleming. But there was something not quite right with what Strong had done. Something that couldn't be explained and, because Campbell was a detective who did everything by the book, he knew he wouldn't be able to let it go.

Chapter 16

Detective Constable Knight had just left her boss's office. She was feeling very pleased and finding it hard to keep a smile off her face. DI Strong's CHIS had come up trumps. Whoever he or she was, they deserved a medal. They'd provided all of the detail of the Boltons' planned hit on Bogdan Popescu. The time, the place, who was going to be there, how they were going to do it. Everything!

Knight couldn't help think that Strong's informer must be pretty high up in the Bolton empire, but Strong said he couldn't tell her anything about the person, which she understood. She just hoped that the CHIS was reliable, that everything they'd told Strong was correct. DI Strong certainly seemed to be pretty sure about it all, he'd said he was absolutely confident in the information he'd received. That was good enough for Knight. She was lucky to have such a brilliant boss as DI Strong. She knew that not every DI would have passed on the information, preferring to keep the glory to themselves, but Strong wasn't like that. He always wanted to help his team and he'd come up trumps once again.

All of what Strong had told her made Knight's planning for the upcoming exercise so much easier. She could get together with her team now and plan exact timings and locations for everyone. Who would do what, where and when. She now knew everything that was needed, including how many firearms officers.

She'd agreed with Strong that they needed to let the thing play out for a bit before they moved in and started to make arrests. They discussed the likelyhood that holding back might not be the best outcome for Popescu. He might take a beating, or worse. But both detectives knew it was their big chance to arrest a number of the key figures in the Bolton gang for a major crime, and finally get them sent to prison where they undoubtedly deserved to be. The two detectives knew that by doing it this way, there was a risk that Popescu might get seriously injured. But Strong's way of thinking was that there was some element of justice in that happening. Bogdan Popescu was undoubtedly a serious criminal who had hurt a lot of people, directly and indirectly, and it was unlikely they would be able to arrest him that night as he was merely there to pick up his daughter, or so he thought. Detective Constable Knight didn't disagree with her boss's thinking but she stayed quiet on the subject, apart from agreeing the approach they were going to take. With the Boltons in prison and the head of the Romanian gang perhaps indisposed, it was likely that the result would be a lot less trouble, certainly in the short term and it would also buy the police time to put in measures that stopped it flaring up again in the future. Try as she might, DC Knight couldn't think of a better scenario for ending the current ongoing violence. And, with all the information they now had, they had the greatest opportunity they were ever likely to get of making a major dent in the area's serious criminal activities.

Although DI Strong had been the source of invaluable information and help, Detective Constable Knight was recognised as being the lead detective on the gang turf war and so she would receive a lot of the credit for resolving it and bringing it to an end, should they be successful. There was no way they couldn't give her the Detective Sergeant role after that surely? She'd be one of the youngest detective sergeants in the force. She could only imagine how proud that would make her mum.

Over in the far corner of the main office, Marsha was sitting at her desk, updating some profiles on the system and, at the same time, watching the clock. She wasn't normally a clock watcher but she was desperately willing the time to go in quickly today so that she could get home and have a proper look at Dylan's diary. She still couldn't quite believe she had it. In her mind she had written it off and reconciled herself to the belief that she would never see it again. That had been hard, giving up the idea of the possibility of a personal connection. Especially along with the disappointment of the laptop. She had thought Jason from I.T. would have been able to get past the password request and gain access to the machine, but apparently not. Marsha had thought about taking

119

it into a computer shop to see if they could do anything, but she hadn't got around to that yet and, if Jason couldn't crack it, then she doubted whether anyone else would be able to either. At the moment it was sitting back in the box at the bottom of the wardrobe in Marsha's spare room.

But, on the plus side, she now had Dylan's diary which somehow seemed much more personal. It wasn't just a hard, shiny piece of metal. It was smaller, softer, smoother and Dylan had handled it, touched it, written in it. Marsha had been imagining that there might be all sorts of things in there. Dylan's personal thoughts and records. Stuff about her, his mum? If there was, maybe she shouldn't look at it. Maybe it would be too personal, things she might not want to read, or shouldn't see. But the temptation was too great and she knew she was going to. She just had to. It was fate that had finally landed it with her and she needed to see what it contained. If anyone was going to read it then surely it should be the mother. The woman who had brought Dylan into the world. Besides, she justified even more to herself, there might be something in there that gave her more insight into how and why Dylan had died.

After what seemed the longest afternoon ever, the clock finally ticked its way around to five thirty and Marsha switched off her PC. She tidied up her desk, before picking up her coat and bag and leaving the office.

Back at her house, Marsha took the diary from her bag and placed it on the coffee table in the living room. On the drive home, she'd planned what she was going to do. She'd get changed as normal, then have her dinner before sitting down to read Dylan's diary. She wanted to take her time, with no distractions so she could give it the time and attention she felt it deserved. It was Dylan's. It was personal, important. It felt like a last link to him and she didn't want to rush it and risk missing something.

It was almost eight o' clock by the time she sat down with a glass of water and picked up the diary again. She read the 'Harry Kane' note once more before placing it back down on the coffee table. It didn't tell her anything new and she wasn't quite sure what to make of it. The name threw her, making her think it was some sort of ruse. The first page in the diary contained Dylan's personal details. Name, address, phone number. Marsha stared at the details and ran her finger across the black ink on the page, feeling that it somehow brought her closer to Dylan. That he was still here. At that address, on the end of that phone. He had written these words. It had been his hand. The same hand she used to hold when he was a child, when she'd be walking him to school. She continued to trace the words as she closed her eyes and thought of the young Dylan. He'd been such a beautiful little boy. A shock of blonde hair and bright blue sparkling eyes.

Marsha's memories were suddenly disturbed by the sound of her phone ringing. She reached forward and picked it up, not recognising the number.

'Hello?' she said hesitantly.

'Hi, is that Marsha?' a brightly sounding woman's voice replied.

'Yes, it is, sorry, who's that?' Marsha replied, still not recognising her caller, but thinking she sounded quite posh.

'It's Catherine Strong, Mo's other half. I've been meaning to give you a call for a while to see how you are,' the woman explained.

'Oh, that's very kind of you,' Marsha replied. 'I'm doing okay thanks, how are you?'

'Oh yes, I'm good. I was just wondering if we might look at getting a date in the diary for a coffee one day. It would be good to catch up,' Catherine replied. 'Sorry I should have asked. Have I caught you at a convenient time, I haven't disturbed you in the middle of your dinner or anything have I?'

'No, no, it's fine. I wasn't doing much. In fact I'm just looking at Dylan's diary,' Marsha replied. 'Do you remember I said we couldn't find it? Well strangely, after all this time, it turned up. A dustbin man had found it over in Greenfield one day and he very kindly returned it to me.'

'Wow, that was lucky,' Catherine replied, while thinking Greenfield, that's a coincidence, that was where she lived. 'I hope you find some comfort in reading it,' she said to Marsha.

The two women then spent the next few minutes going through their own diaries before settling on a mutually convenient date to meet.

After the interruption of the phone call, Marsha turned her attention back to Dylan's diary. She turned to the page of the first diary entry, the first of January. Dylan had come round to see Marsha for lunch that day and Marsha thought back to that day. Of course it was New Year's day and Marsha had always felt she should cook something special on that day so, this year, she'd done roast beef, roast potatoes and a variety of vegetables. There had been far too much food for just the two of them, but sometimes it just felt good to over indulge. After stuffing themselves, the two of them had finished off their wine in the living room while watching a film on TV. It had been a nice day, Marsha could remember thinking it was a lovely way to start the year and she was glad now that she didn't know what was going to happen just a few months later.

She began to read through the following daily entries, then scolded herself for reading them too quickly. She might have missed something, something between the lines. Maybe Dylan was sending out subliminal messages. Perhaps she needed to understand not just *what* he wrote, but *how* he wrote it. Was that possible or was she over analysing things?

Whatever the case, she decided that she needed to take more time and not rush it. She went back to the start and started reading again, this time more slowly, taking in each word, one at a time. Imagining the story behind his short paragraphs, trying to visualise it.

Most of the entries were simple, short descriptions of what Dylan had been doing each day. His work, his social life, seeing Marsha, his mum. It was all there and Marsha could picture him doing these things as she read the words. She paused on the parts that mentioned her and tried to remember them from her point of view. A lot of the time it was just a note about him having called her, but she thought hard to try and remember each and every call. What she had been doing at the time. What they spoke about, how long it had lasted. Often the calls had been pretty short, just a couple of minutes, and Marsha felt guilty as she realised she had sometimes ended them because she was in the middle of doing something else. Nothing should have been more important than talking to her son and if she'd only known how little more time she was going to have with him, she would have kept talking just to have longer with her son. She wished the phone would ring and she could hear his voice now. She wouldn't care what he was talking about, just to hear him one more time would be bliss.

She read through the whole of the January entries and began to experience a sense of calm. In a way it was like he was in the room with her and they were having a conversation. If she tried hard, focusing on the text, Marsha could imagine that being real. He was sitting there, beside her on the settee, just chatting away, telling her what he'd been doing the last few days and weeks.

Marsha looked at the clock on the wall and realised she'd already been sitting there for almost an hour. It had just seemed like a few minutes. She had got lost in her thoughts, her imagination, and the time had just passed. She put the diary down and went through to the kitchen to get another glass of water. As she filled the glass she thought more about what she had just read. There was nothing extraordinary, nothing that would interest anyone else, but to Marsha it was special. It was her son that had written it. Every single word was special. She wanted to read it all and understand it all, consume it, burn it into her brain. Hear him saying the words. It was that important to her.

She walked back through to the living room and picked the diary up again, intending to start reading the February entries but the pages fell open at the month of April. She was about to flick back to February when a word caught her eye. Not a word, a name. 'Strongs.'

It was in the last entry Dylan had made, the twentieth of April. April, that was when he'd gone missing, probably around that specific date, if Marsha thought back. She didn't speak with him every day, but it must have been around that date that she last heard from him. The entry mentioned Fleming and the Strongs, she read it out slowly,

'...Went over the plan for tomorrow. Will see what Fleming's like but think I may need to be tough. He knows about the Strongs. I'll be ready for anything. He won't get near mum, I'll make sure.'

Marsha sat still for a while, thinking. What did it mean? If she was reading it correctly, it seemed likely that Tony Fleming had found out that Dylan had run down DI Strong's parents all those years ago and was going to use it against him in some way. Probably blackmail. But what did '*He won't get near mum*' mean? Why would she be involved? She couldn't make sense of it.

She went back to the beginning of April and read through each entry quickly, but there was nothing relevant, until she came to the entry for Thursday the fifteenth. Once again she read it out aloud.

'Went for usual drink at The White Hart. Met a guy called Ricky. Told me about someone called Fleming who knows about the accident 20 years ago. Could threaten me and mum. Plan to meet him at farm next week and talk him out of it.'

So this guy Ricky, Marsha couldn't think of anyone called Ricky, but he was the one who had told Dylan about Fleming, and only the week before they were going to meet. So Dylan hadn't really known Fleming and there wasn't anything to indicate that he'd been involved in drugs with him in any way. Marsha read the two entries again. Back to back. Somehow she felt vindicated. Dylan wasn't a drug dealer, she'd known that all along. He hadn't known Tony Fleming. He didn't have any connection to him until this guy Ricky appeared. But who was this Ricky and what part did he have to play in it all? Marsha sat for a few minutes thinking, trying to work it all out. Step by step.

Ricky tells Dylan about Fleming. Fleming is going to blackmail Dylan. They meet at the farm and both end up dead, apparently killing each other. That was the simple conclusion but it also raised a lot of other questions. Not least being how would Dylan have a gun? He wasn't the sort of person who would have a gun, or the sort of person who would deliberately kill someone….and why did they have drugs…or did Marsha not really know her own son?

126

Marsha put the diary down on the coffee table and picked up the note again. Maybe Harry Kane could fill in some of the gaps. Maybe he would have some idea of why Dylan was in Greenhill? Did he know him? She didn't have much else to go on and perhaps it was worth a try. She dialled his number and a man's voice answered the phone.

'Hello, is that Harry Kane?' Marsha asked.

'Yes it is, who's that?' Harry replied.

'Oh, hi. My name's Marsha I've got the diary you found. It was my son Dylan's diary, but emm, I've got it now,' Marsha replied.

'Oh right good. I found it when I was working and thought he might have lost it so I just put it back through his letterbox,' Harry replied. 'I hope that was the right thing to do. I wasn't sure. There didn't seem to be anyone in.'

'Yes, no, that was good. Thanks for doing that. I really appreciate it. We thought we'd lost it. Where did you find it exactly?' Marsha asked.

Harry went on to explain to Marsha that he was a bin-man and that he had found it when he'd been emptying a street bin outside a small parade of shops in Greenhill. Marsha asked him if he knew the actual name of the street and he told her it was Ashcombe Road which Marsha jotted down on the note Harry had made previously.

'I don't suppose you knew Dylan at all did you?' Marsha asked. She knew it was a long shot but there were too many unanswered questions and she didn't want to assume anything when she didn't know.

127

'No, I, em, no I don't.. know Dylan,' Harry replied, catching on that this woman, his mum, had said "knew", the past tense. Did that mean...? But he didn't feel it was his place to ask.

'Okay, I didn't think so. Just one last thing,' Marsha asked him, interrupting his thoughts. 'You don't know anyone called Ricky, do you?'

The line went quiet for a few seconds before Harry answered.

'No, I can't think of anyone I know called Ricky, sorry,' he replied.

Chapter 17

The gang of six were back together. Ally Bolton, Charlie, Eddie, Smithy, Chopper and Scotty. They were meeting in a pub on the outskirts of town. Not one of theirs, but Ally knew the landlord well and he'd provided them with a quiet room where they could talk in private. The pub wasn't busy at the best of times. It hadn't really moved with the times and so it was largely serving a diminishing number of elderly clientele. Men who liked to get out of the house, away from their families, and talk about sport with other similar men. The room through the back of the pub was only very occasionally used but it was ideal for Ally Bolton and his trusted men. There was an old dining table and half a dozen dining chairs which were still surprisingly comfortable.

'Why are we meeting here?' Smithy asked as soon as he entered the room, before he'd even sat down. He was the last to arrive and the others had been waiting for him.

'I must have got lost about three times trying to find it, and the bloody satnav took me down a farm road full of potholes,' Smithy complained.

'Yeh, well we needed somewhere different to where we usually meet,' Ally replied, ignoring his mate's grumpiness. 'Grab a chair. I had Chopper give our usual room a good look over and he found a bug under the table. Seems like the police have been listening in to what we've been talking about, so here we are.'

'Shit, the Bobbys. How dae ye ken it's them that's listening?' Scotty exclaimed.

'Our man on the inside told us they knew the date we'd planned for the hit on Bog,' Ally replied, 'as well as a lot of the detail. Everything we'd discussed in that room in fact, so it must have been them that planted it somehow. I've asked Chopper to find out everyone that's been in that room in the last few months to see if we can narrow it down.'

'Bastards,' Smithy exclaimed. 'So what are we gonna do now? I take it that means we can't do the hit on Bog any more? Or at least not like we planned it.'

'Well, no, I don't necessarily think so,' Ally replied. 'Even though they know we were planning to trap him with the false text, they're not going to have told Bog that. I guess they were just going to lie in wait and try and get us before or after it happened. I'm not sure what their plan was. Our man said he didn't know. Apparently his bosses hadn't decided anything yet. So we could stick with the same plan but just change the date, without them knowing.'

'That would be cool. Like in yer face coppers! They'll know it's us though, even if it's on a different date,' said Chopper. 'They know what we were planning to do so if we do that, the text thing, then they'll come straight for us.'

'Yeh, but that's no different to what would happen in any case,' Ally replied. 'If Bog gets beaten up they'll assume it was us, however it happens. But they won't be able to prove anything. They won't be able to admit to bugging our place and so that can't be used. We just need to have our stories straight, just like what we discussed before, and stick to that. We'll all have alibis and witnesses that we were in a meeting in the club when it happened. Eddie will get rid of the phone, they won't be able to trace anything to us. And remember we've got Max Murray on our side. If there is anything we've missed, we can rely on him to make sure we don't get done.'

'I don't know,' Smithy replied, still feeling a bit grumpy from his journey. 'I get it that it would be great to just do it, even though they know our plan. But it sounds risky. They might get us on firearm possession or something.'

'I agree it is risky,' Ally replied. 'But don't forget they have no idea about when we are going to do it. And now we've moved rooms, and aren't being listened to, they've no way of finding that out. But that's why we're all here today, to thrash it out, see if it's still viable and make sure we cover off all of the risks.'

The six men got down to business. They discussed the plan again for another couple of hours. Making little tweaks here and there, making sure their alibis would stand up and, crucially, agreeing a new date for the attack on Bogdan Popescu, this time with no-one listening in.

Chapter 18

'Hi is that Detective Inspector Joseph Campbell I'm speaking to?' a posh voice sounded on the other end of the phone.

'Yes, who is this?' Campbell replied. No-one ever called him Joseph. Only his mum, in a rising voice, when he was a boy and he'd done something wrong.

'Joseph will you get in here and get your homework done this very minute!'

He could still hear his mum's shrill voice shouting out from the kitchen window with her distinctive Jamaican accent. His thoughts were interrupted as he realised the person at the other end of the phone was talking again.

'Oh, hi my love, I'm Tristan Archibald from Moonshine TV and Films. Just call me Tris my dear, everyone else does. You left a message for someone to call you back about our real life crime series. I'm the producer of that, how can I help you Detective Campbell?'

'Oh right thanks for calling back,' Campbell replied. 'I just wanted to have a look at the programme you did on The Anniversary Killer. I can't find it anywhere on TV, or on-line, and there was just something in it that I wanted to check. Could you get me a copy, or tell me where I can get access to one?'

'Sure, no problem my love. What did you want it for, can I ask?' Tris replied.

'Oh nothing much really,' Campbell replied. 'It was just one of the photos you used in the programme. We just wanted to have another look at it. I think it might be better than the one we have on file,' Campbell said, laughing as he spoke.

'Sure okay, shall we set up a meeting then?' Tris suggested. 'It would be good to get your take on the whole Anniversary Killer piece, my love. We didn't get much police input in the original programme as I recall. There were a few unanswered questions and it might be good to do a follow up with your input. It would help solve some of the mysteries. People like that sort of thing, you know, getting it straight from the horse's mouth so to speak. Would that be okay my dear?'

'I'm not sure, I'd have to check with the bosses,' Campbell replied. 'We have all sorts of rules around doing TV stuff. What we can and can't do legally. If you can get me a copy of the original programme I'll certainly ask and let you know.'

'Okay, well, I know my dear. Why don't you find out what you can do and then we can meet up and go through a few ideas,' Tris replied. 'Let me just have a look at my diary and see what we have…'

'Look, as I said, I'm not sure we'll be able to do anything for TV, I'm afraid. My boss doesn't really like publicity. I doubt if he'll agree to us doing a follow up, like you said. But if you can get me a copy of the programme I promise I'll ask him,' Campbell replied, starting to feel a bit frustrated. He'd been expecting this to be a simple request but it was already taking up too much time as far as he was concerned.

'Ah, okay, I understand I've come across your boss's type before, my love. Perhaps I can meet with him, your boss' Tris replied. 'I'm sure I'd be able to persuade him. What's his name?'

'No, he wouldn't agree to that, definitely not,' Campbell replied sharply. Too sharply? He wanted to keep Tris on his side, even though he was finding him very annoying.

'Look I'm being honest with you,' Campbell said, trying to maintain a gentle tone. 'I don't think we'll be able to do a programme with you, I'm sorry but it's just how it is.'

'Oh that's a shame, my dear,' Tris replied. 'I know when we've done real life crime programmes in the past they've sometimes really helped the police. Seeing it on their TVs really seems to identify with the public and they often contact us with things they've remembered from watching the programme. We've also had feedback that it makes the police seem more approachable, you know my love, showing them as human beings, not just people that break your door down in the middle of the night. Do you know what I mean, love? Listen, I'd be happy to give your boss some examples of how we've helped, my love. I remember one that we did with the Lancashire police, in Liverpool I think it was, which helped catch a serial burglar. I can tell your boss about that my dear, give him the name of the detective we worked with. He was very happy with how it went. He was such a sweetie. I think he's retired now. Of course we don't show any confidential stuff my dear, we're always very careful with that. We've done it so often now, these types of programmes, we know exactly what the police rules are, probably better than most of the police do,' Tris laughed.

Campbell had only been half listening to Tris's speech. He was trying to find a gap where he could butt in but this man seemed to be able to talk endlessly without having to pause for a breath. Campbell couldn't quite believe the conversation was still happening and he decided he would have to become a bit more firm to end this conversation and get what he wanted. As Tris began to laugh, Campbell sensed it was his chance.

'Look Tris,' he started. 'I've asked you a few times now, politely. I need to see a copy of the programme as soon as possible. If you won't give it to me now then I'll have to get a warrant and come to your offices. I'm sure you wouldn't want that. It can be very embarrassing having a group of policemen marching through your offices and looking through your files.'

'Oh, well, I don't think there's any need for all of that upset my love,' Tris replied. 'I was only trying to help you, but if you're going to be like that then of course I can send you a copy of The Anniversary Killer programme. It's a shame we can't get your side of the story though. I really think it would have been interesting but, if not, then I just need to get your email and I can send you a link to the programme you want.'

'Great,' Campbell replied. 'How quickly can you do it?'

'I can do it right away, my love, it only takes a second,' Tris replied.

Finally, Campbell thought, looking at his watch. It had taken him half an hour to get something which it turns out only takes a second. As they swapped email addresses and Tris promised that he would send the link straight away, Campbell amused himself by wondering if he should just organise a police raid on the TV production company's offices anyway. Just to ease his frustration and make him feel better. He laughed at his idea as they ended the call.

Chapter 19

DI Strong was sitting at home in his study. It was a bedroom really, but it was downstairs and they didn't need another bedroom so they'd had it converted into a study room. Initially it had been intended for both of them to use, but over time it had become DI Strong's room with his wife graduating to using the kitchen worktop for any paperwork she had to do. Currently the room had a desk, a leather office type chair, a wooden filing cabinet and matching wooden bookcase. There was a small window behind the office chair which looked out onto the rear patio and brought some light into the room.

DI Strong was sitting at the desk and he was feeling concerned. He'd had nothing from the bugging device Jack had planted in the Boltons' meeting room for a few days now. There could be a few reasons for that. The device might have malfunctioned, but that was unlikely. These devices were pretty reliable nowadays. The Boltons might have stopped using that room. Of course that was possible, but Strong thought again it was unlikely. There had been no sound at all for three days now which would have meant no-one had been in the room at all during that time.

Of course another possibility was that the Boltons might have found the device and disabled it. That was the one Strong feared most, but his detective instincts told him was the most likely.

Whatever had happened, Strong seemed to have lost a valuable source of information. He knew the Boltons were planning to do a hit on Bog on Saturday night and some of the plan as to how they were going to do it. But if they had found the listening device, would they still go ahead with it? They would know that the device must have been planted by someone, and the obvious candidates for that were either the Romanians or the police. Both of those would mean that their plan now carried a huge risk. Either Bog or the police would know what they were planning to do and would be able to make their own plans, either an arrest or possible ambush.

Of course Strong knew it was him that had been listening in to the Boltons' plan and it was he who was ready, along with DC Knight and the team, to catch them as they carried out their attack on the Romanian gang leader.

Strong really needed to find out what had happened with the room and the listening device. Had it been found? And, if it had, what the Bolton gang were planning to do now. He needed to get back in control. He would look stupid if he set up a major operation for Saturday night and nothing happened. He was the one who had been providing the information from his secret source, and he had assured DC Knight that it was one hundred percent reliable. If the Boltons changed their plan then, apart from Strong not being able to get the justice he desired, he would also lose some credibility, especially in the eyes of DC Knight. It was that latter part that bothered him. He was confident that he'd get the Boltons and the Romanians sometime, if not this time. But he'd been building up a good working relationship with DC Knight and he regarded her as a good ally, helping him achieve his plans of delivering justice in whatever way they could. If he messed it up for her this time, she might be less inclined to work as closely with him in future and, if that happened, he'd have to be more careful with what he did.

Somehow he needed to find out what had happened. It was risky, he knew, but he couldn't think of any alternative, other than to get Jack Wilson back in there somehow. Strong knew the Boltons were violent men and if they had found the bug, they would be highly suspicious of anyone they didn't really know coming into their premises. Especially someone going into their usual meeting room. Jack had pulled it off once before on the pretext of doing an electrical safety check, but that had only been a few weeks ago and if he went back now, they could easily put two and two together. It wasn't going to be easy and Strong still wasn't completely sure if it was the right thing to do. The last thing he wanted was for Jack to get beaten up.

Strong racked his brains but, not being able to come up with any alternative, he phoned Jack Wilson and told him what he thought had happened, and how they needed to find out for sure. Strong explained how it would be risky for him to go in again, but Jack seemed to think it wouldn't be too bad. He told Strong that he'd actually been in the room a few times already. Firstly to install the device and then he went back a couple of times to check that it was still okay.

Jack explained that if he went in to the club in the afternoon, there was usually just the one girl working on the reception desk. She would always just be sitting there playing with her mobile phone, not really paying attention, and she let him go wherever he wanted to. There never seemed to be anyone else in the club at that time and so he could come and go as he pleased. All he had to do was sign in and out with the girl. Having heard this, Strong felt a bit better. He needed to find out what had happened, and right now he couldn't think of any alternative, so he reluctantly agreed that Jack should go back in and check the room to see if he could find out what had happened with the bug.

As he ended the call, there was a light tap on his study door and his wife Catherine poked her head in to the room. She was wearing a cream coloured jacket with a brown bag hanging from her shoulder.

'I'm just off out for a bit, I'll see you later,' she said, smiling at her husband.

'Okay, where are you off to?' Strong replied, knowing she had probably told him already but, as usual, he had forgotten.

'Oh, just off to meet a friend for a coffee in town,' she replied before closing the door.

On her way out, Catherine wondered why she had said that. Why hadn't she told him she was going to meet Marsha Hughes? After all Marsha worked for him. It had just been a spur of the moment thing. She didn't want to tell him in case he asked her any questions that she didn't want to answer. Quite simply she didn't want to talk about the diary and, at the same time, she didn't want to lie to her husband. Catherine felt guilty at keeping secrets from him, but she was sure it was nothing really, she just wanted to have a chat with Marsha first. That would clear it up.

Marsha was already in the café when Catherine arrived. She was sitting at a table by the window and she gave Catherine a somewhat shy wave as Catherine came through the door. Marsha was wearing a dark blue blouse and Catherine could just see a black jacket hanging on the back of her chair. She already had a coffee and so Catherine ordered one for herself and walked across to Marsha's table. Marsha stood up and the two ladies hugged before Catherine sat down on the wooden chair across the table from her. Catherine's coffee soon arrived and the two women began chatting about their everyday lives. Marsha soon realised that Catherine's was much busier than hers. She seemed to be involved in a lot of local activities. There were gym classes, she was a member of several local organisations and she also did some voluntary work. It made Marsha's life seem dull by comparison, which she knew wasn't far from the truth. She had slipped into a bit of a lazy routine lately and she knew she needed to shake herself out of it, do an

142

evening class or something, maybe in photography. She'd always been interested in that.

'Where do you live?' Marsha asked Catherine, thinking she might be able to piggy back onto some of the many things Catherine did.

'Greenhill,' Catherine replied. 'We've been there quite a few years now, in fact we moved there not long after Sophie was born. We needed that bit more space and a nice garden.'

Greenhill, where had Marsha heard that before? It was somewhere quite recently and then suddenly it came to her.

'Oh, Greenhill.' Marsha said. 'I knew I'd heard that somewhere recently but I couldn't think at first. That was where the bin man found Dylan's diary, you know the one I mentioned to you?'

'Oh yes, I remember,' Catherine replied, happy that the conversation had fortunately moved on to the subject she really wanted to find out more about. The diary. And its connection to her husband, if any.

'I think you'd just got it that evening when I called you,' Catherine said.

'Oh yes that's right. I'd just got it that very day,' Marsha replied. 'It's funny, I'd given up on ever finding it and then suddenly the estate agent gives it to me. I don't know how long he'd had it but he said he found it in Dylan's hallway. He presumed someone had pushed it through the letterbox and there was a note inside from this guy, Harry Kane, saying he'd found it.'

'Harry Kane, where do I know that name from?' Catherine pondered.

'Oh, you're probably thinking of the footballer,' Marsha laughed. 'That's what I thought too, but this one doesn't earn as much I don't think. He's a bin man.'

'Was it, was it any help, I mean reading it.' Catherine asked. 'Did it give you any comfort?'

'A bit I think,' Marsha replied. 'I felt a bit closer to him, just reading his words and imagining him in the places he was talking about. I think it helped. I was also keen to see if there was anything that explained how he had been killed at the farmhouse. You know, anything that might have led up to that evening. Why it all happened.'

'And was there anything like that?' Catherine asked, keen to know.

'Not really. There were a couple of entries I suppose that might have meant something but nothing I could figure out,' Marsha replied. Knowing Catherine was DI Strong's wife she didn't want to say any more as the diary entries showed an obvious connection between Dylan's death and the accident which killed DI Strong's parents twenty odd years before that.

'Did you show it to Mo?' Catherine asked. 'Maybe he could make something of it? Him being a detective and that. You never know.'

'No, I didn't,' Marsha replied. 'To be honest some of it is a bit too personal and I decided to just put it away after I'd read it. Time had gone by and I think I needed to move on. I'm pretty sure there was nothing in there that the Guvnor, sorry I mean DI Strong, would have been interested in.'

'Of course,' Catherine replied, 'I understand. If anything changes and you'd like someone else to take a look at it and see if they can make any sense of it, of course I'd be happy to do that for you. You just need to ask.'

'That's very kind of you, thank you,' Marsha replied. 'But as I say it was a bit personal and, how can I put it, it's like something that only Dylan and I have and I don't really want to share that.'

'No, I understand,' Catherine replied, whilst wondering if there was something in the diary that Marsha didn't want anyone else to see and, at the same time, wondering if her husband had seen that very thing.

For her part, Marsha was keen to move the conversation on. She liked Catherine, but she was too close to DI Strong to be able to trust completely. Marsha was sure that anything she said to her would find its way back to the detective and she didn't want that as there would be a risk that the whole story about Dylan running down Strong's parents would then be exposed. She took a drink of her coffee and smiled at Catherine.

'So tell me all about this yoga class you go to. I've been thinking of taking it up but I need a bit of encouragement,' Marsha said, laughing at her friend.

Chapter 20

DI Campbell had watched The Anniversary Killer programme on his laptop. Three times now, although he'd skipped through it the last couple of views. He'd seen himself, DI Strong and Andy Austin in the programme and wondered how the TV company had got the photographs they'd used.

He recognised the main one they'd used of him. It was the photo he'd submitted for his police security badge many years ago. How would they have got hold of that? It wasn't a great photo, but, on the plus side, at least it made him look a bit younger. He had more black hair then, less grey, and a much thinner face, more chiselled. He'd definitely put on a bit of weight during his stint in Leeds. Too much living off takeaways and not enough exercise. Now he was working back down South and living at home, his aim was to get into a healthier routine again. Better food and more regular visits to the gym. That was the plan.

The photos of Andy Austin on the television programme were much clearer than the ones he'd had access to in the police database. Yet another limitation of the system that the police had to work with. The police didn't have the time or resources to find multiple photos of their suspects, or the digital technology to enhance any they did get to get a better image, not as standard anyway. The standard process is they'd get one reasonably good photo and scan it in to their central database, and then that would be it. That was good enough normally.

The one photo they had of Andy Austin wasn't terrible, but it wasn't great either. The TV company had several photos of him and they were much better, much clearer, which is why Kyle Smith had sat up and taken notice when the programme was first shown. And why he hadn't recognised him when Campbell had previously shown him the blurry photo of Austin from the police database.

DI Campbell didn't have any plausible reason to return to Leeds at the current time. He was too busy, as they all were, trying to sort out the increasing violence between the two gangs. The Boltons and the Romanians. He knew there was no way that DI Strong would let him, or anyone else in the team, have any time off without there being an exceptional justification for it, and he couldn't very well tell Strong the real reason he wanted to go to Leeds.

Ideally, Campbell would have liked to have been sitting with Kyle Smith when he watched the programme and saw the photos of Andy Austin again. It would have been interesting to see Kyle's immediate reaction so he could judge it for himself. Did it look genuine? How certain was he that the man he was looking at on the TV was the same man that had attacked him? Campbell felt if he was there, with him, he would be able to tell. But the fact was

147

he couldn't get away, and it could be weeks or even longer before he would be able to. Campbell wanted to know quicker than that. He wanted to know now. He needed to know. It was nagging away at him and he needed to get it over with. One way or the other.

He phoned Kyle and arranged to email him a link to the programme. Campbell stressed how important this was. He told Kyle that he needed to take his time and really look at the man on the screen. Was it the man who had attacked him? How certain was he? Campbell told him to set some time aside and watch it on his own, with no distractions. Watch it a couple of times, Campbell had suggested. Make sure you get a good look and then, when you have done that, to give DI Campbell a call.

Kyle called him that evening. Campbell had just left the office and was on his way home. If the traffic was clear, he was hopeful that he would be home in time to bathe Rosey and read her a story as he put her to bed. He'd already phoned Femi and told her he was on his way. So far the journey had been good and so he was in a positive mood.

Then his phone rang. It was hands free, plugged into his car dashboard, so he could answer it while still driving. Having made such good progress, he feared this would be a distraction. It would most likely be a work thing and it would probably be something that would delay him somehow, missing the chance of him seeing his baby daughter that night. He glanced at the phone and saw the name Kyle on the display. He hit the answer button and said hello.

'Hello, it's, emm, Kyle Smith from Leeds,' Kyle replied. 'Are you okay to talk?' he enquired, aware of the background noise.

'Yes, sure. I'm driving, but hands free, so please go ahead,' the detective replied, hoping it was going to be a quick call but at the same time very keen to hear what Kyle had to say.

'Okay, so I, emm, I had a look at the link, the programme you sent me. I looked at it in the office then I've just looked at it again now, back at my flat,' Kyle replied.

'Yes, okay, and what do you think?' Campbell asked, glancing to the side of the road, wondering if he should pull over.

'It was definitely him,' Kyle replied.

'Andy Austin? You're absolutely sure?' Campbell replied, setting his indicator and pulling into a layby at the side of the road.

'Yes, one hundred per cent. The guy looked me straight in the face. I'll never forget that. His eyes. If it's not that Andy Austin bloke on the programme, then he must have an identical twin brother, I swear,' Kyle replied.

'Okay, okay,' Campbell replied, sitting in the layby, engine idling and thinking. Just thinking.

'Are you still there?' Kyle's voice came out the speaker, bringing him back to reality.

'Yes, sorry I was just thinking,' Campbell replied. 'Have you any idea why Austin would have attacked you? Did he say anything to you at all?'

'No, I've racked my brains. I can't think of any reason. He just took my phone and I managed to fight him off and escape.' Kyle replied. 'I can't

149

remember him saying anything,' he added, knowing that wasn't exactly what had happened, but he couldn't change his story now.

Austin had taken Kyle's phone, that part was true but Kyle hadn't fought him off. Austin had just let him go after warning him to show more respect to women. Kyle had assumed he must have been the boyfriend or husband of one of the women he'd befriended at some point. Kyle knew he'd sometimes used his position as an estate agent to manipulate women with a view to getting them into bed. Although it wasn't always one sided. He often came across lonely housewives who enjoyed his company and would regularly come back for more. It was all a bit of fun for Kyle, he had been a single man at the time. It had all happened well before he'd met Karen. However the incident with Austin had been a warning sign. He'd always known he was taking a bit of a risk, especially when the women were married. There was always the chance that a husband would find out and come after him, and he guessed that's what had happened. It had definitely scared him, and the threat from Austin had been enough to make him change his ways. However he couldn't tell any of this to detective Campbell without potentially getting himself into trouble, and he had too much to lose now.

'And you'd never heard of Andy Austin before?' Campbell asked, drumming his fingers on the steering wheel, trying to make some sense of it.

'No, never. Not until I saw him in that programme. That was the first time I'd even heard of him,' Kyle replied.

'Okay and what about a Jack Wilson? Does that name mean anything to you?' Campbell asked.

'Well he was spoken about in the programme too, wasn't he? He drove the car didn't he? But no, I'd never heard of him before that,' Kyle replied.

'Okay, leave it with me,' Campbell replied, glancing at the clock on his dashboard. 'I'll be back in touch if we need anything else from you. Thanks for your help,' he said, ending the call and pulling back out into the traffic, estimating that he should still be able to make it home in time for the bedtime story if he was lucky, but doubting that he'd be able to focus on it following the call he'd just had with Kyle.

Chapter 21

It was mid-afternoon and Jack was approaching the door to Club Extream. It was a nice sunny day for a change and he was feeling optimistic. Confident, and a little excited at the same time. He liked doing these jobs for DI Strong. As Strong always put it, he was doing something good for society. In a small way he was helping to reduce crime. That could only be a good thing.

It had been a few weeks since Jack had last been in the club, and on that occasion everything had been pretty straightforward. He'd made a quick check of the listening device to confirm that it was still securely in place and then he'd wasted some time in the cupboard that held the fuse boxes on the pretext that he was doing a standard electrical safety check. Leila, the girl on reception, was the only person he had seen on that visit and she hadn't taken any notice of where he had gone or what he was doing. As usual, she was too engrossed with her mobile phone.

Jack knocked firmly on the solid black door. It was about the same width as a normal house door but beyond it there lay a very large interior with a main dance hall, a smaller club room and, towards the rear of the building, several rooms serving as offices or store rooms. You would never have imagined that from the outside.

There was a buzz and the door unlocked and opened a few inches. Jack pushed it further inwards and stepped into the club, carrying his small canvas tool-bag in his left hand. To his right there was a glass window and behind that sat Leila, in her normal position, head down with phone in hand. She looked up, as Jack approached and gave her normal non-committal smile. No underlying message, just a straightforward smile as she pushed a ledger through the gap underneath the window. It was a routine. There was a pen lying on top of the ledger and Jack picked it up and signed his name, date and time in the relevant columns before pushing it back towards Leila. Routine over.

'Everything okay?' Jack asked her and she nodded before returning her attention to the phone in her hand.

It was a well worked process which had taken thirty seconds at most. Jack was happy that everything was just the same as usual.

He walked along the corridor towards the back of the building, past the ladies and gents toilets, one red door and one green door, until he reached the cupboard door, behind which were the fuse boxes. He opened it up and stepped inside, placing his tool-bag at his feet. It was just about big enough for one man and a tool-bag. Anything more would have been uncomfortably cramped. Jack switched on the light and closed the door behind him. There was nowhere to sit, so he leaned against

153

the bare cupboard wall on his right hand side. He checked his watch and decided to give it five minutes. That should be long enough to convince anyone that he was actually doing something. Even though he knew there was probably only Leila out there, he didn't want to take any chances. From what DI Strong had told him, the people who owned this club were not to be messed with and so he certainly didn't want to get caught. He took out his mobile and checked his messages. There weren't any new ones. He thought about sending a message to his girlfriend Lucy, but then she might text back asking where he was or what he was doing and he didn't want to have to lie to her. Best just not to say anything. Instead, he scrolled through his social media feed and watched a couple of TikTok videos one of his friends had posted, with the sound turned down. After a few minutes he looked at his watch again and decided he'd been in the cupboard long enough to convince anyone that he'd actually been doing something electrical. DI Strong had advised him to be careful, not to take any chances, and that was what he was doing.

He exited the fuse box cupboard, picked up his bag, and looked around before making his way further into the building until he came to another door on his right. This one was painted black, similar to the main entrance door. He looked around again, making sure no-one was there, before turning the handle and entering the room. He closed the door quietly behind him and quickly walked across the room to the large wooden table sitting in the middle. He put his bag on the floor and crouched down beside one of the wooden table legs. He reached under the table and felt around with his fingers. Nothing! He felt again before crawling completely under the table and rolling onto his back to get a better look. He checked all the legs, just in case. There was definitely nothing there. The listening device was gone. Damn. He thought he'd hidden it really well but someone must have found it.

He could have planted another one, there and then, but Strong had told him not to. The detective said he just wanted to know if the device was still there or not. Well, it wasn't.

Jack got up, brushed himself down, picked up his bag and quickly left the room. There was still no-one around and he walked back down the corridor and past Leila on reception calling out 'bye' as he went past. Leila looked up briefly from her phone and reached across to make a mark against Jack's name in the ledger, before returning her attention back to her phone. Jack pushed open the solid black door, screwing his eyes up as he stepped out into the bright daytime light outside.

Chapter 22

DI Campbell got up from his seat and stretched his arms high up above his head. He was feeling stiff, too long just sitting at his desk staring at a screen. Now that he was living back down South he really needed to get back into the gym, like he used to do. Get back into the routine. He was letting himself go. When he got dressed in the morning he could feel his trousers were that bit tighter and his stomach was beginning to drop over the top of his belt, straining his lower shirt buttons.

He pushed his chair back in under the desk and walked across the general office, heading towards the kitchen. He fancied a coffee, although that was something else he needed to keep an eye on. He was drinking much more coffee now than he used to. It was becoming a habit. He knew he should cut back, but maybe from tomorrow. Right now, he felt he badly needed a caffeine kick.

As he was standing in the kitchen waiting for the kettle to boil, Marsha Hughes came in with a glass tumbler in her hand. He had seen Marsha around the office and he'd nodded and smiled to her a couple of times since he'd returned, but they'd not really spoken since the day of Dylan's funeral.

'Hi Marsha, how are you doing?' Campbell asked, smiling at his colleague.

'Yeh, not bad, you know,' Marsha replied. 'Getting there. Thank you for asking.'

'Yeh I understand. These things are never easy. Losing someone so close like that. I think you just have to take things a day at a time and hopefully it becomes a bit better,' Campbell replied.

'Yes, I think so,' Marsha said. 'That's what people tell me anyway.'

'I'm sorry I had to rush off after Dylan's funeral,' Campbell said, 'but I told DI Strong about the flat and maybe getting some of his stuff from it. Did he emm…' Campbell stopped as the kettle clicked off and he picked it up to pour water into his mug.

'Yes, the Guv went over and checked it out,' Marsha replied. 'He's been really helpful. He picked up the mail and some other bits and pieces. I've been there myself since, but I've actually sold the flat now.'

'Oh that's good,' Campbell replied, as he opened the fridge door and retrieved a bottle of milk. 'Did you manage to get any of Dylan's personal things? You said he kept a diary didn't you?'

'Emm, yes, that's right,' Marsha replied laughing. 'I did get the diary, but that wasn't exactly straightforward.'

Marsha went on to explain to Campbell how she had finally come into possession of the diary through the kindness of the bin-man, Harry Kane.

'You don't know anyone by the name of Ricky do you?' Marsha asked Campbell after she'd finished her story. 'I know it's a bit of an unusual question but it's just someone Dylan mentioned in the diary, shortly before the end, and I'd never heard of him before. I've always been wondering who he was.'

'Ricky,… Ricky,' Campbell murmured away to himself. 'Not emm…Red Ricky is it? That's the only Ricky I can think of.'

'No, well it didn't say that, just Ricky,' Marsha replied. 'Why? Who is Red Ricky?'

'Oh, just someone I know,' Campbell replied. 'Nobody really, bit of a stab in the dark, it was just he was the only Ricky I could think of when you said it. I doubt it would be him though,' Campbell said, shaking his head.

In fact, the more he thought about it, he didn't even really know who Red Ricky was. He'd only heard the name through DI Strong. He was a CHIS, somebody who provided the police with useful information from time to time in exchange for a small token of appreciation. Usually a packet of cigarettes, or a couple of pints of beer. Campbell had a couple of people he used regularly in a similar fashion and there were some others that the whole team used from time to time, but as far as he could remember Red Ricky was solely affiliated to DI Strong. Campbell had certainly never met him, and he didn't think any of the others had either.

'What did Dylan say about this Ricky in his diary?' Campbell asked, picking up his mug and taking a sip of his hot tea. 'Do you want one?' he asked Marsha, holding up his tea towards her.

'No. I'm fine thanks. I just popped in for a top up of water. I'm trying to drink a couple of litres a day. The doctor said it would help me to sleep better. I'm not sure it's making much difference though. I ought to get back to my work really,' Marsha replied and she stepped across to the kitchen sink, her glass held out in front of her.

'So, what did Dylan say about Ricky in the diary?' Campbell persisted. He wasn't sure why he wanted to know, but something was nagging at him. That old detective instinct again.

Marsha had her back towards Campbell, filling up her glass with water from the tap. She was beginning to wish she hadn't mentioned Ricky now, it had just been a spur of the moment thing. She didn't really want to tell anyone what was in Dylan's diary. It was a personal thing. Something she wanted to keep to herself. She felt it was somehow part of the special connection that only she had with her son Dylan. Besides that, she didn't want to run the risk of opening up the whole thing around Dylan's accident twenty years ago. But as she filled her glass and turned back around, she could see DI Campbell was waiting for an answer.

'Well from what I could see it seemed this Ricky character introduced Dylan to Tony Fleming the week before....before, you know..' Marsha replied, still struggling to talk about what had happened to Dylan.

'Oh, I see,' Campbell replied.

159

That's interesting, he thought. If this Ricky guy knew Tony Fleming then he must have been involved in the criminal world in some aspect. A criminal, or a policeman, or a CHIS? If it was Red Ricky, then did that mean that Strong was involved in some way? But Campbell couldn't think of any reason why Strong would ask Red Ricky to introduce Tony Fleming to Dylan Hughes. There wasn't any logical explanation, unless Campbell was missing something. He could see why Strong would be happy that Tony Fleming was off the streets, but how would Marsha's son fit into that? He wasn't anybody, no criminal record, just a normal guy as far as Campbell knew. Campbell took another sip of tea and mentally scolded himself for letting his imagination run away with him again. Just because Marsha had mentioned this guy Ricky. There must be hundreds of Ricky's out there?

Marsha turned to leave the kitchen, the conversation had made her feel anxious and she wanted to get back to the safety of her desk and her work to take her mind away from it all. But before she could leave, DI Campbell had one more question for her.

'Where did this bin-man find the diary…did you say?' Campbell asked, again something nagging at him, but he didn't know what or why.

Marsha was half way out of the door, but she turned her head back to look at him.

'I, emm, didn't say, but it was in a bin outside a shop in Ashcombe Road in Greenhill, he said,' Marsha replied and then she was gone.

160

'Mmm…Greenhill….' Campbell murmured to himself. A nice area. Nice houses. He'd only ever been there once before when he and his wife Femi had been invited to dinner at DI Strong's house.

<u>Chapter 23</u>

There was a knock on the door and Ally Bolton shouted 'Come in.' The door opened and Chopper stepped inside the room. He was wearing his usual black padded jacket, a blue t-shirt, blue jeans and a pair of black boots. His dark hair was swept back over the top of his forehead.

'Ally, Charlie,' he said nodding towards the two Bolton brothers who were sitting at a small round table in the centre of the room. On the table sat two half full bottles of lager alongside two mobile phones.

Chopper picked up an aluminium chair from the side of the room and placed it at the table, sitting down between the two brothers. Chopper didn't drink alcohol. Not any more. He hadn't had a drink now for over five years and was much the better for it. Better, not necessarily health-wise, but more so psychologically. He was more in control of himself now. When he had been drinking he could turn very violent. Sometimes for no obvious reason. A bit like Scotty did now, although the Scotsman didn't seem to need a drink to be like that.

When Chopper had been younger, after a few drinks he would just suddenly switch, and if you were the unlucky one with him, he could suddenly turn on you. He could be a very violent man back then, and he'd spent quite a bit of his young adult life in prison because of that. He could still be violent now, but in a much more controlled way. Nowadays he knew exactly what he was doing, and that had largely kept him out of prison for the last five years.

'So, I think I might have some news on our bug man,' Chopper said, tapping his fingers on the table in front of him.

'Oh yeh? What have you found?' Ally replied, reaching forward and taking a sip from his bottle of lager.

'Well, a couple of days ago, about three o'clock in the afternoon, an electrician by the name of Jack Wilson came into the club,' Chopper started. 'We got him on CCTV. He goes into the fuse box cupboard and then about ten minutes later he comes out of there and goes into the meeting room. He's in the meeting room for around three minutes, then he comes out and leaves the club.'

'So, what….was he planting another device in the room?' Charlie asked.

'No, I gave it a good check earlier today. It's definitely clear,' Chopper replied. 'And I can't see anything out of place in the fuse cupboard either. But, the thing is, there was no need for him to go into the meeting room. There's nothing particularly electrical in there he would need to check, so maybe he was checking to see if the bug was still there. If it was him that planted it in the first place he wouldn't have got anything from it

163

since we found and removed it. Maybe he's come back to check on it.'

'Is there any CCTV showing him going into the meeting room before then, on any other day?' Ally asked

'Well no, we normally only turn on the CCTV at night when we actually open the club,' Chopper replied. 'There's never really been any need for it before that, during the day. But since we found out about the bug thing I've told Leila to switch it on when she comes in now at twelve, which is how we saw him this time. But we do have a signing-in book at reception and I've had a look at that. This Jack Wilson has been in the club a few times over the last couple of months. I'm not sure why. No-one has requested an electrician and we don't have any problems with our electrics as far as I know. Even if there's nothing else, he could be ripping us off with call out charges. I've asked Bernice in Accounts to have a look but she's not come back with anything so far.'

'Yeh, it all looks a bit suspicious,' said Ally. 'Do we know anything about this Jack Wilson? Is that his real name?' he asked.

'I think it is,' Chopper replied. 'I haven't had much time yet to get any more detail on him but I will do in the next couple of days.'

'Yeh, do that. Then maybe we should get him in for a chat, see what he has to say,' Ally said, banging his bottle down on the table.

'Yep, no worries, I'll get that sorted,' Chopper replied.

Chapter 24

DI Campbell looked around the office, it was pretty empty. Most people were either out on jobs somewhere, or in meetings elsewhere in the building. Detective Constable Harris was still sitting at his desk though, facing away from Campbell. He could see the detective's back. He was hunched forward reading something on his laptop. Probably the latest health and safety email. They seemed to come out very regularly. More rules and regulations.

The two detectives hadn't spoken much since they'd gone out for a coffee and Harris had voiced his concerns about DI Strong's methods of working. But Campbell was keen to keep him on side to see if there was anything else he could tell him about Strong. He was starting to build up a file on his boss, just a few notes, but for what reason he didn't know yet.

Campbell had looked at the SOCO report on the Fleming murder and it was just as Harris had told him. There was a lot of detail in the report, but the two key points were there. The report suggested that the two bodies might have been moved and they were pretty certain it had been a murder/suicide. It was the most likely explanation for the angle and entry points of the two bullets that had been fired. But they weren't absolutely sure. Not a definite. When everyone is dead, there's no-one you can ask. No-one can tell you exactly what happened, so some of it has to be guesswork. Based on some logic, yes, but still with a few guesses and assumptions thrown in to the mix. And although Campbell would have accepted the SOCO findings and worked the case from those, Strong's explanations were still plausible and there wasn't enough to make anything more out of it on its own.

Campbell rose from his chair and walked across the office to where his colleague was sitting.

'Fancy a coffee?' he asked DC Harris. 'My shout this time and I could do with stretching my legs a bit.'

Harris smiled and got up from his seat. He had been in the middle of writing up a report from a witness interview concerning a fight that had taken place outside a pub the previous evening, and ideally he would have liked to carry on and get that finished. However he was keen to nurture his relationship with DI Campbell, knowing that it might be useful for his future career aspirations.

A few minutes later the two men were back in the café, sitting at the same table they had been at just a few days before. It was late afternoon and the café was quiet. The café owner was furtively clearing things away, trying to minimise what would need to be done when the café actually closed forty minutes later, but trying not to give anyone the impression that she was actually doing that, so as not to make her existing customers feel

166

uncomfortable. There were only two couples sitting at other tables and Campbell recognised one of them. They were a man and a woman from the police support and administration team. Jonathan and Sally, Campbell thought, although he wasn't certain that was their names. Generally Campbell wasn't one to listen to office gossip, but he knew that these two were supposed to have been having an affair for as long as he'd known them. They were sitting closely together, talking quietly, their knees touching under the small round wooden table. Campbell caught the man's eye and immediately looked away.

'So how's it going?' Campbell asked as he and his fellow detective got settled at their table. 'The Guv isn't causing you any more problems I hope?' he asked, taking a sip of his coffee and enjoying the sensation of the warm liquid as it trickled down his throat. He was starting to cut back on his caffeine intake and he had signed up at the gym again, so things were heading in the right direction. But sometimes, when he was beginning to flag, he felt he still needed that shot of coffee.

'Ha-ha, no. I haven't had much to do with him lately,' Harris gave a short laugh. 'As you know I'm running the general day to day on-goings, the usual domestics, drunken fights and stuff, while you lot focus on sorting out the bigger issues with the gangs. I think that's definitely the Guv's top priority for now so we haven't spoken much lately. I did have an interesting conversation with one of the ladies in the support team though.'

'Oh? Who was that?' Campbell asked, taking the opportunity to have another drink of his coffee.

'Marsha Hughes, you know the quiet one that sits in the corner, always smartly dressed but doesn't say much. Mother of the now infamous Dylan Hughes,' Harris replied, reaching for his mug.

'Yes I know Marsha,' Campbell replied, thinking back to his recent conversation with her about Dylan's diary.

'Oh yes, of course you do,' Harris replied, as he took a quick drink of his coffee. 'Well, we were in the pub last Friday. It was Carol Dobbs leaving do, one of the admin team. I don't think you were there?

'No, I was invited,' Campbell replied, 'but I had a family thing on, so I couldn't make it.'

'Ah right, yeh. Well I stayed a bit longer than I meant to and at some point I found myself sitting at a table with just Marsha,' Harris replied. 'I think she'd had a few drinks because she was quite chatty and we'd never really spoken that much before. Anyway I asked her how things were going and all that, you know after her son's…well, and I can't remember how we got onto it, but she started talking about the Guvnor,' Harris stopped to take another drink of his coffee before carrying on.

'So it turns out Marsha really likes him. Not in, …you know, ..that way,' he added as he realised what he'd just said and he could feel himself beginning to blush slightly. 'More as a sort of boss I suppose. She said he really helped her with what happened with Dylan and other stuff. And then she went on to say that she'd done a few jobs for the Guv over the last couple of years. To be honest, I wasn't really listening that closely by this point, I had other things on my mind. But, just to keep the conversation going I suppose, I asked her what she'd done for him, thinking maybe some admin tasks, a bit of filing that sort of thing. But she started to tell me about things that the Guv had asked her to do, it seemed like he used her to do secret little jobs for him, research on potential criminals, tracking people down, stuff like that. She mentioned Andy Austin at one point, but when I tried to ask her more about what she actually did for him, she seemed to realise that maybe she shouldn't be saying anything and so she just sort of clammed up, made some excuse about having to go to the ladies and that was that. To be honest I didn't think any more about it until you asked me about the Guv now.' Harris stopped talking and took a big mouthful of his coffee.

'Mmm... that's interesting,' Campbell replied. 'I didn't know that, about Marsha helping him I mean. Doing things for him. I'd seen her go into his office a few times I guess, but I didn't realise she was doing specific jobs for him.' Campbell stopped and took a sip of his coffee, his mind beavering away as he drank.

'It seems strange using one of the admin staff to do that,' Campbell continued. 'Why wouldn't he just use one of the Serious Crime Team? That's what I would have done. That's their job. Make sure it was visible to everyone working on the case,' Campbell shook his head. 'And you say she mentioned Andy Austin, what did she say about him, can you remember?'

Harris took another drink of his coffee, trying to remember how the conversation with Marsha had gone. It had been pretty short and he hadn't listened that closely to what she was saying. He was wishing he had now as DI Campbell seemed to find it interesting. What had she said about Andy Austin again? Was it something to do with names? She had a list of names or something?

'Ah, yes that was it,' Harris suddenly exclaimed as the memory came back to him. 'She said she had a list of names she had to check out to see if any of them came up on any of the police systems, I think that was it. I think the Guv gave her the names. I think she meant they were names that Andy Austin might have been using, different identities I mean, although she didn't say that exactly. That was just my guess.'

'Mmm…that's interesting,' Campbell replied. 'We knew Austin had multiple identities he used at various times, but I can't remember us having a list of the names. Of course I could be wrong, it was a very hectic time, as you know. There was a lot of pressure on us to find him and things were moving quickly. I might have just missed that, or even forgotten about it.'

However, Campbell knew that wasn't the case, but he didn't want to share too much of his suspicions with Harris or anyone else. Not at this point. Not until he'd pieced together enough to make it something definite, something more

170

substantial. Campbell had never been aware of any list of false names Austin could have been using and if there was one, and Strong knew about it, then Campbell couldn't think of any reason why that information wouldn't be shared with the rest of the team on the case. It was a significant piece of information and would have become a major area of focus as they tried to track Austin down. Why would Strong only show that to a member of the support team? It didn't seem to make sense unless DI Strong was hiding something, something he wanted to keep to himself.

'You know, it's funny,' Harris began, interrupting Campbell's thoughts. 'Now that we're talking about Andy Austin, I just remembered something else. Something that I thought was a bit strange at the time but I just forgot about it.'

'What was that?' Campbell asked, keen to hear anything more about Andy Austin. The double murderer had taken up a lot of Campbell's thoughts and time during the previous couple of years and he still wasn't satisfied with the way it had ended. Furthermore, a lot of his suspicions about DI Strong seemed to have some connection with Austin.

'Well, you know he was apparently killed in a hit and run accident but we never managed to find the driver. There weren't any witnesses or CCTV or anything,' Harris continued, 'and so it just remained as an unsolved incident.'

'Yes, I remember hearing that,' Campbell replied.

'Well one day, not long after we'd found out it was Andy Austin. Remember we didn't have

171

any ID on the body for a while, not for a few months,' Harris went on.

'Yes, yes,' Campbell replied, knowing all of this background detail and keen to hurry Harris along to whatever he was about to reveal.

'Well, the Guv asked me to go round to see Jack Wilson and put a bit of heat on him about the hit and run,' Harris said. 'Wilson had the same type of car we thought could have been involved in it, but, as far as I know, nothing more than that.'

'Wait, wait, wait,' Campbell said hurriedly. 'Let me get this straight. The Guv asked you to talk to Jack Wilson about the Andy Austin hit and run. The same Jack Wilson who killed Austin's family in the first place and started off this whole thing, Austin's whole mission of revenge?'

'Yes, that's right. I thought it a bit funny at the time,' Harris replied, 'but he's the Guv and I think he said he'd had a tip or something so I just went along with it. I guess there was some logic to it because of the connection between the two of them, Wilson and Austin. Maybe Wilson getting revenge? Austin did kill Jack Wilson's brother.'

'And what happened? What was Wilson like when you saw him?' Campbell probed further.

'Well, as I told the Guv, he seemed a bit nervous, but not any more than most people are when a policeman is asking them questions and examining their car,' Harris replied.

'And what did the Guv say afterwards when you told him?' Campbell asked his colleague.

'Nothing really, Harris replied. 'He just said something about it being a long shot but worth asking. I don't think we did any more with Wilson or anyone else for that matter. It's not a current case any more.'

Campbell nodded and took a long sip of his coffee. Lots of things were shooting around in his head. DI Strong, Andy Austin and Jack Wilson. They were all connected somehow, something other than the obvious, but Campbell couldn't work out how. It was another piece in the jigsaw, it might even be a key piece, but at this point in time Campbell just didn't know.

Chapter 25

Jack Wilson and Detective Inspector Strong were sitting at their usual table in their usual pub. The one which tried its best to look like a country pub, with various pieces of agricultural equipment dotted around outside and in the bar area, to try and give that impression. It was also the pub which was far enough out of town for it to be unlikely that anyone would ever recognise either of them there. It wasn't a place you would just stumble across or even make a plan for a special visit. In truth it was just an ordinary pub with no redeeming features, despite the agricultural decoration. It was just the type of place DI Strong needed for a private rendezvous and so it had become his and Jack's normal meeting place.

Jack had told the detective about his most recent visit to Club Extream and him finding that the listening device was no longer hidden under the table in their meeting room. Strong had suspected that might be the most likely explanation. So the Bolton gang had found it. But they wouldn't know who had put it there, who had been listening in on their conversations, or how long that had been going on for. However, if Strong had been a Bolton, he would have assumed the worst - that it was either the Romanians or the police who had been listening in on their conversations. Whichever way, their plans to take out Bog were blown. If the Romanians had planted the device, Bog would just ignore any text sent and not turn up, simple as that. Or, if he was clever, somehow lay a counter trap for them. Alternatively if it was the police who had planted the bug, then presumably they would be lying in wait for the Boltons.

And of course it had been Strong, and that had been his plan. Somehow Strong needed to find out what the Boltons were planning to do now, but he wasn't sure how he was going to do that.

'I could go back and plant another device,' Jack suggested, but Strong shook his head.

'Nah, that would be too risky. They'll be on the lookout for anything, or anyone, suspicious now,' Strong replied. 'And don't forget these are not nice people.'

'I know but I don't think they suspect me at all. In fact they actually called me the other day and asked if I could come in and have a look at some problems they're having with the lights in the main dance hall,' Jack replied, pausing to take a sip of his orange juice. 'They wouldn't have done that if they thought I'd planted a bug in their building, would they?' he added.

'Wait,' who called you exactly and what did they say,' Strong asked, suddenly alert.

'It was just the girl on reception, Leila. She's the only one I've met in there,' Jack replied. 'She's a bit dippy really, always on her phone, but she called me and said she'd overheard some of her bosses talking about the lighting problems in the main hall, and how they needed it fixed, and so she'd suggested me. They told her to give me a call and that's what she did.'

'Okay... and how did she have your number?' Strong asked.

'I think the first time I went in I had to fill out a form with some details, you know, name, address, phone number and the like,' Jack replied. 'I think Leila told me they had to have it on record or something for health and safety purposes in case there was a fire or something when I was in the building and they needed to know who was there.'

'Mmm...I'm not sure about that,' said DI Strong. 'It sounds a bit strange that they've never contacted you before and then suddenly, out of the blue, they ask you to come in, just after they've found the listening device. It's a bit suspicious. I think it might be a bit risky. They might suspect you planted the bug and this is just a ruse to get you in so they can interrogate you. Remember these people have a history of violence. If they suspect you've done this, or had anything to do with it, they won't hold back. They've probably got CCTV in the club and perhaps they saw you going into their meeting room.'

'Yeh they have got CCTV,' Jack replied, 'but I remember Leila telling me they only used it at night-time after I joked about them seeing her being constantly on her phone.'

'Yeh, well I think it's still too much of a coincidence,' Strong replied, taking a sip of his Coke. 'And I don't believe in coincidences. I'd

176

recommend you stay away from the club for a while till we get a better idea of what their thinking is. We'll have to think of a different approach. What did you say to Leila when she phoned and asked you to come in?'

'I told her I'd get back to her,' Jack replied. 'The truth is those club lighting rigs are a bit beyond my level of expertise and I wanted to buy some time to read up on them before I went back. I planned to watch a few videos on YouTube, so I had an idea of what I was facing.'

'Good,' Strong replied. 'Okay, so what I'd suggest is you just don't call her back and if she calls again, tell her you're sorry but you're too busy and those lights are a bit outside your skill set anyway. Tell her they'd probably be better getting someone else in to look at them. Someone with a bit of experience of those things. Then you should lie low for a bit. Don't go back to that club. Maybe take a few days away with your girlfriend Lucy until this dies down and we get a better idea of what the Bolton's might be planning next.'

'Okay, if you're sure,' Jack replied. 'What are you going to do to keep tabs on them then?'

'I don't know yet,' Strong replied and at this very moment he knew that, unfortunately, that was the truth. The plan he'd been formulating was now in pieces. It had been dependent on the Boltons' plan to attack Bog happening, giving him the chance to manipulate the scene to clear out as many of both of the gangs as possible. Now that wasn't happening, he'd have to think again but at this point there was no plan B and DI Strong was feeling pretty dejected.

Chapter 26

DI Campbell was back in the police station, sitting at his desk. He'd got in early today, skipping his gym session, and he was busy reading emails on his laptop, but with one eye on the far corner of the office. The corner where Marsha Hughes was stationed. He'd seen her come in a few minutes ago and sit down at her desk. He was now waiting for an opportunity to "bump into her", probably in the kitchen when she went to get herself a coffee. Campbell wanted to have a chat with Marsha to see if he could find out any more about DI Strong, following the conversation he'd had with DC Harris.

Of course he could just go over to her desk and ask her or even take her to a meeting room and question her there. But he knew he was unlikely to get anything from her if he did it that way. She would probably just deny everything. He couldn't make her talk. She wasn't a suspect in any crime. And there was also the likelihood that she would tell DI Strong that he had been asking questions. And that was the last thing he wanted. That could really backfire on him. He couldn't afford to make an outright enemy of Strong at this point. He didn't have enough on the Guv, even if there was anything to prove, and he knew he would lose credibility and probably his career if Strong found out Campbell was investigating him. DI Strong held a lot of power and also had powerful allies in the police force.

Campbell knew he needed to be subtle with Marsha. He needed to make her think that he was on her side, that he knew more than he actually did, that Strong and him had been working closely together when she'd apparently been helping the Guvnor.

He noticed some movement and, looking up, he saw Marsha pick up a white cup and walk across the office floor towards the kitchen. Campbell waited a few seconds, not too long, then he did the same, entering the kitchen, cup in hand, pleased to see there was only Marsha in the room.

'Oh, hi Marsha,' he said in a possibly over-friendly way, but Marsha didn't seem to notice.

She had her back to Campbell, carefully filling her cup with hot water from the silver kettle. Only when she was finished did she look around.

'Good morning,' she replied, smiling back at Campbell. 'How are you? How's your little baby, Rosey? I bet she's growing up isn't she?'

'Yes, she sure is,' Campbell replied, pleased that the conversation had started off in such a friendly manner and, keen to keep it that way, he put his cup down on the counter top and took his phone from his pocket. He walked towards Marsha as he tapped a couple of icons on the device.

'Here, I took some photos of her at the weekend. We went for a walk to the swing park,' he said, standing next to Marsha cupping his phone in his left hand as he scrolled through his photos with his right.

'This is probably the best one, she's smiling here, look,' he said raising the phone so Marsha could get a better look.

'Aww, she looks beautiful,' Marsha replied, looking at the screen and smiling. 'Make the most of it, they grow up quickly. I bet you're glad you're back working here again so you get to spend more time with her and your wife.'

'Yes, that's definitely been a bonus,' Campbell replied. 'It was difficult when I was in Leeds. I couldn't really get much time to see her, or Femi. Technology is great, we used to face time a lot, but it's not the same as being with them. I'm glad to be back here. Also, I really like working with DI Strong. I seem to learn so much from him, how he works, you know, stuff like that.'

'Yes, DI Strong is great, isn't he?' Marsha replied. 'He was so good to me with what happened to Dylan, you know. He was very kind. Everyone was. But the Guv especially. He didn't need to be really, but he was.'

'Well I think he wanted to,' Campbell replied, putting his mobile back in his pocket. 'He knew how you'd helped him in the past, you know with some of the cases we worked on. The stuff you did. He was always telling me how good you were at finding things out.'

Campbell reached up to the top cupboard and took out the coffee jar, putting a spoonful of the brown granules into his cup. He didn't really like instant coffee, but it was all that they had in the kitchen and it was better than nothing.

'Did he really?' Marsha replied, smiling, as she bent down to dispose of her tea bag in the bin below the sink. 'I didn't know that, that you knew I mean, or that he'd said anything.'

'Oh yes, we worked pretty closely together on some of the cases,' Campbell replied, as he filled his cup with boiling water from the kettle. 'I think he liked to use me as a bit of a sounding board on some of his thoughts and ideas. Like with some of the tasks he used to ask you to do. We would often discuss it first.'

'Oh, right,' Marsha replied, picking up her cup and taking a sip of her tea. This wasn't how she had understood the arrangement she had with DI Strong. The "*Strong and Marsha*" programme she used to imagine in her head. It was never *Strong and Campbell and Marsha*. He was never a major part in the series as far as she was concerned, so it was a bit surprising now to hear how much he had been involved.

'As I say I didn't really know what I was doing a lot of the time. Oh, that doesn't sound right does it?' Marsha laughed. What I mean is that he'd just ask me to do something or have a look for something. He didn't really tell me why, although sometimes I could guess, but I assumed if he wanted to tell me he would have done. He was, still is, the Guv.'

'Yes, that's right,' Campbell replied. 'He said you were very good at finding out bits of information for him, especially on the Anniversary

Killer case, which of course we worked closely together on. I remember, didn't he give you a list of names to look at one time? He wanted to find out where they were or something?'

'Well, I, emm, …he asked me to do a few things. Mostly just simple database searches and the like, but I was glad to help. It made a break from the normal daily routine,' Marsha answered, picking up her cup of tea. She was feeling a bit uncomfortable with DI Campbell's line of questioning. The Guvnor had never mentioned that he had told Campbell about their arrangement. In fact he had stressed, on several occasions, that it was just between the two of them. Strong and Marsha, which is where the idea for her fantasy TV series had come from. She decided she didn't want to say any more.

'I'd better get back, I'm supposed to be on a call in a few minutes,' she said as she eased her way past Campbell and left the room.

Campbell took a drink from his cup of black coffee, contemplating the conversation he'd just had with Marsha. She hadn't told him much really, but then again she hadn't denied any of it which was just as interesting. He sensed that she didn't want to say too much to him about what she had done, maybe Strong had sworn her to secrecy. Strong had definitely been using her for something though, and it was something that he didn't want anyone else in the team to know about. Could he have used Marsha to help track down Andy Austin? And then what? He took Austin to Leeds to mug an estate agent and take his phone? It just didn't make any sense. Maybe there was more to it than that. And where

183

did Jack Wilson fit in, if anywhere? Campbell was convinced there was something there, but he didn't know what. It was like having a jigsaw puzzle with no picture on the box and half the pieces still missing.

Chapter 27

'Where are we with that electrician guy, it all seems to have gone a bit quiet? Have we not been able to get a hold of him yet?' Ally Bolton asked his brother Charlie, as they sat together in one of the smaller rooms they used as an office at the rear of the Club Extream building. The room contained two silver aluminium chairs, a wooden desk and a tall coat stand in the corner. Pretty sparse, but a good venue for a one to one chat. It was one that Ally and Charlie used a lot, when it was just the two of them.

'Yeh, it has been a while hasn't it? The last I heard from Chopper was that we were supposed to be getting him in to have a word and see if he was the one that planted the bug in the meeting room,' Charlie replied. 'But that must have been a week or so ago now. I don't know what's happened. Let me give Chopper a call now and see what he says.'

Charlie dialled a number in his mobile phone and sat back in his seat, stretching out his legs and crossing them at the ankles. These aluminium chairs were okay for sitting in for a short while, but after a few minutes, Charlie's back began to get sore and he could feel the cold metal pressing into his spine. A few seconds later his call was answered and he began talking. Ally sat back in his own seat, waiting, while catching one half of the conversation. After a couple of minutes Charlie ended the call, placed his phone on the table, and looked across the room at his brother.

'So apparently we made up some story about an electrical fault with the lights and called him to come back in and fix it,' Charlie began. 'But he rang back and said it wasn't his area of expertise and that maybe we should get someone else. Leila has tried calling him a couple more times but she just keeps getting his voicemail and he's not calling her back.'

'Mmm…do you think he's smelt a rat?' Ally asked his brother.

'Yeh, that's what Chopper thinks, and it sounds like it might be the case,' Charlie replied. 'I don't see any other reason why he wouldn't take Leila's call. But Chopper knows where he lives and so him and Scotty are going to grab him one day. They'll chuck him in the van and bring him in and we can see what he's saying then.'

'Bloody hell, tell Chopper to keep Scotty under control,' Ally replied. 'You know what he can be like. We need to do this softly, softly. The guy might not be the one. The last thing we want is the police sniffing round accusing us of GBH or worse. I don't want him hurt at all. Not yet anyway, not until we've spoken to him. We need to keep him on our side if we can.'

'Yep, I'll have a word and I'll talk to Scotty myself too,' Charlie replied. 'I'll make sure they go gently on him. There's no point in asking him questions if he can't reply because his face is smashed in,' Charlie said, laughing at his own joke.

'Definitely not,' Ally replied, laughing along with his brother. 'And if we are clever about this, and he's a smart lad, we might be able to get some use out of him, especially if he's connected to the police or the Romanians. He might be able to tell us something about their plans and we also might be able to use him to feed them with false information about us. Let's get him in though and we'll see how it goes.'

Chapter 28

DI Strong and DC Knight had taken a break from the police station and were sitting closely together at a little table in the back area of the local café. Knight had been surprised when Strong had suggested going there, but she readily agreed. The way things were going, she needed all the help she could get and DI Strong had been nothing but helpful so far.

'It's good to get out of the office sometimes,' Strong explained. 'Some days I feel like I'm living my life in there, with meeting after meeting. I used to come here quite often when I was a DC like you, but I haven't been for ages. Getting out gives us a break from the norm and sometimes just a different location can help generate fresh ideas.'

DC Knight nodded and took a sip of her coffee, letting her boss steer the conversation.

'But, anyway,' Strong continued, 'I just wanted to have a more informal update on where we are, just you and me. Sometimes it's easier to do that outside the office. We can speak more openly here, without any interruptions or formalities. Obviously the Chief is still putting us under a lot of pressure to sort out the current disturbances at the clubs and elsewhere. It doesn't look good for us, and the newspapers are beginning to pick it up and make something out of it. Last week's fighting at the two town centre clubs made the front page of the local papers again and some of the national red tops are beginning to sniff around too. They like it when the police can be seen as apparently not doing a good job. It makes a good headline. The Chief hates when that happens. It's his worst thing, I think. The thing I've seen him getting most upset about.'

'The new PCC, Ms Gordon, is also causing a fuss,' Strong continued. 'She's trying to prove her worth by stirring things up a bit. The Chief can't stand her. He says she's just a career politician. She's never worked for the police and doesn't understand what it means to be a modern day police officer. No doubt he's right, but that doesn't mean she doesn't have any influence, and so he has to treat her carefully, with respect, and not say what he really thinks.'

'So, tell me Laura,' Strong continued, now smiling across the table at his colleague. 'As you can see it's not a pretty picture from the top. Where are we in reality with these gangs? Give me a quick update will you?'

Knight took another sip of her coffee, savouring the taste, while deciding how best to answer her boss's question. It was unusual for him to call her by her first name, but she was pleased that he had. It had been a tough day so far and it didn't seem to be getting any easier. She'd bumped into Marsha that morning and it brought back the memories of seeing Dylan's body lying there on the farmhouse floor along with Tony Fleming. Knight still felt a bit guilty about how they had closed that case, with Marsha not really knowing the truth about how her son had died. Marsha was a colleague and a good woman and maybe she deserved to know. But, as Strong had said, sometimes it's best not to know the whole truth, especially if it's only going to cause more pain. Knight didn't doubt that Marsha wouldn't have wanted her son to have committed suicide, what mother would? So maybe Strong was right. Maybe it was best that she would never know that. DI Strong had a lot of experience in these types of serious cases and how best to deal with the victims, and Knight was learning a lot from working with him. He also seemed to like working with her, which she hoped could only be good for her career. She still had her eyes on the vacant Detective Sergeant role but she knew it would be very dependent on how quickly she resolved the current gang problems.

As she sipped her coffee, hoping for some inspiration, she knew there were a couple of options. She could answer Strong optimistically and exaggerate some of the progress they had made, or she could be honest and own up to the fact that it was looking like it was going to be a long slog.

She chose the honest route, trusting that Strong would understand and continue to support her in any way he could. DI Strong was a powerful ally to have and Knight knew she had to keep him on her side. As she looked across the table at him smiling at her, waiting for her answer, she knew honesty was her only real choice.

She knew that Strong knew most of what was going on but experience had taught them both that it was often useful to go over things from the start again. Occasionally something could pop up that they'd missed initially. Early days of any investigation were usually pretty hectic and it was easy to overlook something that could turn out to be important.

DC Knight explained to Strong that it was definitely the Romanians who were causing the trouble in the clubs, but they were being very clever in their approach which made it extremely difficult to catch any of them. Their method seemed to be to start a random fight in the middle of a crowded dance floor, then throw a few bottles around to incite even more people to get involved. Once the fighting had got going, they'd then cleverly get lost amongst the mass of people and confusion and leave the club before any of the security staff caught them, or the police arrived. The trouble always happened in clubs that were run by the Bolton gang and those clubs were now beginning to get a reputation of not being safe places to go on a Saturday night. That would undoubtedly be harming the Bolton business in a number of ways. Not just the admission money at the clubs but, as the police knew, some of the clubs were also used as locations to carry out drugs and prostitution trade and so there would be a negative impact on that too. But, so far, the Boltons didn't seem to have reacted. At least not in any obvious way to the police.

191

'Have you managed to get any more information from your source Guv?' Knight asked her boss as she finished her summary of the current position. 'The one you had on the inside? He was very useful. Do you know if they are still planning to do the hit on Bogdan Popescu?'

DC Knight took a sip of her coffee. She was desperate for some good news. Something that would help them get a lid on the current situation, and hopefully put a couple of the senior gang members from either gang in prison. She didn't care who, but they needed to make some sort of arrest. She feared that anything less than that would reflect badly on her police record and her reputation as a detective. It would definitely harm her chances of getting a detective sergeant role anytime soon. At least Strong still seemed to be on her side, looking to help her, and that was critical if she was going to progress up the ladder. But she knew she couldn't rely on him unreservedly. Being the lead detective on this case, DC Knight knew that she needed to show some progress soon. The Chief had already brought in DI Campbell to work alongside her and the team, but they had let her continue to be the lead, so far. Knight guessed that if she didn't come up with some breakthrough soon, they could easily replace her with DI Campbell as the lead detective. They might even be looking at that now, she didn't know, but she desperately didn't want that to happen.

'No, unfortunately we've had a problem there,' Strong replied to Knight's disappointment.

She'd been desperately hoping Strong would have some information that could help them.

'In fact I've had to pull him out, temporarily at least,' Strong said. 'They were getting a bit suspicious and it was getting too risky to carry on with him at the moment. I think we can still use him, but I need to think about what the best way is to do that. But what it means is that the information we had about the hit being on Saturday night is now likely to be no longer valid. They may still be planning to attack Popescu at some point, but I'm pretty sure it won't be on Saturday.'

'Okay, well we are making some progress on the Romanians,' Knight said, trying to find something positive to add. 'At least we know who most of the main guys are and we have some information from our Romanian counterparts on their background. They're not a nice bunch, as you might expect. Most of them have pretty violent backgrounds and have spent time inside. The problem we're facing is because they're Romanian, they're pretty tight. They stick together and won't let any non-Romanians into any of the senior positions. And they won't talk to us in English, although they're perfectly capable of doing so. So although we know who they are it's still very difficult for us to get any inside information, or build up a real picture of what their long term plans are. Of course we can make some assumptions and guesses but….' Knight stopped talking and took another drink from her mug.

Likewise, DI Strong took a long sip of his coffee, thinking through possibilities. There wasn't an easy answer but he knew he had to do something and he needed it to be done quickly before things got completely out of hand. These scum, Bolton's gang and the Romanians should all be where they belonged, locked up in prison for a long time. Either that or dead, and Strong was going to have to do something about that before the Chief Constable ran out of patience and took it out of his hands.

Chapter 29

Chopper and Scotty were sitting in a dark grey transit van in the far corner of the Greenhill recreation centre car park. The car park was pretty full, with only a few empty spaces left.

It was almost eight pm on Thursday night and Jack Wilson was inside the large building to their left, playing six a side football with his mates. It was something Jack did every Thursday, unless the Thursday happened to fall on Christmas day or New Year's day. That was the only time that the Recreation Centre was closed.

Chopper and Scotty had arrived earlier that evening and watched Jack park his car and take his kit bag out of the boot, before walking across the car park and disappearing into the sports hall. Scotty was eager to make a move then, but Chopper had persuaded him to wait until later when it was a bit darker, and the car park would be less busy.

While Jack was inside the Centre playing his game of football, the car park began to get less busy as people finished their evening's activities and drove off in their cars. Jack's car was soon sitting pretty much on its own and so Chopper drove the van forward to an empty bay, a couple of spots away from it. He switched the engine off and the two men waited.

Chopper was leaning back in the driver's seat with Scotty sitting alongside him. Scotty was impatiently fiddling with the radio, trying to find a station that played music he recognised.

'What is it wi' aw this crap radio?' he complained. 'It's aw just noise noo-a-days. Whit's happened to real music, like Sinatra, Dean Martin, Sammy Davis? Ye never hear them any mair.'

'No, maybe it's because they all died years ago mate. You need to get into some of the more modern stuff Scotty,' Chopper replied, laughing at his friend. 'Like the stuff they play in the clubs. Just put it on Heart or something, they play some good music.'

Scotty fiddled with the radio some more, before giving up, leaving it on a sports station where they were discussing the latest England cricket match. Scotty slumped back into his seat with a sigh.

'And the sport, its aw English stuff, they hardly ever mention any Scottish teams,' Scotty exclaimed.

'Have you ever thought of moving back to Glasgow Scotty? I think you'd like it up there,' Chopper said laughing. 'You might find other people just like you, although I'm not sure that's a good thing!'

Scotty sighed, wriggled in his seat, and closed his eyes. In truth he'd love to go back to Glasgow, his home town, and one day he would. One day. But not just yet. He loved the city. The

196

streets, the people, the smell of it. Even the weather! Despite what people said, it didn't rain all the time. There were some dry days too! But overall, he knew where he was in Glasgow, and who he was.

But he also knew it was still too dangerous for him to return there. The last time he had been in his beloved city had been around ten years ago. He could still picture it as if it had been yesterday. He'd been working as a doorman at a city centre nightclub, The Blue Bottle. It wasn't a great job, and didn't pay very well, but it gave him enough to be able to do the things he wanted, which wasn't much. A few games of darts in his local pub, a daily trip to the bookies and some food and drink. Maybe an occasional football match. A Saturday afternoon watching his favourite team, Celtic. That was about it. He wasn't interested in much else. That was everything he needed.

At that time of his life, Scotty had only ever been out of Scotland once. That had been on a day trip to Newcastle with a woman he was seeing at the time. But it had been a disaster. She wanted to go shopping. He didn't. So Scotty had spent the afternoon in a city centre pub before getting the last train back to Scotland on his own. And he'd pretty much been on his own ever since. Most of the time he preferred it that way. He could come and go as he pleased, do his own thing with no-one else to worry about. He was living a simple life, but it was the life he wanted to live. But then everything had changed that one night ten years ago.

It was raining, as was usual for that time of year, early spring, and Scotty was doing a late shift on the door at The Blue Bottle, when a fight broke out inside. That wasn't an uncommon occurrence. A lot of young people who didn't know how much booze they could drink often ended up fighting. Boys and girls. It didn't seem to matter. Too much alcohol, a wrong look, and that was it. Cue for a fight.

They had a set routine at the Blue Bottle to deal with any trouble arising inside. Firstly they shut the front doors and then the doormen, usually there were three of them, joined up with the rest of the security staff to sort out the trouble inside the club. Normally it was pretty easy. A couple of slaps would calm the perpetrators down, before a quick march along the corridor, followed by ejection out the rear door of the club. A little nudge in the back to help them on their way. They were often too drunk to resist. If they wanted to keep fighting, they could carry on outside, alongside the rubbish bins, without disturbing anyone else. Usually though, they got the message and disappeared into the darkness. Hopefully going home to sober up. The doormen would then return to their station at the front of the club and the doors would be re-opened. Sorry for the slight delay.

This particular night had turned out differently though. As Scotty entered the main dance hall he could see four men facing each other in the middle of the floor, two on each side. The music had stopped playing and everyone else was standing back against the walls of the room, watching and waiting. It reminded Scotty of fights in the school playground where those not directly involved couldn't resist staying to observe.

The night club lights were still flashing as if nothing had happened and the club was carrying on as normal, but it wasn't. Scotty saw the light reflecting off something in two of the young men's hands. As Scotty got closer to them, he was able to confirm what he had suspected. Two of the men were holding knives, one on either side of the opposing factions. He could see the long, narrow silver steel blades, pointing down towards the floor. Scotty hated knives. In fact he hated weapons of any kind, except maybe a wooden club, if necessary. In general he believed a fight should only be carried out with fists and other parts of the body. Feet mainly, but his head had often been a useful weapon too. Using knives or guns wasn't right. It was a cop out as far as he was concerned, a coward's fight, and it often left a mess. Too much blood. It wasn't how he'd been brought up. His dad had never used weapons on him, just his fists and occasionally a leather belt, with nothing to clear up afterwards.

The four young men were too much in their own little world and didn't seem to be aware of the club's security team approaching them from the edge of the floor. The young men were too focused on each other, waiting to see who was going to make the first move. Who was brave, or stupid, enough to make that first stabbing lunge. Scotty could imagine the thoughts going through their heads now, weighing up the options. The ifs and buts. Attack or retaliate – which was it to be?

While the young men had their stand-off, considering their options, four of the security men, including Scotty, had split up so that one was now approaching each of the young men from the rear. When they were a few steps away, there was a slight pause before one of the security men gave an almost imperceptible nod of his head and, in complete synchronisation, the four security men each stepped forward and grabbed one of the young men from behind. It was like a training exercise, all done to clockwork and the whole thing was over in a matter of seconds. It was a well worked routine which they had all practiced a few times, as well as having had to do it once or twice in real life situations, although thankfully not too often. The two knives clattered to the floor as the young men's wrists were squeezed to almost breaking point. Scotty had taken one of the knife wielders, making him drop his knife and he now had him in a bear hug, his arms wrapped tightly around him, pinning the young man's own arms to his sides. Scotty started to march him across the floor, step by step, to the dance hall exit, his legs forcing the young man's legs to walk forwards. The other three men were being similarly escorted from the club ahead of Scotty. One of Scotty's colleagues had retrieved the two knives and the rest of the club clientele were beginning to move away from the walls, back onto the dance floor. The noise level in the room was gradually increasing as everyone found their voice again and started excitedly discussing what they'd just seen.

The man Scotty had grabbed was struggling, trying to break free, and shouting at his captor. It was mostly indecipherable, but undoubtedly non-complimentary. Scotty was trying to tune out, concentrating on just getting the job done, but he did catch quite a few swear words.

The man tried to turn his head to look at Scotty but Scotty sensed the movement and bit down hard on the man's ear, tasting the warm blood on his lips. That made the man scream and struggle even more, desperate to loosen himself from Scotty's grip. Scotty laughed and kept moving forward. They were now out of the main hall and Scotty forced his man to turn to the right and along a narrow corridor. He could see one of the other Security men a few yards in front of him moving more quickly, his hostage seemingly less problematic.

'Do you fucking know who I am?' the young man screamed, trying to turn his head again, but Scotty just ignored him and kept marching, forcing the man forward, step by step. He didn't care who he was. To Scotty he was just a stupid kid who needed to be taught a lesson by being thrown out of the club. And that was what he was going to do.

The two of them were now half way along the quiet corridor, heading towards the rear door. Scotty tightened his grip on the man's body, not wishing to give him any hope of being able to escape, which caused him to scream again. Scotty continued to frogmarch his captive as quickly as he could towards the door. His legs were pressed against the backs of the young man's legs making them move as if they were bound together as one.

Scotty smiled, he always enjoyed this part of the job. The physical bit. It didn't happen very often, usually he was just stood on the door all night getting bored. Having the same conversation over and over again as the young people filed past him into the club. So when there was a chance to get involved physically, Scotty relished it.

As he continued to move along the corridor with his hostage, he passed the three other security staff heading back towards the main dance hall, having already disposed of their own men.

'Need a hand with that one Scotty?' one of his colleagues asked as they passed by each other.

'Nah, yer okay.' Scotty replied and he kept walking slowly forwards, enjoying the moment, but especially looking forward to the ejection. That was always the best bit.

He could see the black rear door up ahead now, just a few metres away and he readied himself to push down on the metal bar so the door would swing open and he could dispose of this annoying little idiot. The young man seemed to have come to his senses and quietened down, probably realising there was no point in carrying on with his struggles. He was going to be thrown out, there was no two ways about it. Scotty tightened his grip with his right arm and loosened his left hand so that he could reach down to the metal bar. Sensing a slight pressure change, the young man managed to twist around slightly and, with his new position, he threw his head back, head-butting Scotty fully in the face.

'Yah wee bastard,' Scotty growled as he pushed the bar down and kicked the door open, still holding the man tightly with his right arm.

He grabbed the man with both arms again, turning him back around to face away from him and squeezing him tightly, despite his head aching and blood running down his face. That wasn't a new sensation to Scotty and he just carried on, stepping out into the yard outside. The other three ejected men were nowhere to be seen and Scotty pushed his man forward and started running with him still holding him tightly from behind. The man was taken by surprise and had no option than to move with Scotty forcing him forward at a pace. Scotty ran the young man straight into the side of a metal skip, full on, face first, the man unable to put his arms up to protect himself as Scotty only released him at the last second before impact. Scotty could hear the crunch of bones as he ground him further against the metal skip from behind. After a few seconds Scotty let go and the man slid down the side of the metal container, ending up prostrate on the cement slabs, his face resting against the bottom of the skip. Scotty gave him one more kick for the head-butt, and then a final boot in the face for luck, before he turned around and went back into the club.

The rest of the night passed peacefully without any further incident and Scotty thought no more about it. It wasn't the first time he'd had to teach someone a lesson and it wouldn't be the last. Hopefully the young man would get the message, but to Scotty it was all part of the job. A part that he quite liked.

The following day Scotty was sitting in the Horseshoe bar in the town centre, it was almost mid-day. Scotty was studying the horses in the Racing Post, when Malky sidled up next to him. Malky wasn't exactly a friend, more of an acquaintance, just someone that Scotty knew. In fact someone that everyone seemed to know. Malky always seemed to be around somewhere – in the pub, in the bookies, at the football. Scotty had even bumped into him in the supermarket once and jokingly accused him of being a stalker. But, in truth he seemed harmless and he had occasionally been a useful source of information. Malky was dressed as he always was, in a well-worn brown suit, cream coloured shirt and brown brogue shoes – scuffed at both front and back. His hair used to be ginger but it was now a mix of light brown and grey, swept up and back from his forehead.

'Ony tips fir the races this afternoon?' Malky asked him looking across at the paper spread out on the bar in front of Scotty.

'Aye, dinnae waste yer money,' Scotty replied. 'That's ma best tip,' he laughed.

'I heard guid things aboot The Lord's Hat runnin' in the three twenty at Kempton,' Malky replied.

'Oh, aye, where did ye hear that from?' Scotty asked.

'Oh jist somebody that knows somebody in the stable. Ye ken hoo it goes,' Malky replied, signalling to the barman to get his usual drink. 'Can I top ye up?' he asked Scotty.

'Aye go on then. Whit's happenin' then?' Scotty asked. Malky always seemed to have the latest gossip from the street.

'Well the big news is that Jackie McNeill's youngest boy got badly beaten up last night,' Malky started, stopping to take a sip of his drink and handing a ten pound note over to the barman. 'He's in the Royal Infirmary, apparently in a critical condition. They're no sure if he's gonna make it. Jackie's on the warpath. If he finds oot who did it, well…lets jist say I widnae want to be in his shoes.'

'Oh aye, where did it happen?' Scotty asked, trying to appear somewhat disinterested by not raising his head from the paper.

'They found him oot the back o' a club in town. Apparently he'd had a right good kickin', Malky replied. 'He probably deserved it like, everybody says he's a mouthy wee git but Jackie won't see it like that. He'll do anything fir his wee boy and he'll want his revenge.'

Scotty knew Jackie McNeill, not personally, but he had seen him around a few times and he certainly knew of his reputation. He was a big man in many senses of the word. He was also a violent man who headed up one of the main gangs in Glasgow and he was thought to have been responsible for a number of murders and assaults over the years. But nothing had ever been proven. The word was that he had a number of senior people on his payroll. Policemen, judges and politicians, that sort of thing. He was either paying them or he had something on them. Something he could use against them if he needed to. Although Scotty

205

wasn't averse to a bit of violence himself, he'd heard that Jackie McNeill could take it to another level with stories of men being brutally tortured for no particular reason, before then being killed. Scotty didn't want to get involved with a man like that. You would never know when he might turn on you. So far he'd managed to give him a wide berth.

'Mind ma seat a minute,' Scotty said, 'I've jist got to make a call.'

Scotty got up and walked through to the payphone in the back corridor of the bar. The light was gloomy as he dialled the number of the Blue Bottle and a man answered. Scotty recognised the voice as that of his boss, the club manager

'Dan, it's me Scotty.' Scotty said.

'Where are ye?' Dan replied.

'In town, havin' a pint,' Scotty replied.

'Ye better make it yer last and get oot of town, somewhere far away. Jackie McNeill's lookin' for ye. It was his boy ye threw oot last night and he's in a bad way. The word is McNeill's no takin' any prisoners. Ye better go now, but don't say I told ye to,' Dan advised, and hung up the phone.

Scotty walked back to the bar, picked up his paper and told Malky that something had come up and he had to go.

'Ye can have ma pint,' he shouted back to Malky as he left the pub.

Malky nodded knowingly as he watched Scotty go, and he murmured to himself 'Good luck Scotty,' as he turned his attention back to the two pints of beer now sat in front of him on the bar.

Scotty left the pub and headed straight to the main train station. He knew it would be too dangerous to go home, they'd have someone there waiting for him. There wasn't much in the flat anyway, just some clothes and old bits of furniture that weren't really worth much.

And that was the last time he'd set foot in his beloved hometown of Glasgow. He knew Jackie McNeill would never forgive him for what he'd done to his son, even if he had deserved it. Since leaving Glasgow, Scotty had heard through the grapevine that the young lad had suffered some sort of brain damage and he had been confined to a wheelchair ever since coming out of hospital. He'd also heard that McNeill knew it was him that had done it and if he ever found him, or if Scotty ever set foot in Glasgow again, he was a dead man. McNeill wasn't one for forgiveness and Scotty knew it wouldn't be a quick ending for him if McNeill managed to find him. So far, Scotty had managed to avoid that fate and he hoped that one day he would still be able to return home to Glasgow.

Scotty was suddenly awoken from his nap, and his thoughts of home, as he became aware of someone shaking his arm. For a split second he feared Jackie McNeill had found him.

'Wake up,' Chopper said. 'Jack Wilson will be out in a couple of minutes. We better get ready for him. You won't need that,' he added as he saw Scotty reaching for a leather cosh lying between the two front seats. 'Ally and Charlie said they didn't want him hurt or anything that might bring the

207

coppers sniffing around. We want him safe, in one piece, so we can see what his game is.'

Scotty made a face and put the cosh back down again. The two men got out of the van and walked round to the back of the vehicle, opening the rear door slightly. They stood to one side of the van, out of sight of anyone approaching from the sports centre but with a good view of the entrance door. A few minutes later they heard voices and watched as Jack and his mates came out of the bright doorway and headed into the darkness, towards their separate cars. After football they always met up in the pub for some post-match analysis and refreshments. Usually this involved picking on anyone who had had a particularly bad game.

'How did you miss that open goal? What a shocker!'

They all knew it was just friendly banter though and it was usually someone different each week. They were all pretty much the same standard which meant they all made the same mistakes.

Jack had his sports bag slung over his shoulder, and he pressed his key fob as he approached his car, the indicator lights flashing in response. As he was about to open the car door he heard a voice call his name and he looked up to see a man standing by the van which was parked next to his car. The man was wearing a dark sweatshirt with the hood up, and his face was in darkness. Jack couldn't make him out and he took a step towards the man to see if he could recognise who he was. Just then he was suddenly propelled forward as someone grabbed him from behind, wrapping their arms around his body, pinning his arms to his sides. It all happened in a moment, and before he could call out he was bundled into the back of the van. He ended up lying on the cold dark floor with someone else still holding him tightly and now lying on top of him. He opened his mouth to shout and felt something being pressed into it. A handkerchief, or some sort of rag. It made him cough. He sensed another person entering the van and, between them, the two men tied his hands and feet together and put some tape around his mouth, holding the gag in place.

Jack's eyes were slowly adjusting to the dark interior of the van but he still couldn't really see what was happening, or make any sense of it. It seemed he was being mugged, but why was he in the back of this van? He could make out the shapes of two men as they dragged him across the van floor and attached his wrists to a bar on the side of the vehicle. Jack tried to call out, but the mouth gag and tape were too tight for any noise to come out. The effort made him cough again and for a moment he thought he was going to be sick. He saw the two men leave through the rear door of the van, closing it behind them, making everything dark again.

Jack tried to bang his feet up and down on the van floor to make some noise and hopefully attract someone's attention. There must be other people in the car park? But he realised the men must have moved him onto a pile of sacks or blankets and the sound of his banging was muffled. He could hardly hear it himself so there was no chance anyone outside would.

The whole incident had taken less than a minute, the two men had carried it out like a military operation and Jack guessed it wasn't the first time they had done this. But why him? He heard the van engine start up and he banged his head against the side of the van as it suddenly lurched forward.

'Mind oot, ye almost hit that ither car,' Jack heard a voice say from the front of the van.

A Scotsman? What was this all about? Jack wondered. His prevailing thought was that it could only be something to do with the work he'd been doing for DI Strong. Strong had warned him that it could be risky and that the guys who owned Club Extream were not to be messed with. He knew they'd been trying to get him in and he'd just ignored them, not returned Leila's calls. Hoping they'd give up. It appeared they hadn't.

Maybe they'd found out that he'd planted the device? A shiver ran down Jack's spine. What would they do to him if they had found out? He thought this sort of stuff only happened in the movies, but here he was trussed up in the back of a van and God knows what was going to happen to him next. He needed to get his story straight and he thought back to what he and Strong had discussed.

Jack guessed he would soon find out who it was, and what they wanted, as the van came to a stop about ten minutes later and he heard the two men get out. He tensed up waiting for them to come and get him, wondering if he would have a chance to escape as they got him out the van, but nothing happened. It was all quiet and he realised the two men must have gone somewhere else, leaving him in the van. But for how long? He writhed around as much as he could trying to loosen his bonds but they were too tight. These guys had definitely done this before.

Chopper and Scotty had parked the van around the back of one of the clubs run by the Bolton gang. Chopper gave a sharp knock on an anonymous black door and it was slowly opened from the inside, a man's bald head poking out to see who was there. On seeing it was Chopper, he opened the door further and Chopper and Scotty stepped inside. Nothing was said and, as it was only the evening on a week night, the club was still fairly quiet. It would be nearer midnight before it started to get busy, even at weekends as people filled up on drinks in the pubs before heading into the club.

As the two men walked along the dark corridor they could hear music faintly playing somewhere in the distance, the volume not yet turned up. They stopped outside a dark wooden door and Chopper gave it a knock before reaching for the handle and opening it inwards.

They stepped into a large room with a long, rectangular table in the middle and a desk at the far end with a computer monitor positioned on it. Ally Bolton and his brother Charlie were sitting at the far end of the table, across from each other. They both looked up as Chopper entered the room with Scotty a few steps behind.

'Did you get him?' Charlie asked as they approached the table.

211

Chopper pulled out a chair and sat down before replying. Scotty remained standing.

'Yep, he's trussed up in the back of the van. What do you want us to do with him?' Chopper asked.

'Any problems?' Ally asked. 'Anyone see anything? You didn't have to hurt him at all?'

'No, it all went like clockwork,' Chopper replied. 'Even Scotty behaved himself this time,' he said, looking back at his colleague and laughing.

'Aye, lucky fir him, the wee man behaved himself', Scotty replied, laughing along with the rest of the room.

'Okay, so I think let's bring him in here. Don't let anyone see you though,' Ally replied. 'Shut the far corridor door and tell John not to let anyone in until you're done. When we get him in here, me and Charlie will have a chat with him and see what he is saying.'

'Dae ye want me to gie him a slap, soften him up a wee bit first?' Scotty asked hopefully, smiling.

'No,' Charlie replied, laughing. 'Just bring him in, unharmed please. We want to keep him on our side at this point. He might be useful for us. Did you get his phone?'

'Yep,' Chopper replied. 'I've passed it to Eddie. He's gonna have a look through it and see if he can find anything on it that might help us.'

A few minutes later, Chopper and Scotty re-entered the room pushing Jack in front of them. They made him sit in a seat at the table and removed his ties and gag before both of them left the room leaving Jack to face the Bolton brothers. Jack didn't know what to do or say and the room stayed silent for a few seconds until Ally Bolton spoke.

'So, Jack Wilson, the quicker we do this the better for all. We can all get back to what we were doing and everyone is happy. I'm sorry we had to bring you in like this but you did seem to be avoiding us. If you're smart, which I think you are, you'll be out of here before the pubs shut. But if you piss me about then you'll be spending some time with my Scottish friend and he can be a bit nasty sometimes. Believe me you don't want to do that. Do you understand?'

Jack's mouth was dry and he licked his lips and nodded his head in response, not yet trusting himself to speak. He wasn't sure how much danger he was in and he didn't want to do anything that might make things worse. At this point he thought it was best just to let these two guys lead and see where it went. That was what Strong had said. The two guys both looked quite tough and Jack guessed they weren't to be messed with.

'Good,' Ally replied. 'I knew you was a sensible lad. So, we know you planted a bug in one of our meeting rooms. I need you to tell me who asked you to do that and why? And also what you, or someone else, heard from the device.'

Jack lipped his licks again, thinking, trying to buy some time. Apart from looking a bit tough, the two men across the table from him looked normal enough. Just the sort of men you might pass in the street. But then they couldn't be normal could they? They'd kidnapped him and brought him to

213

somewhere, god knows where, and had issued veiled threats of violence, which he was pretty sure they would carry out if needed. He definitely didn't want to take the risk. From that perspective these men weren't normal.

Jack and DI Strong had discussed this sort of scenario, getting caught, and the policeman had advised him what to do. He had the basis of a story ready which was largely the truth.

'Just tell it a bit at a time, make it look like they're getting it from you,' Strong had advised him. 'But if it looks like they're going to get violent, don't take any chances, don't hold anything back. If they're clever they'll be thinking they might be able to use you to help them in the future, so they'll want to keep you sweet.'

But Strong had also stressed that these guys were not to be messed with. Now that he was here with these two men sitting in front of him, Jack thought that was probably the best approach. He hoped that if he told them some of the truth, a refined version of it, a bit at a time, then they'd let him go. He remembered Strong's advice to let them draw it out of him, otherwise it would seem too easy and less believable. He looked towards the man that had spoken.

'I'm a sparky, an electrician. It was just a job I was asked to do,' Jack began. 'They paid me cash and I didn't ask any questions. That was it, Nothing else.' Jack stopped talking.

The other man leaned forwards, his elbows resting on the table in front of him. Jack could see he had big, solid looking hands, both heavily tattooed with blue ink.

'Who asked you to do it?' Charlie asked, staring straight at Jack.

'I'm not sure,' Jack replied. 'Someone called me up when I was on another job. I scribbled down some details and that was it really.'

Charlie sighed loudly and Jack shifted uncomfortably in his chair. Had he said enough, or too much already? It was difficult to judge. He imagined one of these men could suddenly just punch him in the face without him being able to do anything to defend himself. They were sitting that close to him, he wouldn't have time to react. What would he do then? Just tell them everything? Plead for mercy?

'You said they paid you cash. How did they do that?' Charlie asked, his bright blue eyes burning into Jack's face.

'Emm, well, emm, not cash I emm, they transferred the money I meant,' Jack replied realising he was floundering, and hoping that they bought it. The story he and Strong had come up with had a few "mistakes" in it so it would look like they were catching him out and making him gradually confess to the truth. He hoped it was working but he might have messed up already. Maybe he had been too obvious? His body tensed up waiting for the punch.

Ally made a point of looking at his watch and then smiled at Jack.

'Okay, look Jack. I know you're in a difficult position here,' Ally said. 'All we need to know is who you were working for and what they know. Just tell us that and then you can go. That'll be it all over. I promise you. No-one will know what you told us.'

'Was it the police?' Charlie asked him, again directly.

Jack paused for a second then nodded. 'Yes, yes… it was,' he said, nervously. 'They made me do it. They threatened me with something. It was something I did in the past, a while ago.'

'Okay, who was it?' Ally asked him.

'I honestly don't know,' Jack replied, shaking his head. 'He said his name was Detective Smith but I don't know if that was his real name. I think he might have just made that up. He said the less I knew about him the better.'

'Mmm, Smith. And what did this Smith ask you to do exactly?' Charlie asked.

'Just put in the device, under the table in that room you found it in,' Jack replied. 'That was all, nothing else. That was about a month ago and I haven't heard anything from him since.'

'Did he tell you why he wanted you to plant the device?' Ally asked Jack.

'No, he didn't say,' Jack replied. 'He said the less I knew the better, but if I didn't do it, well then he was going to charge me with something I did a while back. I didn't have a choice really. I thought if I did it then that would be it. It would get him off my back and that seems to have been the case. I'm sorry I, emm, did it to you guys. I didn't know whose place it was. He didn't tell me and I didn't want to know, to be honest.'

216

'Did he tell you anything at all about what he'd got from the bug, or what he was hoping to find out?' Ally asked Jack.

'No, nothing at all,' Jack replied. 'He said up front the less I knew the better.'

'Why did you come back into the club a few weeks ago and go into the room?' Charlie asked.

'He, Smith, called me and asked me to check the bug,' Jack replied, nodding his head. 'I guess you guys must have found it then and he wasn't getting anything from it but he didn't tell me why. Just do it he said.'

Ally relaxed back in his chair. He knew Jack wasn't telling them everything, but that was fine for now. He had confirmed that he was the one who had planted the device, and that it was the police who had been listening in on it. That was good to know and it was enough for now. At least Bog and the Romanians didn't know what they were planning for him, unless they also had someone on the inside, but Ally doubted that. They were new on the scene and it took time and knowledge to find out enough about the police to be able to use that to get a police source. Someone on the inside who could provide them with any useful information.

Ally was content that he'd learned enough from Jack for now and, although he knew there was more to come, he didn't want to force it at this point through threats or actual violence. He could see that Jack Wilson could potentially be useful to them in future with his connections to the police. He looked across the table to his brother and they both nodded.

'Okay Jack. We're done for now,' Ally said. 'Don't tell anyone about this meeting. And I mean no-one,' Ally emphasised, leaning forward, his face a few inches from Jack's. 'Not your mates or family. Not the police. If you do, we'll get to know and I promise you, you'll wish you hadn't.'

Ally Bolton sat back again and smiled.

'You're a sensible guy Jack. Keep it that way. The lads will drop you back. Don't worry you can sit up front this time,' he added laughing. 'Sorry about the ride last time but it was proving difficult to get you here. I'll get them to give you a few VIP tickets for the club for you and your mates. We'll give you a few of the girls as hostesses too. I'm sure you'll all have a good time,' Ally laughed.

Charlie got up and left the room leaving Ally and Jack sitting in silence. Jack was frightened to speak in case he messed anything up. It seemed he'd got off pretty lightly, although he wasn't out yet and he was still nervous something else was going to happen. He wasn't sure he could trust these people. Would they keep their word?

A short time later Charlie came back into the room with Chopper. Chopper was holding a mobile phone and he handed it to Jack before taking his arm and leading him out of the room. Jack recognised it was his own phone. Chopper closed the door behind them.

'Did Eddie find anything useful on the phone?' Ally asked his brother as he sat down at the table again.

'Nothing obvious, he says,' Charlie replied. 'He's taken a copy of some stuff and says he'll have a proper look tomorrow but nothing jumps out to him at the moment.'

'Okay, well I think we've got enough from Jack Wilson for now, but we'll get him back in soon,' Ally said. 'He knows more than what he told us, like who his police contact really is, I'm sure of it. But we need to go easy on him. He could be a useful guy to us, another inside line to the police, when we persuade him it's in his best interests to co-operate with us. If not, then it's his loss.'

Chapter 30

Although Jack had sat alongside Chopper in the front of the van on the way back to the recreation centre, and the mad Scotsman hadn't come with them, he still didn't feel totally confident that Chopper was just going to drop him back at his car. But that's exactly what he did. They hadn't spoken throughout the journey, the only noise being the radio which was tuned into a sports station. Jack couldn't concentrate on it, he was still on edge. He'd been able to get a better look at Chopper on the return journey and he could see he was a big man with a full head of black hair brushed back over his scalp. Jack knew he'd be no match for him if things got physical.

But, despite Jack's fears, when they arrived back at the recreation centre car park, Chopper just smiled and handed Jack an envelope before letting him out and then driving off.

Jack stood by his car for a few seconds looking around. He'd been here just an hour before and so much had happened in that short period of time. He'd been abducted, bundled into a van, tied up, threatened with violence and then questioned by a couple of thugs. That's what they were – thugs.

Although they were dressed smartly and looked like normal people, normal people wouldn't do that sort of thing. He suddenly realised he had an envelope in his hands and he stared at it for a few seconds before tearing it open. Inside there were a dozen silver and blue, embossed VIP tickets to Club Extream, all with Jack's name on them. Oh well that was something, he thought. Some compensation for what he'd just been through. He looked at the time on his phone, wondering about going to the pub to join his mates, but he guessed they'd have gone by now. They usually only stayed in the pub for one or two drinks, with it being a week night and the fact that they were all driving. And, even if they were still there, they'd only want to know where he'd been. Questions. Questions he didn't want to have to face at the moment.

He noticed he'd had a missed call from Jason, one of his group of friends, obviously wondering where he had got to. He decided to make up some sort of story about problems with his car or something and call him back tomorrow. Right now he had another, more important call, he wanted to make. He got into his car and dialled a number. As he waited for an answer he watched two young women walk across the car park wearing pink and black leggings and baggy grey sweatshirts with branded sports bags hanging down from their shoulders. They got into a dark blue car parked in the far corner of the recreation centre car park and a few seconds later the car drove off.

'Hello,' a voice spoke into his ear, bringing him back to focus.

'Detective Strong? It's Jack Wilson. Can you talk?'

Chapter 31

Strong was feeling worried after hearing Jack's story. It had always been a risk putting Jack back in to the club, and so it had proved. Maybe he shouldn't have done it. They were now back at square one, the only good thing being that at least he knew what they knew now. The Boltons would know that the police were aware of what they had been planning for Bog. They would undoubtedly change their plans and the difficulty now was that Strong would have no way of finding that out. What they were planning next. He fully expected they would still carry out some sort of attack to disrupt the Romanians, to warn them off, but now he didn't know what, where or when.

It was also interesting to see that Jack hadn't been physically assaulted in any way. The Boltons had threatened him, but the way Jack told it, the meeting had been quite civil after they had got him there. Jack hadn't known who he had encountered, both in the car park or at the meeting room. No names were mentioned but he did remember one of them had a Scottish accent and DI Strong assumed that would have been one of the Bolton's gang, known as Scotty. One of the gang's heavies. From his description of the two men Jack had met in the room, Strong assumed it would have been the Bolton brothers. They would have been the most likely ones to question him.

The fact that Jack hadn't been beaten up, not taught a lesson for helping the police, led Strong to suspect that they hoped to use Jack again sometime in the future. It made sense. They effectively had him where they wanted him and they knew he had some sort of connection into the police which they might think they could use to their advantage at some point. So they would want to keep him safe for now, keep him onside, but Strong knew that wouldn't always be the case. He had a shelf life of usefulness to them. There was no doubt Jack was in danger and it was Strong's responsibility to make sure nothing happened to him, if he could. He needed to get Jack off the scene until he sorted out these gangs and got some of them locked away. And that was something he now needed to do even more quickly.

DI Strong still had a nagging thought about how the Boltons had found the bug in the first place. From what Jack said it was well hidden and secure, not something that would have been easily found unless you were specifically looking for it. Unless you knew it was there, somewhere in the room. Had someone told them? It was only Strong and Jack that knew about the device. It wasn't particularly legal and Strong hadn't even told Knight about it, preferring to let her think that he had a CHIS in on the inside.

Strong considered that one of the ways they might have found it was if someone had told them that the police knew about their plans to attack Bog. They'd then put two and two together, realised where these plans had been discussed, and searched the room, finding the device. If that was the case, the worrying thing was that "someone" could be a member of the Serious Crime Team. Very few people outside of the team knew that the police had the details of the planned attack and so it was possible that the Boltons had a mole in Strong's team. He was going to have to be careful what information he shared going forward and he also needed to get that message across to his senior team.

He called DI Campbell and DC Knight into his office to explain his concerns. He felt totally confident that he could trust them both. The three detectives took their seats at the long table in his office, Knight sitting across from Strong and Campbell positioned to his right.

'Okay, so here's what I think. The Boltons somehow found out that we knew of their plan to take out the Romanian gang leader Bogdan Popescu,' Strong began. 'Without giving too much away, I believe one of the possible scenarios is that they got this information from someone in our team.'

'What? You think we've got a mole in the team?' Campbell asked.

'I don't know for sure, but it's certainly a strong possibility,' Strong replied. 'I know we all hope there isn't, and we believe they are a good team, but it wouldn't be the first time someone in the police has had something used against them. When I was a younger detective we had a DS leave suddenly. The rumour was he had a gambling addiction and had fallen into the hands of a major criminal.' Strong paused and took a breath.

'I think at this point we just need to be a bit careful on what we tell any of the team,' Strong continued. 'It's a need to know basis, which is why I've kept this meeting to just the three of us for now. I may be wrong, and I hope that I am, but I'm not taking any chances until we get this gang mess cleared up.'

'Have you had any more information from your CHIS again, or is he still out?' DC Knight asked her boss.

'Yes, I'm afraid so. I think we may have lost him for a bit, the situation is a bit too risky at the moment,' Strong replied.

'So what do we do now then?' Campbell asked. 'We know the Romanians are causing trouble and the Boltons would like to run them out of town, but we don't know what their plan is any more. I assume they'll have to come up with something different now that they know we know about their original plan to get Bog.'

'Yes, I think you're right,' Strong replied. 'So it was for that very purpose that I called the meeting of we three today. I wanted us to bang our heads together and see if there was anything else, anything different perhaps, that we can do to stop this current round of trouble. Let's go back to basics and see if we can come up with any fresh ideas.'

The three detectives spent the next two hours discussing the situation. DC Knight summarised where they currently were with the investigation, which, in a nutshell was making some progress, but only very slowly. Neither of the other two detectives were able to come up with any great suggestions, no golden nuggets, to improve what the team were already doing. It was just good basic police work, but that was never quick, and this was a time when they needed to make some sort of leap forward.

After coming to a dead end on any improvements to the current activities, Strong then steered his colleagues towards brainstorming any alternative ideas they might have. Both he and DC Knight came up with the embers of a few possibilities, ways they could do things differently that might expose some of the criminal activities, but they were quickly doused by DI Campbell who pointed out the legalities of what was being proposed. Strong thought if they played it cleverly they could work their way around any areas of concern, but he didn't want to push it too far with Campbell in the room. He knew Campbell had already had his doubts in the past about some of his methods and he didn't know the full picture. Strong didn't want to give him any more to worry about and he half wished he'd just held this meeting with DC Knight. They might have been able to take some of their alternative ideas a bit further and maybe make something more of them, but he knew he couldn't exclude Campbell without him becoming suspicious about what was going on. After all, although Knight was leading this case, Campbell was a more senior detective.

So, by the end of the meeting they hadn't been able to agree on any new major approach to ending the gang war. In fact the only thing they had managed to agree on was to keep doing what they were currently doing and reconvene in two days time to review the situation once again. DI Strong watched the two detectives leave his office, knowing they were all running out of time and the team, or he on his own, needed to do something more quickly.

Chapter 32

Chopper and Ally Bolton were sitting at a table in The Horse and Groom. It was a pub Ally often came to when he wanted to meet anyone for a quiet chat. It wasn't busy today and Chopper and Ally had a choice of tables, opting for one they regularly used in a corner of the bar, by the large stained glass window. There was no-one else within earshot of them so they were able to talk freely.

Ally was pissed off. Chopper had just told him that their plans to attack Bog would have to be put on hold for a while. He had found out that Bog's ex-wife had taken her daughter and son on holiday. It seems they'd gone to Portugal for a couple of weeks.

'Apparently it was a spur of the moment thing,' Chopper explained. 'Her cleaner is one of our girls at the club. One of the dancers, and she said the wife had just decided the day before and that was it. She told our girl that she was going away to Portugal for a few weeks and she'd be in contact when she was coming back, so she could have the house ready for her. You know, nice and clean. That was it, nothing we could do. I guess we'll just have to wait till she comes back before we do our hit on Bog. The plan's still good, but obviously we will need to change the date.'

'Yeh, meanwhile Bog and his crew continue to mess us around and try and nick our business,' Ally replied angrily.

He stood up and paced around the room, thinking about the news Chopper had just brought him and what they could do about it.

'I was really hoping we could put an end to this now,' he said. 'We need to have a think and see if there is anything else we can do. I'm not happy at waiting another few weeks, and we don't even know how long she's going to be away do we?'

'No, it seems pretty open ended,' Chopper replied. 'Obviously we're hoping it's just a week or two but we don't know. I suppose the kids will need to come back to school or college or whatever at some point. As soon as our girl hears, she'll let us know.'

Ally had stopped pacing and was now sitting back in his seat. His elbows were wedged on the table, his hands cupping his chin, his head bowed forward. He was thinking, but getting nowhere. After a few moments, he sat back up straight, with a sigh.

'Okay, I can't think of anything else we can do at the moment and I need to get going,' Ally said, looking at his watch. 'Charlie and me have got a meeting with a potential new supplier. It could be good business and definitely something we don't want the Romanians getting their dirty fingers on. Can you contact the rest of the guys and tell them what's happened? Tell them we need to meet up tonight at the club and see if there's anything we can do meantime, while the wife's away. I don't like the idea of us just sitting around doing nothing. The Romanians will be laughing at us.'

'Yeh, I know what you mean. I'll let the guys know and see you later,' Chopper replied as the two men got up and left the pub.

Chapter 33

It was only eight o' clock and Scotty was on his fourth pint of beer. He had felt angry and frustrated when Chopper had told him that they weren't going to do the hit on Bog just yet. He'd been looking forward to it. A bit of excitement. Now it had been put off for a few weeks, maybe longer. Nobody seemed to know. And all they were going to do was meet up and talk about it! Again! What was the point of that? Scotty had a lot of time for Ally Bolton and his brother Charlie. They'd been good mates to him and helped him a lot after he'd started working for Tony Fleming. But Tony would have sorted the Romanians out quicker than this. All this talking, it was just a waste of time. And it was letting the Romanians get more settled, letting them build up their resources. Why couldn't they just get on and do it? Take Bog out, or smash up the snooker hall, just do something!

Scotty hadn't really understood the whole idea of the mobile phone and text and all that stuff. He'd switched off during the discussion. It had all seemed unnecessarily complicated. If it had been up to him he would have just gone out and shot the guy. That's how they used to do it in on the telly in the old days. None of this flaffing around with technology and setting traps. It wasn't needed. It was simpler than that to kill someone. You just pointed a gun at them and pulled the trigger. Or kicked them until they stopped moving. It was pretty basic stuff.

Scotty had done it before, once, when he was back in Glasgow. It had been a drunken dispute over his football team, Celtic. Scotty had been minding his own business, just having a few drinks on a Saturday night, when this guy had taken some sort of dislike to him. Apparently because Scotty was wearing a Celtic football shirt, green and white hoops, and the other man didn't like it. He was insistent that Rangers were a better team and he started pushing Scotty and calling him all sorts of names. A few of the other people in the bar tried to calm him down, but he wouldn't listen to them. He was like a dog with a bone. He'd challenged Scotty to "come outside" so Scotty had obliged, taking a sip of his pint before climbing down from his bar stool and following the man towards the pub door. The two men walked around the side of the pub, down an alleyway and, before the man had time to say anything, Scotty had head-butted him. Hard. There was a loud cracking sound and the man's legs gave way. He fell forwards onto the ground, onto his knees then his body, and finally his face hitting the wet pathway with another loud crack. Scotty stood behind him and kicked him once in the groin before walking around his prone body and then jumping on the back of his head, bending his knees as he landed to deliver the maximum force. He looked at the man lying there, crumpled up, before turning and going back into the pub to finish his pint. He heard some days later that the man had been found dead, but there were no witnesses. Although the bar had been busy, nobody had seen anything. That's how it was.

Scotty finished his pint and decided to have a walk to the Snooker Hall. He thought he had a bit of time before Ally's meeting and, even if he didn't, he wasn't that bothered about missing the meeting anyway. It would just be a waste of time and Chopper would tell him what had happened without him needing to waste a couple of hours of his life being there.

Scotty hadn't played snooker for a long time, probably not since he'd been a teenager, but from what he could remember, he hadn't been bad at it in his younger days. If he'd kept playing, who knows he could have been a superstar!

There was a lot of money in snooker now. They were never off the telly, there was always some competition going on. But not back then when Scotty was in his teens. At that time it was only played by men in dark, smoky rooms, often for a bit of cash, but nothing like the amount they could make now. Still, Scotty fancied a game today. Maybe he'd find someone to play against, perhaps even make a bit of money from it, just like when he was a teenager. He smiled as he thought about those days, back in Glasgow, and he wished he was back there now.

Soon Scotty was at the Snooker Hall and he entered the building and walked upstairs to the first floor, pushing open a couple of heavy wooden doors and stepping into the main snooker room. He stood for a second letting his eyes adjust to the dim light. It was still dark, but not smoky any more. Not since they'd banned smoking indoors. Although Scotty didn't smoke himself, he never saw the point of it, he still missed the smoky atmosphere you used to get in places like this, snooker halls and pubs.

Inside the large room, there were twelve snooker tables, set in three rows of four brown and green tables. Ten of them were occupied, a bright overhead light shining down on each of the busy tables, reflecting off the multi coloured balls and the dark green baize. The snooker players were walking around the tables, wooden cue in hand, sizing up their next shots. All of the players were men. The other two tables stood alone in the darkness, as if they'd gone to sleep. At the far end of the room there was a countertop, where a man stood leaning on the counter, with a rack of cues on the wall behind him. To the right of that, there was a small bar with a dim light and a few people standing around with drinks.

Scotty walked along one side of the long room, eyeing up the players at the tables as he passed them to see if he recognised anyone. There didn't seem to be anyone he knew and no-one acknowledged him. He heard a few snippets of conversation as he made his way towards the bar, but nothing that he could make out. In the old days, back in Glasgow, he would have known everyone in a place like this. And everyone would have known him. It was much more friendly there, unless there was a fight, but even then they'd all be mates again the next day, until the next fight.

As he approached the bar he recognised one of the men standing there. It was Kenny Mac and he was on his own. Not his favourite person in the world, but at least it was someone he could stand with while he was having a drink. He didn't want to be a "Billy no mates." Kenny saw him coming towards the bar and beckoned him over.

'Hey Scotty, how's it going mate? I haven't seen you in here before,' he said, smiling at Scotty.

'Yeh, no been in for a wee while,' Scotty replied and he nodded at the barman who started to pour a pint.

While Scotty waited for his drink, Kenny prattled on about something or other, but Scotty had tuned out. He quickly remembered why Kenny Mac wasn't his favourite person. Basically, he just talked a lot of crap. He seemed to have an opinion on everything, be it politics, sport or just some random TV programme. Luckily Scotty's pint arrived quickly and he took a sip of it, letting the cool liquid stay in his mouth, savouring the bitter taste, before swallowing it down. Kenny had stopped talking so Scotty nodded at him, as if he had been listening.

'So shall we have a game then? Scotland versus England? Twenty quid for the winner?' Kenny asked smiling at Scotty.

Scotty couldn't resist a challenge.

'Twenty quid? Make it forty an' I'll play ye,' he replied.

The two men walked across to one of the unlit tables and put their drinks down on the ledge at the side of the room. There were two cues lying on the table and Scotty took hold of them, sizing them up before he decided which one he wanted. He pressed his thumbnail into the tip of the other cue before laying it back down on the table. Kenny had switched on the overhead light and was setting up the balls as Scotty chalked his cue.

'You can break,' Scotty said, conscious that he hadn't played for many years and didn't want to risk missing the whole pack on his first shot.

Kenny bent down, pulled his cue back and lined up the white ball in front of him. He pushed his arm forward and the ball sped down the table, crashing into the triangle of reds at the far end, balls cannoning off each other, hitting cushions and moving in every direction. He stood up smiling, seemingly satisfied with his shot.

'Your go,' he said, standing at the end of the table with his cue held vertically in front of him.

After a few minutes, both men had potted a few red balls and Scotty was beginning to relax and enjoy himself. He was feeling like a teenager again and he'd actually played a couple of half decent shots. A red and a black, followed by a red and a pink. Not bad at all. Kenny had just missed an easy one and Scotty was growing confident that the forty pounds would soon be his. He might even be able to tempt Kenny into a "double or quits" game to get him up to eighty pounds. He potted another red ball, and as he leaned over the table to play his next shot, a black for seven more points, he saw two men walking towards the table out of the corner of his eye. As they got closer to the table, Scotty stood up

237

from his shot, holding his cue in front of him. One of the men walked right up to him and said,

'We're on here.'

Scotty looked at him. He had a strange accent, definitely Eastern European. He was slightly taller than Scotty and, under his tight fitting t-shirt, he looked more muscly. Definitely a regular at the gym. He was an ugly bastard though.

'There's a table over there,' Scotty replied, disinterestedly, pointing at the other unused table with his cue.

'This is our table,' the man replied, calmly. 'Fuck off.'

He stepped forward a pace so his face was up close to Scotty's. Scotty could feel the man's breath on his face. It was too good an opportunity to pass up. With barely a movement, Scotty head butted the man on the nose and he staggered back a few paces. A Scotty classic. The man shook his head and ran at Scotty in a rage but Scotty was ready for him and he stepped aside and whacked him on the back of his head with the snooker cue as the man ran past him and into the table. Scotty laughed, but then he felt someone grabbing him from behind, circling their arms around him and gripping him tightly. He struggled to break free but the man's hold was too tight. He kicked back with his right foot, trying to catch the man's shin but it was just clean air. Suddenly there was a group of men in front of him and he winced as he saw them all raise their snooker cues and start to rain blows down on him. He tried to break free, but could feel himself weakening as he was repeatedly struck on

238

the head and body. After a while he lost consciousness and the man who was holding him let go and he slumped to the floor.

It had all taken less than a minute and Kenny had just stood there, on the other side of the table, transfixed, still holding his own cue. He slowly sat down on the bench, sinking into the darkness, keen to stay anonymous. He quite liked coming here for a drink during the week.

'Let's get him out of here,' one of the men said and a big man stepped forward and picked Scotty up. He slung him effortlessly over his shoulder and waited.

'What do we do with him?' the big man asked.

'Let's take him to Bog and see what he says,' the other man replied.

Kenny watched as the two men walked out of the snooker hall, the big one with Scotty draped over his shoulder, unconscious, following the other man. The rest of the snooker players had all returned to their tables and were getting on with their games as if nothing had happened. Kenny took another sip of his drink before quietly making his way along the dimly lit side of the room till he reached the door. He opened it as quietly as possible and slipped through the gap. He cautiously looked around and was relieved to see that there was no-one else in sight. He guessed the men had taken Scotty to see their boss in another room in the building and he silently exited the building before marching quickly down the street in search of a friendly pub.

'Do we know who he is?' Bog asked as he looked at the slumped body, still unconscious, lying prone on the chair in front of him.

They were in an office at the back of the snooker hall. Bog was sitting behind a wooden desk and the rest of the room was pretty bare apart from a few chairs dotted around on the wooden floor. It was the room Bog used to conduct most of his growing business, his empire as he liked to think of it. He thought that was funny as he was taking the business away from the British, who always seemed to go on about how great they were, and how they had a British Empire. Great Britain they called themselves. Bog laughed at that too.

'We think he's one of the Bolton gang. We think his name is Scott,' the other man replied. He was in fact Bog's cousin, Alexandru. Alexandru had come to England at the same time as Bog and his family, and he was now more commonly known as Alex. He was widely seen as being second in command to Bog in the Romanian gang.

'He's supposed to be a bit of a hard man. A bit of a wild man, they say,' Alex added.

'Do we know why he was here? Just looking to cause us some trouble?' Bog asked, partly answering his own question.

'Yes probably,' Alex replied. 'What should we do with him?'

'Just dump him somewhere. In a skip or something, maybe some waste land,' Bog replied. 'But not somewhere near here and make sure no-one sees you. I'm not ready for an all-out war with the Boltons yet.'

240

The big Romanian who had brought Scotty in had been standing by the door waiting. He nodded and stepped forward, picking Scotty up again as if he was just a dish towel, throwing him back over his shoulder as he walked out of the room.

<u>Chapter 34</u>

It was all Alice Mountjoy's doing. She was the one to blame. Alice had called Laura the week before and somehow persuaded her it would be a good thing to do. A thirtieth birthday school reunion at Danesborough High School, the school Laura and Alice had both been pupils at fifteen years ago.

Laura had received the official invite through the post a few months ago. It was one of those over the top cards, all fancy writing and lots of colour.

'Ooh look how exciting I am?' it was calling out in brightly coloured fonts.

But it wasn't at all exciting to Detective Constable Laura Knight. The invitation had gone straight into the bin. To be recycled. Into what? Maybe toilet roll, that might be appropriate. Laura had no desire to meet up with the people she went to school with. Especially not now they were all turning thirty. Too many years had gone by and she had no desire to rekindle old relationships. She'd moved on. Alice Mountjoy was her only friend from her schooldays. The only one she'd really kept in touch with, and there was a reason for that. Laura didn't feel she had much in common with any of the others. Yes, she'd sometimes bump into one of them in a supermarket or maybe at a local restaurant, but it was just a quick smile or a polite hello and then she would walk on. It wasn't that she hadn't had friends at school, it was just that she'd grown away from them. She'd got on with her life, got her own place, made new friends, and she was now making a career for herself in the police force.

To Laura, most of the others seemed to have just stayed where they were, treading water, not doing anything exciting. Not making anything of their lives. Some of them were still living at home with their parents. At thirty! Quite a few of the girls had got married and had children. Not that there was anything wrong with that, but there were so many other things you could do first. Her old schoolmates didn't seem to have the same spirit as Laura, not the same sense of adventure, of wanting to achieve something with their lives.

Alice was different though. She was an aspiring actress. Not very successful so far, but at least she was giving it a go. Chasing her dreams. Not content just to settle for a husband, two kids, a nice semi-detached house and a holiday in the Greek islands every summer. Not Alice. She was making her way up the acting ladder. Frustratingly slowly, but that was how it was sometimes. You just had to keep plugging away.

There was no doubt that Alice was very pretty and so far she had appeared in a couple of TV adverts for shampoo, and toured the country as part of the ensemble in a popular musical. She was the understudy for one of the lead parts in *We Will Rock*

You, but the girl playing it had remained unnaturally healthy throughout the tour, which meant that Alice had only been asked to step up once for an afternoon matinee performance. Alice had the talent, but just needed that one bit of luck to break through and get that bigger role. Maybe in her next musical, the lead won't be so healthy and maybe come down with a throat infection, giving Alice her chance to shine. But, whatever happened, Alice's time would come, Laura had no doubt about her friend's talent.

It was Alice's eternal optimism, her general enthusiasm for everything in life, that had eventually persuaded Laura to agree to go to the school reunion.

'Come on. Don't be a Debbie Downer. It'll be fun finding out what everyone else is doing. Seeing how much weight they've put on, how many of them are going bald. And then there's the boys too!' she'd shrieked and, in a moment of weakness, after a few glasses of wine, Laura had given in and agreed to go.

It was a Friday night and Laura had the weekend off, although she knew that if there was any more gang trouble then she'd most likely have to go in. She was the lead detective after all, but up till now most of the trouble had been on Saturday nights so she hoped she might be okay. In reality, she was always on call. Sometimes because she actually was, and other times because she had a fear of missing out. FOMO they called it. If she was the lead she didn't want anyone else getting the glory of solving the problem when something happened. She wanted to be there, at the centre of it. Luckily she

244

had her phone with her and so she could regularly check it for any incoming messages.

Thankfully the school reunion was being held in the function room of a local hotel and not in the school sports hall. If that had been the location then Laura definitely wouldn't have gone. Nothing could persuade her to revisit that airless, sweaty smelling room. When Laura was a teenage girl, P.E. lessons were like a weekly punishment session on her school timetable. Although she quite enjoyed the competitive nature of sports, the whole getting changed in a communal changing room, becoming all sweaty and then all showering together, standing in someone else's dirty water, and dressing back in that changing room with all the other girls again. That was something that Laura never looked forward to. Then, on top of that, for two weeks every year the hall was also used for exams, which again brought back bad memories for Laura. Although she'd actually done well in her exams, she still remembered the anxiety of waiting outside the hall and then waiting again to see what problems the paper held when you were allowed to turn it over.

Alice and Laura had decided to meet in a bar across the road from the hotel. They arrived at the same time, both wearing long, flowery dresses which was the current, springtime fashion. Alice's dress was set against a light pink background and Laura's was mainly baby blue. The dresses showed off the two women's slim figures which they had managed to keep, partly due to the physical demands of their jobs. Both of the women had visited the hairdressers earlier that day and they were also wearing high heels to match their dresses, with Alice being the slightly taller of the two. They'd made an effort for the reunion. There was no way that any of their former school-friends were going to be able to say that they'd let themselves go!

Alice and Laura's plan was to have a drink or two before they ventured across to the hotel where the reunion was taking place. A bit of Dutch courage. At the bar, they ordered a couple of cocktails, two Pornstar Martinis.

'Mmm…these are good,' Alice said as she slowly sipped her cold drink. 'I think a couple of these and we'll be set to go. Meet the rest of the gang.'

'Yeh, I might need more than a couple before I'm ready to meet the likes of James Snowdon again,' Laura replied, laughing. 'I wonder if he still picks his nose and eats it? That was his party trick, wasn't it?'

'Oh my god, we'll have to be careful what we say,' Alice said. 'Especially with you being a serving police officer. You know what we're like when we've had a few drinks.'

Both girls laughed and took another sip of their cocktails. Laura took advantage of the brief break in their conversation to have a quick look at her phone. There were no messages and no important emails either, just the usual routine stuff. She took another drink of her cocktail and then looked up at Alice.

'Actually, do you know who's going to be there?' Laura asked her friend.

'No, not really. I did email Jenny Broughton,' Alice replied, 'she's the one that seems to be organising it all. But all she said was that it was going to be a good turnout. I was thinking, there were four classes in the year, all with about thirty pupils, so I guess there could be up to a hundred people there.'

'Blimey,' Laura replied. 'I'll definitely need a few drinks before that then!' and the two girls laughed again. Laura had left her phone on the bar and she automatically reached for it again, but Alice grabbed it first.

'Why do you keep looking at your phone….have you got a secret fella you haven't told me about?' she asked, laughing at her friend.

'Haha, no, I wish. It's just work stuff unfortunately. I know I should just leave it but….' Laura replied.

'Ooh, who's this DI Strong bloke? You seem to get a lot of messages from him. Is he fit? He sounds like he should be!' Alice exclaimed.

'He's my boss!' Laura replied laughing. 'He's probably old enough to be my dad.'

'Oh yeah, I've just googled him,' Alice replied. 'He's not bad you know, a bit of a silver fox. I bet you've been tempted!'

'No, well…I know he's good looking,' Laura replied. 'But he's a lot older than me. I think he's married as well, but to be honest we don't really talk much about our personal lives, it's all work stuff really.'

A few cocktails later, Laura conceded they couldn't put it off any longer and so they settled

247

their bar bill and set off across the road to the hotel. All the single men, and a few of the married ones, watched the two women leave. They entered the bright hotel reception area of the hotel and walked up to the front desk. A woman, hair tied up, wearing a blue jacket, white blouse and a red and white cravat smiled at them from behind the brown and cream coloured counter.

'Good evening ladies, how can I help you,' she asked with a well-practiced smile on her face, underneath a layer of make-up. It was hard to tell her age, she could have been anything from twenty five to forty five.

'We're looking for the Danesborough High School reunion party,' Alice replied, smiling back, her acting skills on display. 'I think it's being held here.'

'Oh, yes, it's in the main function hall. Just go down the corridor there,' the receptionist said, indicating with her right hand, 'then turn left at the end and you'll see a set of double doors. It's in the function room there.'

'Are there many people in there already?' Laura asked, still not sure she wanted to be here and looking for a reason to turn around and go.

'Yes, I think so,' the receptionist replied, still smiling. 'I only came on shift half an hour ago but there's been a few people come in since then.'

Alice took Laura's arm and, following the receptionist's instructions, the two women soon found themselves standing outside the doors to the main function hall.

'Are you ready?' Alice asked.

'Ready as I'll ever be,' Laura replied, knowing it was too late to back out now and, besides, Alice had a tight grip on her arm making it impossible for her to do a runner.

Alice pushed one of the doors open and stepped inside with Laura by her side. Laura squinted her eyes as they were immediately hit by the bright white light, a contrast to the dimly lit corridor they'd just walked along. The function room was large, with a bar on the left hand side, several sets of tables and chairs on the right hand side and a wooden dance floor in the middle. In the far left hand corner, past the bar, there was a small stage and she could see, what looked like a deejay setting up his equipment. Lots of electrical stuff with black boxes, buttons and cables. The room was about half full with groups of people standing around the tables and a few waiting at the bar for their drinks. The dance floor was empty, too early Laura reckoned, and no-one was sitting down at the tables yet although a few of the chairs had jackets and handbags hanging from them.

Laura did a quick headcount and guessed that there must be fifty to sixty people in the room. All around thirty years old, all her ex-schoolmates. There was some low background music playing and Laura half recognised the song as being one from her teenage years, although she couldn't quite place it. Was it Madonna? Or the Spice Girls? Laura was never very good at pop quizzes. She always knew the song, but couldn't remember what it was called, or who the artist was, which, in a quiz situation, wasn't very helpful.

'I know it, I know it.'
'What is it?'
'It's....emm...oh it's thingy... you know.'
'Who?'
'Oh...emm...it's ...whatshisname.'
'Who?'
'Wait, emm...
'Quickly, who is it Laura?'
'Oh God, I can't remember. But I definitely know it.'

'And the answer was Madonna singing Vogue.'

'That was it. I knew it!'

Back in the hotel function room, there was a desk positioned immediately to their left, inside the door, and the woman sitting behind it smiled up at them as Alice and Laura stood looking around.

'Hello,' she said, 'come on in. It's Alice and Laura isn't it? Neither of you have changed,' she said, still smiling. 'We've got these name stickers, just in case, you know, to avoid any embarrassment. We've just done first names as we know some people will be married now and have changed their surnames. If you could just stick them on your tops, that would be great,' she said, a sticker with the name Jenny firmly fixed to her own green blouse. 'I'll catch up with you both later, but I expect you both want a drink first. A bit of Dutch courage I guess. The bar's over there,' she said, nodding behind her, over to her left.

Alice and Laura took their stickers and walked across to the bar, aware of several pairs of eyes watching them as they went. They ordered their drinks and then turned around to face the room. Most of the people were standing close to the tables in mixed groups of varying sizes. Alice and Laura surveyed a few of the groups to see who they could recognise.

'Look, over there,' Alice said, nodding towards a group standing in the middle of the tables. 'Isn't that Katie Fraser and Sarah Mann? Shall we go and join them?' she asked. 'We can talk about the old netball team. How we should have won the league,' Alice laughed. 'I'm sure I heard Sarah married an older guy and they've got a couple of kids, as well as him already having had two before. Shall we go and get the gossip?'

'Okay, why not?' Laura replied, unenthusiastically, taking a long drink from her large glass of white wine, knowing she had little choice other than to follow her friend.

The two women walked across to the group and it automatically opened up to allow them in to the circle.

'Wow, you look good.'

'I can't believe how long its been.'

'Where do you live now?'

'Are you married?'

'Any kids?'

'Do you remember Mrs Walton, the Geography teacher?'

Laura was quickly getting bored with the retrospective chat. All trivial stuff that happened a long time ago. Nothing important or even that interesting. She checked her phone again, but there was nothing new. She half hoped something would happen that she would have to leave for. This was exactly what she'd imagined the school reunion was going to be like, a look into the past, and she was now wishing she hadn't let Alice change her mind about coming. She looked over Debbie Stringer's shoulder, which wasn't hard as she was only just over five feet, even in high heels. She seemed to have stopped growing when she was only fourteen. Laura raised her empty glass towards Alice who mouthed back "yes please", seemingly engrossed in Katie Fraser's life story, but then Laura knew Alice was a good actress.

Laura made her way back to the bar and while she was trying to catch the barman's attention, she became aware of someone else arriving at the bar and standing next to her, their arms almost touching and she subconsciously moved her arm closer to her body. The barman was proving hard to get hold of, he seemed to be engrossed in telling one of the barmaids a funny story by the cash register. Laura hoped it was a short story, she could do with another drink. Just as it looked like he was going to turn in Laura's direction, a head leaned forward and a smiling face appeared in front of Laura's, blocking her view of the elusive bar tender.

'Hi Laura,' the face said to her, still smiling as if they both shared some sort of secret.

Laura recognised the man as Bradley Smith, or an older version of the Bradley Smith she remembered from school. He still had curly brown hair but it had crept further up his head now. A few less curls, a bit more forehead. He'd also put on a bit more weight, giving his face a much rounder look. It reminded Laura of an old leather football. An old leather football wearing a curly brown hairpiece.

Bradley Smith had never been the slimmest person though. Even at school he was probably the chubbiest in the year. In fact, Chubby Smith, wasn't that what they used to call him? Aside from that, Bradley had just been one of those boys who was there, but was never really noticeable. There was nothing that really made him stand out, be it his looks or his personality. He'd always just been one of the group. In the background somewhere.

'Oh, hi Bradley, how are you?' Laura said, turning to face him, giving up on the barman and returning her old school-friend's smile. Alice wasn't the only one who could act.

Bradley stepped forward and gave Laura a tight hug, running his hands up and down her back, before letting go and stepping back. She could feel his stomach pressing into her own.

'Yeh, I'm good. People call me Brad now, Bradley seems a bit formal,' he laughed.

Laura wasn't sure what he was laughing at but she laughed along with him, just to be polite. Brad then spent the next five minutes telling Laura what he'd done since he'd left school. How he'd got a job in the local supermarket and progressed to manager level.

'You might have seen me in there,' he suggested, 'although I'm often in the office doing management work, making sure it's all running smoothly, you know.'

Of course Laura knew. It was vitally important to make sure there were enough mangetout on the shelves. And tomato puree. Who knew management did such a fantastic job?

She finally caught the bartender's attention and ordered drinks for her and Alice, hoping that when she turned back Bradley Smith would have disappeared. But no such luck.

Having completed his employment story, there was more. Brad went on to tell Laura how he'd managed to buy a new flat in a nice part of town. In a lovely new development, he said.

'Is that where the council waste recycling place is?' Laura asked him. Otherwise known as the dump.

'Emm, well, yes, it's near there, but you don't notice it really, not if the wind's blowing the other way. And of course it's handy if you've got any rubbish to get rid of,' he added. 'It's just a two minute drive.'

Laura was looking for a break in his monologue, which she suspected he'd written and rehearsed in advance of the reunion. He'd done his work bit and his property bit. Hopefully there wasn't much more. Relationships? Holidays? Laura hoped not, she wanted to re-join her friend Alice and hand over her drink which the bartender had just placed in front of her. She checked her phone again, but all was quiet. She looked up, hoping, but apparently Brad wasn't quite finished yet.

'Do you know, I probably shouldn't say this, it's a bit embarrassing,' he said. 'But when we were at school, you were the one I always fancied.

But I never had the balls to ask you out. I always wish I had done.'

'Oh, I thought you were going out with Alison Kirkbride at school,' Laura replied, looking over Brad's shoulder to see if she could catch Alice's attention. This had taken a weird turn and she was keen to escape.

'Well, yes, for a bit we were. But it was nothing serious, you know,' he said and he touched Laura's arm with his hand. 'I always thought you were the best looking girl and, seeing you here tonight, well …you still are. I just wish I'd….'

'Is Alison, not here tonight?' Laura interrupted him, looking around the room. 'I don't think I've seen her.' Bradley and Alison, the Chubsters, wasn't that what they used to call them. Or Mr and Mrs Chubby? A bit cruel maybe, but it was just playground fun, wasn't it?

'What, no, she's emm not no, I don't think so,' Brad stammered in reply. 'I haven't seen her for ages. It was just a school thing we had, nothing more serious than that if you know what I mean.'

Laura had a fair idea of what he meant and she thought Alison Kirkbride must have had a lucky escape. I mean who would want a little chubby, curly brown haired baby?

'Oh, I'd better get back to Alice with her drink, she'll be gasping,' Laura said, holding up the two glasses of wine to let Brad see them, before stepping quickly past her old school mate, like an old netball move, and making her way back to the safety of her friend Alice.

Laura successfully managed to avoid Brad for the remainder of the evening, getting through a number of common discussions with a variety of people she vaguely recognised from years gone by. Thankfully none as weird as Brad though. As she got more and more bored, her mind started to drift back to her police work and how that was going. None of her old school-friends seemed to be as into their work, their careers, as she was. When they found out she was in the police, they laughed and told stories about noisy neighbours and minor traffic offences. Laura laughed along with them, not telling anyone that she was a detective constable in the Serious Crime team. They all just assumed she was an ordinary copper. A uniformed constable. Was that because she was a woman? Still at least it stopped them asking questions about serious cases she'd been involved in, which she didn't really feel like discussing with anyone tonight.

Most of her old schoolmates admitted they were just working to pay the bills, with hopefully enough left over for a weekly night out or a takeaway, and a summer holiday in the Mediterranean. The men were all especially disappointing. None of them seemed to have any ambition to make something of their lives. Laura couldn't understand that. Why would you work five days a week in a job you didn't like, or a job that wasn't providing any great service to the general public? It was a great chunk of their lives wasted as far as Laura could see.

Her career in the police was completely different. She loved the job and she was doing something good for society as a whole. Every morning she woke up, keen to get into the police station and carry on with whatever case she was working on. Sometimes it was hard and frustrating, but she could never see herself wanting to do anything else. She was catching criminals, cutting down crime. Helping ordinary, law abiding people get on with their lives. In contrast, none of her ex-school friends seemed to have the same attitude about their work. It was yet another way she felt she had outgrown them. None of the girls were like her, and none of the men had the same ambition or personality of the likes of someone like her boss, DI Strong. They just didn't compare.

As the evening came to an end, Laura found herself back at the bar, having a last drink with Alice. Both women were a bit drunk, but just happy drunk. Laura was glad she'd made it through and the evening was coming to an end. There was no way was she ever going to let Alice persuade her to do anything like this again. Still, at least she'd had a laugh with Alice, which she always did.

'What do you think of Bradley Smith now?' Alice asked her friend, smiling widely, before taking a sip of her Baileys.

'Yeh, he's okay, I suppose. A bit....you know. Wait, why do you ask?' Laura replied, sensing something her friend hadn't said.

'Well I didn't really remember him that well from school. Like I remembered him, his name and that, but I couldn't really remember him much as a person. Didn't they use to call him something? But, anyway, we were just having a chat earlier and he

257

told me that when we were at school he'd always fancied me, but he'd been too shy to ask me out,' Alice replied. 'I never knew that. It was quite sweet really.'

'Mmm…he probably didn't ask you out because he was going out with Alison Kirkbride at the time?' Laura suggested. 'Mr and Mrs Chubby.'

'Oh that was it. Well yes he was for a bit, but he said it was never serious,' Alice replied. 'Do you know what else he said?' she asked her friend, before taking another drink from her glass.

'That you were the best looking girl at school and you still are?' Laura suggested with a mischievous grin on her face.

Alice almost choked on her drink. She slammed her glass down on the bar and looked directly at Laura.

'How did you…wait…did he say the same to you?' Alice asked open-mouthed, staring at her friend with big eyes, the realisation coming to her.

'Yes, I'm afraid so,' Laura replied laughing. 'I think it was a well-used script. I'm sure I saw him trying the same with Jenny Broughton a little while ago too, even though she's married.'

'What a bastard. Why are men like that? He gave me his phone number and I was seriously thinking of giving him a call sometime, just for a drink, you know?' Alice laughed. 'God, I am so gullible when it comes to men,' she said before picking up her glass and finishing her drink. 'I need someone reliable. I need you to introduce me to your silver fox boss, he'll do,' she laughed.

'Yeh, right, there's no way that's happening,' Laura replied. 'Come on. It's time we went home I think. Let's go outside and grab a taxi.'

The two women walked along the corridor, past reception and out through the revolving door. They waited by the taxi rank and a few minutes later a black cab came around. As they sat together in the back of the taxi, Laura's mind drifted back to the events of the re-union. As well as Bradley Smith, all the other men had been equally disappointing to Laura. None of them seemed to have any oomph. They weren't inspiring at all. Just ordinary boring men, with boring lives. Those seemed to be the only men she ever met nowadays.

In her mind, she often compared her potential men to her boss, DI Strong. Now there was a real man. He was inspirational, clever, handsome, someone you could look up to and admire. But he was much too old for Laura, wasn't he?

If only he had been twenty years younger, not her boss, and not married, probably with a family, then he might have been the ideal man for her. As she sat back in the taxi, she couldn't stop herself from bursting out laughing at the thought of her and DI Strong as a couple.

'What are you laughing at?' Alice asked Laura, giving her a poke in the ribs.

'Oh, nothing…just… men,' Laura replied and the two women laughed along together as the taxi made its way through the dark, quiet streets.

Chapter 35

It was the cold that woke Scotty up. He was shivering when he came to, but he lay still, trying to get his senses in order before he was ready to make a move. He remembered what had happened up until the attack in the snooker hall. After that, it was just a blank. He guessed he must have been knocked unconscious and dumped on the waste ground where he now found himself.

Scotty sat himself up and felt pains shooting through his upper body and head. He gingerly touched his head and face and could feel a number of cuts and bumps. No fresh blood though, so nothing too serious. On the positive side, his legs seemed okay and so he slowly stood, looking around to see if he could recognise anything that would give him an idea of exactly where he had been dumped.

There wasn't anything much around, nothing to see, just hedges and fields. None of the fields seemed to be in use. Just bare land. There were no crops or animals, and there was no-one else to be seen. In the distance he could make out some buildings, houses he thought, and so he decided to start heading in that direction.

As he walked across the fields, the pain in his body started to ease and he guessed there was nothing broken, probably just bruising. He could live with that. Scotty had been in enough fights to know when something was broken. It was a different type of pain. Sharper and more persistent. It stopped you doing things, like walking. Stiffness and a dull ache usually just meant tissue damage. The bones were still whole. Tissue damage would repair quite quickly.

As he neared the end of the fields, the houses became clearer and he saw some cars passing on a road to his left. He changed course and headed for the road, walking along the side of a field towards a wooden gate at the far end. As he approached the gate, he checked his pockets and was relieved to find that nothing had been taken. He still had his phone, wallet and keys. He hadn't been mugged, just beaten up.

Scotty went through the gate and found himself standing on a pavement at the edge of a road which led towards the houses he had seen from the fields. Looking in the other direction, it appeared to be just more countryside with even more hedges, trees and fields. Coming from Glasgow and living in other cities since he'd left there, Scotty found the countryside a bit alien. He wasn't used to the nothingness, no people, no noise. It didn't seem right. He preferred the hustle and bustle of busy city life.

Scotty took out his phone and pressed the maps app icon. A few seconds later the screen kicked into life and he looked at it to determine his current location. According to the app he was on the edge of a relatively new residential suburb about ten miles out from the centre of town. He walked along the road towards the houses until he came to a road sign which said "Farrah Road". He remembered hearing some time ago that there had been a new development planned for this area and they were going to name the streets after famous Olympic athletes. He guessed this must be it. He sat down by the street sign and called Chopper's number.

Half an hour later he stood up again as he could see Chopper approaching in the transit van. He still felt stiff but less painful. That was a good sign. No long term damage. The van pulled to a stop beside Scotty and he pulled open the door and stepped inside.

'Jesus Christ, what happened to you?' Chopper asked him, staring at his friend's face.

Scotty pulled down the sun visor and looked at his face in the mirror. He wasn't looking his best, that was certainly true. His face was covered in cuts and bruises. Scotty reached up and gently touched it with his fingers, wincing once or twice as he found a sensitive part. Nothing seemed broken, not even his nose. The cuts and bruises would fade in a few days and he'd soon be back to normal. He took out his handkerchief and spat in it before wiping his face, getting rid of the worst of the dried blood.

As they drove back into town, he told Chopper what had happened, or as much as he could remember.

'What were you thinking of going to the snooker hall?' Chopper asked. 'You know that's where they all hang out. They'd know you were one of our team. You were just asking for trouble. You're lucky they didn't finish you off.'

'Ach, I jist fancied a wee game of snooker. That wis all,' Scotty replied laughing. 'I didnae go there to cause any trouble. They should've jist let me play. That wis all I wanted to do. Noo they've made it personal.'

'You'd be better staying away from there unless you want another kicking,' Chopper replied. 'And next time they probably won't be so lenient. Anyhow, Ally and Charlie have still got plans to deal with Bog and his gang when the family return from their holidays.'

'Aye right,' Scotty replied, smiling to himself.

Plans, plans. Ally and Charlie Bolton might have plans but he had plans of his own. Better plans. Simpler. The Romanians had crossed the line as far as Scotty was concerned. They'd made it personal. All he had been doing was having a nice game of snooker, taking some of Kenny's money from him, and they'd come along and attacked him. There was no need for it. He wasn't causing anyone any problems, apart from Kenny and his wallet. But now, well now, he was going to have to sort them out. Get his revenge. He couldn't let them get away with that. It wasn't right. And once he'd done the business, Ally, Charlie, Chopper and the rest of them would see that he had been right all along and they'd thank him for it.

263

'Jist drop me aff at ma flat,' he said to Chopper. 'I need ti git cleaned up.'

Chapter 36

Catherine had opened a bottle of wine, a white, Chilean pinot grigio. She preferred the South American wines, although she didn't quite know why. She was in no way any kind of wine expert and she freely admitted that she usually bought wine based on what the label looked like. She helped herself to a glass of the wine while she cooked dinner, savouring the ice cold taste. She would normally wait until they were both sitting at the table before she had a drink, but tonight she felt a bit different. Maybe she just needed a bit of Dutch courage, something to help her with what she was planning to do. She could hear Mo talking to someone on his phone in the other room but not loud enough for her to be able to make out what he was saying.

Not that she ever listened in on any of his phone calls. She trusted him absolutely, and in all the years they had been together she had never had any doubt that he was a good, honest man.

That was why she was going to talk to him tonight about her meeting with Marsha Hughes. Catherine was feeling guilty. She still didn't quite know why she hadn't told him she was going to meet Marsha at the time. It had been something to do with when she had seen Mo reading a diary in the study. That, and how he'd acted when she saw him. Suspiciously. Or was it? Maybe it was just Catherine's imagination. Yet everything that she'd learned since had given further substance to the possibility… or was it probability?...that it had been Dylan Hughes's diary Mo had been reading that day.

Marsha had told Catherine where the diary had been found and it wasn't far from where Mo and Catherine lived. Mo could have easily put it in the bin outside the newsagents shop when he'd gone for a paper one day, as he often did.

Marsha had also told Catherine that reading the diary had given her some comfort, but there wasn't anything of any significance in it and that, after reading it, it had helped her move on. She hadn't shown it to DI Strong, or even told him that she had it, so Mo was none the wiser.

It was all yesterday's news really, but if it was Dylan Hughes's diary that Mo had that day, Catherine couldn't shake the question from her head as to why he had it, and why he hadn't given it to Marsha. She'd thought long and hard about it and decided that now was not the time to start keeping secrets from her husband. Not after all these years. She was going to have to tell him what she knew and what her concerns were and listen to what he said. Otherwise it was just going to continue to nag away at her.

She gave the food another stir. It was a spicy vegetable stew which they were having along with some boiled rice. It smelled delicious. Catherine had cooked it a number of times before, having got the recipe from one of her friends. Both her and Mo really liked it.

'Dinner's ready,' she called through to the other room as she began serving up the food.

Catherine took another mouthful of wine before walking through to the dining room, carrying the two plates, her wine and the bottle, all on a large wooden tray. They sat at the table in their usual seats, directly across from each other at one end of the table and began to eat their food. Whilst eating they chatted about the day's events, what each of them had been doing, and what they had planned for the rest of the week. Catherine was waiting for the right moment to introduce Marsha into the conversation. She wanted to do it casually, just something else to talk about, nothing that important. There was a sudden lull in their conversation and Catherine leaned over to fill up Mo's wine glass.

'How's Marsha Hughes doing?' she asked with as casual a tone as she could muster. 'Is she getting over the death of her son, do you think?'

'Marsha? Yes I think so. I don't see her that often to be honest but I've seen her in the office a couple of times. She looks okay,' Strong replied. 'I know what you're going to say. I should make time and check in with her. I know. I promise I will,' he added taking a sip of his wine and smiling at his wife.

'Yes, you should,' Catherine replied laughing. 'Actually I, emm, bumped into her a few days ago and we ended up having a coffee together.'

'Really? You didn't tell me that,' Strong replied, with a quizzical look on his face.

'No, I think it was one of those crazy days,' Catherine replied confidently. She'd rehearsed this bit. 'You know, you were working long hours and I had evening classes or something. I meant to say, but it must have slipped my mind.'

'Well, you probably know more than me then,' Strong replied. 'How did she appear to you?'

Catherine took a long drink of her wine before replying. So far it was going to plan.

'I think she seemed okay,' Catherine replied. 'She said she'd found something that had belonged to Dylan and that had helped her.'

'Oh what was that…did she say?' Strong asked.

'Yes it was his diary,' Catherine replied, looking closely at her husband's face as she spoke. His cheeks seemed to be reddening a bit, or was that just the effect of the wine? And did his left eye twitch slightly when she mentioned the diary? It was hard to tell. Maybe it was just her imagination.

'She found his diary?' Strong replied. 'Did she say where she'd got it from?' He picked up his glass and took another drink.

'Well, yes, from quite near here actually,' Catherine replied. 'Apparently it was in a bin by the Newsagents.'

'Really? That's strange. How did she find it in a bin?' Strong asked.

'Well, no, she didn't find it in a bin, but the bin-man did and he'd returned it to her. It must have had Dylan's name and address in or something I guess,' Catherine replied.

'I see. Did she say what she's done with it? I take it she read it?' Strong asked his wife.

'Yes, she said she read it and got some comfort, as she put it, from doing that. Then she said she put it away,' Catherine replied. 'I think she felt that was enough and she was now ready to move on. I did ask her if she'd shown the diary to you, but she said she hadn't.'

'No, she hasn't said anything to me about it,' Strong replied. 'I'm glad she's got it though. I thought it was lost.'

Strong turned his attention back to the food and Catherine took another long drink, letting the cool wine stay in her mouth for a while before swallowing it and asking the question she'd been waiting to ask.

'Did you have it then? Was it the one I saw you reading in the study one evening?'

She could feel herself blushing as she looked at her husband, not knowing if she'd done the right thing. Maybe she should have just kept quiet. She'd never questioned him about any work related thing before. Perhaps she should have kept it that way. Strong had put his fork down by the side of his plate and was looking at his wife. He seemed to be thinking.

'Ah, yes, it probably was,' Strong replied confidently after a few seconds. 'I wanted to look through it as part of the investigation into her son's death and I brought it home so I could do that without being disturbed. It was DC Knight's case

269

really but because it was Marsha's son, I wanted to protect her and just check it first.'

'Who's DC Knight? Is she the pretty one with long dark hair?' Catherine asked.

'Yes, that's right,' Strong replied. 'Laura Knight. It was her case and I wouldn't normally do that, bring anything home I mean, but because it was to do with Marsha's son I wanted to make sure there wasn't anything in there that could cause her any more distress or pain.'

Strong stopped talking and took a drink of his wine. Catherine did likewise, sensing that he wasn't quite finished.

'I looked through it that evening and it was fine,' Strong continued. 'There was nothing in there that would help us with the case or give Marsha any further worries. It was just your usual diary stuff. What he did that day, who he met. That sort of thing. Just brief notes.'

'But how come you didn't give it to Marsha or DC Knight then?' Catherine asked. 'How come it ended up in the Newsagents bin?'

'Well, I don't really know,' Strong replied. 'I put it in my jacket pocket so that I wouldn't forget to take it back in to the police station the next time I was in. All I can think of is that it must have fallen out of my pocket and someone else picked it up and put it in the bin.'

'Yes, I think you did go to the shop for milk that next morning,' Catherine replied. 'Maybe it fell out then.'

'Yes, I guess it must have,' Strong replied. 'Ah well, it's good she's got it now and it's helped her a bit. If you see her again, best not to mention that I had it though, she might think it funny I didn't say anything. But, to be honest, I was a bit embarrassed when I discovered it had gone missing. No-one knew I had the diary so it was easier just to stay quiet and as I said there was nothing in it relevant to Dylan's death.'

Catherine took another sip of her wine and smiled. She was pleased she'd discussed Marsha's diary with Mo now. It had been worrying her, but of course she should have known there would be a perfectly reasonable explanation. As usual, Mo was looking after someone, protecting them. It was what he was good at and Catherine knew she should never have had any doubts that would be the case. It was how her husband had always been and why she still loved him so much.

DI Strong took another sip of his wine and thought about the discussion they'd just had. Initially he was surprised that Catherine had brought it up and that she had met Marsha for a coffee. His wife had never talked to him much about his work before and he preferred it that way. The less she knew the better. It could often be a very unpleasant job.

However, now that she had spoken about it, he was pretty confident that he had managed to reassure Catherine and that she still trusted him. Between them they'd managed to come up with a plausible explanation for what had happened with the diary.

Strong was also pleased to hear that Marsha had read the diary and had made nothing of it.

Especially with regard to the entries that referred to Strong's parents and the events leading up to Dylan's death. Of course he was pretty sure that Marsha knew that Dylan was responsible for the deaths of his parents twenty years ago and that she always had done, but that obviously wasn't something she wanted anyone else to know. Nor was it something she could discuss with DI Strong. It all sounded like Marsha had literally closed the book on Dylan, which suited DI Strong.

Chapter 37

Scotty had been sitting in the pub for the last hour, which wasn't an unusual thing for him. But what was different this time was that he wasn't in one of his normal drinking haunts, and he'd had the same pint sitting in front of him, now still half full, for the whole time he'd been in the place. Normally he'd have polished off three pints of strong lager in that hour.

But today was different. He wasn't here to have a drinking session, he was here to do a job and for that he wanted to stay sharp and focused. Although he had been tempted by the array of different beers on tap, there were risks involved in what he was planning to do and he needed to stay sober, at least until it was all over. Then he could have a few pints to wind down.

Scotty was sitting on his own at a table by the bar window. It was an old-fashioned pub with a stained glass, bay window, but some of the staining had come off. Enough so that Scotty could see out, without anyone being able to see him looking. He was keeping an eye on a hairdressers shop across the road. He knew that his nemesis Bog went there most Thursday afternoons on the pretext of getting his hair trimmed, but in reality it was well known, at least amongst those that had an interest in him, that he went there to have sex in the flat above the salon with the salon owner, Trudi. He didn't really try to hide it, certainly everyone in the salon knew, and Trudi was one of the women Bog's wife had found out about a few months ago, signalling the end of their marriage.

Trudi was an attractive young woman in her mid-twenties. She had long blond curly hair and she always dressed in a way to show off her curvy body and long slim legs. Usually tight, short, bright coloured dresses with matching high heels. Not really what you would call work clothes, unless your job was simply to get admiring looks from men, and a few envious looks from the women.

Trudi was born, and brought up in Liverpool but had moved South two years previously to make her fortune, or at least enough money to have a good time. She'd quickly lost her Scouse accent and now spoke like a local, as if she'd always lived here.

One night a few months ago, Trudi had found herself in the same bar as Bog and, knowing who he was, and sensing an opportunity, she had approached the big Romanian man and made sure he got to know who she was and what she could offer him. Trudi was nothing if not a confident young woman, and she knew how to use all of her female skills to get a man's attention, and more. A few weeks after that first meeting she became the proud owner of a new hairdressing salon, which was something she had always wanted. *Trudi's Salon.*

She thought about calling it something else, something catchy, but she wanted everyone to know it was hers. That was important. She was now her own boss and she immediately moved into the flat above her salon. The real salon owner, Bog, visited her once a week and she was happy with that arrangement for now, but she had other plans too.

Scotty had spotted Trudi at the salon window a couple of times, and once she had stepped outside on to the pavement to chat with one of her customers as the woman left the salon. She was dressed in her usual style and Scotty could see the attraction. There was no doubt she was a beautiful young woman.

Bog hadn't arrived yet, he usually turned up later in the afternoon, but Scotty didn't want to take any chances and so he had got to his vantage point early and was happy to just sit and wait. He knew what he was going to do and he could bide his time. No rush.

Scotty sat forward in his seat and leaned in towards the pub window as he saw a dark saloon car slow down and finally come to a stop outside the hairdressers shop. Two men, smartly dressed in dark suits, got out of the front doors of the car and stood on the pavement looking around for a few seconds. They were big men who looked like they spent a lot of time in the gym. Or took steroids. Or both. Scotty thought he recognised them as doormen from one of the Romanian run clubs. He'd definitely seen them before with Bog, they seemed to be his regular team of bodyguards. Scotty ran his tongue across his lips before taking another sip of his beer.

One of the men moved to the rear of the car, on the pavement side, and opened the door. Another man emerged, he too in a dark suit, and Scotty immediately recognised him as Bogdan Popescu, or just simply Bog. He was of similar build to the other two men and he said something to one of them before he entered the hairdresser's salon. The man nodded and the two bodyguards stood for a minute before they both got back in the front of the car. That was Scotty's signal to move. He took a last gulp of lager from his glass and put it back down on the table, still a quarter full.

Scotty left the pub and walked across the road in the direction of Bog's car. He stopped by the rear door on the passenger side ensuring he was visible to the man sitting in the passenger seat, via his wing mirror. Scotty could see the man sitting there watching him and he took an iron bar from his inside jacket pocket and pressed it against the rear car door, pulling it downwards, leaving a deep gouge, exposing the shiny silver metalwork underneath the dark paint. It made a screeching noise which reminded him of his schooldays and the sound of chalk on the blackboard. His action had the desired effect though, as the passenger door was thrown open and the Romanian bodyguard started to emerge. His legs swung out, shiny black brogues hitting the tarmac. Scotty was ready for him. As soon as his head became visible, Scotty hit him hard on the crown with his iron bar. The man immediately slumped back into the car and Scotty heard a shout coming from inside. He quickly ran around the back of the car and as the driver's door opened he gave a repeat performance on the second Romanian as he too tried to get out of the car. One hard hit and he also slumped back into his seat, out stone cold. Scotty leaned into the car and manoeuvred his victim until he was sitting upright, the back of his head resting on the headrest, his arms by his sides. Scotty closed the door and walked around to the passenger side and did the same with the other man before closing the passenger door. Anyone walking past would just think it was two men sat in their car, probably waiting for someone in the hairdressers, which actually wasn't that far from the truth.

Scotty took a few seconds to look around and he satisfied himself that no-one had seen him carry out his attack. There was no-one else in the street. Job well done. Those two would be out cold for at least an hour which would give him plenty time to carry out the second part of his operation. He leaned against the car and smiled. These things were so easy if you didn't complicate them. No need for false text messages and hoping that Bog would respond. It was much more straightforward than that. Wait till Ally and Charlie found out.

Satisfied with his work so far, Scotty walked back across the road, past the pub door and on into the pub car park where he'd left his car. He got in and drove the short distance back to Trudi's salon where he parked at the side of the road, closely behind the Romanian's car.

He got out and stood by the window of the chemist shop which was next door to Trudi's hairdressing salon. The chemist's shop had a blind that overhung the shop window and Scotty positioned himself underneath it so that he was partly in the shade. He wasn't all that bothered if anyone saw him, but it was probably best to stay as concealed as possible. He looked at his watch and settled down to wait. Ten minutes, he reckoned.

Sure enough, almost exactly ten minutes later, a bell sounded, signalling the door to the hairdresser's salon being opened, and Bog appeared. Scotty let him walk a couple of steps across the pavement, towards the car before quickly stepping forward and hitting him from behind, hard on the back of his head. He felt the man's skull crunching, with a noise similar to that as if he had just stood on a packet of crisps. As soon as he'd hit him, Scotty reached out and caught Bog under the arms before he fell. He walked his victim forwards and, opening his car boot, he bundled him inside, quickly closing the lid. The whole thing had taken less than a minute and Scotty looked around, again satisfying himself that no-one had seen what he'd done.

He got into his car and set off, turning the radio up loud and singing along with the music as he drove.

Chapter 38

Bogdan Popescu's wife, or to be more precise, his ex-wife - since she'd caught him playing around with other women, was enjoying her holiday in Portugal. 'Other *women*' might even be stretching it a bit. Some of them looked like they'd not long left school, maybe they'd just made it into their early twenties at a push. Okay, Maria might be in her mid-thirties now, but she was still attractive. She could see all the men's eyes following her as she walked around the pool to her chosen spot. Let them look, she thought as she sat down, sunglasses on, stretching her long slim legs out on the grey, cushioned sunbed.

It had been a snap decision to take a vacation but she was glad she had done it. The sun was shining brightly and the cocktails were flowing nicely. She'd flirted a bit with the young, handsome barman, yes she still had it, and the kids seemed to be enjoying themselves too. What was there not to enjoy?

This was the most relaxed Maria Popescu had felt since she'd found out about Bogdan's infidelity. Of course, she'd suspected him for a while. After all he was a man. And worse than that, a man with power who thought he was untouchable. He believed he could do whatever he wanted, but not to Maria he couldn't. The late nights and smell of perfume from his clothes had become more and more frequent and his excuses lamer and lamer. Maria had hired a private investigator, not a Romanian, but a rather dishevelled English man she'd found through an advert in the local paper. She wanted someone completely anonymous. Someone from outside of Bogdan's criminal world who she could trust not to shop her, and Colin Kerr fitted the bill. I mean, what sort of business advertises in a local paper nowadays? He didn't even have a website. He said he didn't see the need for modern technology, it just confused things.

So Colin Kerr preferred the old ways and if his office was anything to go by, that certainly seemed to be the case. He was located in a narrow alley off the High Street. Maria had never even noticed it before. It was so narrow, Maria suspected you couldn't even ride a bike down it. The outside door to Kerr's office was completely anonymous apart from a number three, painted in blue on the dark brown background of the door. Inside was like going back in time. There were two rooms, an outer office with a worn down brown, leather settee. It looked so soft and saggy that Maria thought if she sat on it, she might not be able to get up again. It would just swallow her up.

Kerr's office lay behind a half frosted glass door to the left of the settee. Through that door, there was an old wooden desk, two wooden chairs, one on either side of the desk, and, in the corner, an old green metal filing cabinet with four drawers. The rest of the room was bare. It wasn't what you would describe as homely. More functional.

Kerr was an ex-policeman who'd retired from the force and set up his own business a few years ago. Maria guessed he was in his mid-fifties but he could easily have passed for ten years older. He didn't actually have a beard, but somehow he looked like he always needed a shave. And a new suit – one that fitted him. Colin Kerr was a strange man, but he was just what Maria needed.

He had only taken a week to come back to Maria with evidence of Bogdan Popescu's infidelity. The Private Investigator had met Maria in his office and handed her a plain brown envelope which contained a series of revealing photos. Maria had only looked at them once before handing them back, asking Kerr to destroy them. She didn't ask him how he had got them. In her mind she counted three different women, two blondes and a brunette, but that was just over a period of one week, and so she assumed there were probably even more. What a stupid man. She paid Kerr in cash and left his office, knowing exactly what she was going to do.

Although she knew it would make things harder for her and the two children, there was no doubt that she would leave him. The marriage was over. As far as Maria was concerned, infidelity was a definite no. A red line. Maria had made that clear to Bogdan right at the start, when they'd first got together. She had experienced enough of that when she was growing up. Enough for a lifetime. Her father had treated her mother badly, leaving her for

281

other women many times, but she always took him back. Maria had told Bogdan that if he was ever unfaithful to her then that would be it. Game over. And so it was. If he wanted to sleep with some young blond bimbo then he could do. He could have as many as he wanted. But he would never share a bed with Maria Popescu again. No way.

The first few weeks of separation had been tough for Maria and the children. They'd had to find another place to live and she'd cried more than once, but she knew she'd get through it. She was tough and so were her kids. They knew what was going on and they understood. She was doing the right thing. Setting them an example and hopefully breaking the chain. After a while they all settled into a routine, Bogdan had access to his son and daughter and that worked well. Maria was happy with things as they were for now. Some of her friends had tried to set her up on dates with other men but she wasn't ready for that yet. Maybe in a year or so, but for now she was happy to be on her own and do things the way she wanted to.

Maria was lying on her front on the sunbed by the pool. She had her bikini top undone so she didn't get a strap line ruining her all-over tan. She was about to turn over again on to her back, when her mobile phone started to ring. She held her bikini in place and picked up the phone from the table beside her sunbed, looking at the number. It wasn't a number she recognised and she was tempted not to answer, but she decided to anyway. The man on the other end was a policeman from the UK who told her that her husband, technically ex-husband, was in hospital with a head injury. It wasn't clear what had happened exactly but the policeman said he'd been found in a field by a dog walker who had then alerted the police. It was possible he had been attacked and then dumped in the field, but he was still unconscious and so far there were no witnesses to the incident. The policeman gave Maria his contact details and told her which hospital Bogdan was in. When she told him she was currently on holiday in Portugal, he replied.

'Okay, well I expect you'll want to come home as soon as possible to see him. I'm sorry to have brought you this news, but please let me know when you're back in the U.K. so we can come and talk with you.'

After the call ended, Maria remained sitting on her sunbed for a while, sipping her cocktail and continuing to soak up the lovely warm sun. She didn't want to leave this and go back home, but she knew, if only for the children, she had to. He was their father. Maria wasn't interested in seeing him though and she certainly didn't want to have to take any responsibility for his ongoing business or personal affairs. She'd left him and, in her eyes, there was no going back. Maria wasn't surprised that he'd been beaten up, but she wanted nothing to do with him or his crooked businesses, no matter how badly injured he was. In all the time they'd been together Maria had kept out of Bogdan's business activities as much as she could. She knew he dealt with some unsavoury characters, men who could be violent and she suspected Bogdan could be like that too, although he'd never been physical with

283

Maria. But he didn't need Maria now, he had family, Romanian family. They could deal with it all. He wasn't her responsibility.

Maria finished her cocktail, picked up her phone and called his cousin, Alex. She hadn't spoken to him since she had left Bogdan and she didn't particularly want to now, but she knew he would be the best person to sort things out. He answered quickly and Maria explained what had happened. He seemed shocked but relieved that Bogdan was still alive. He told Maria how no-one had seen him for twenty four hours and that his two bodyguards had been violently attacked in their car. Although she felt a bit sorry for them, Maria wasn't really interested and she cut Alex short, telling him which hospital he could find Bogdan in and that she would be back sometime in the next few days when she had organised a return flight. Maria ended the call as quickly as she could and relaxed back on her sun lounger closing her eyes, trying to blank it out and think of happier times and wishing she hadn't answered her phone.

Chapter 39

After getting the call from Maria, Alexandru had driven straight to the hospital to see his cousin Bogdan. He was still alive, but he didn't look well. He was lying in a hospital bed, covered with a white sheet, with all sorts of tubes and wires attached to him, keeping him going. There were a couple of monitors by the side of his bed and every now and again a nurse came around and had a look at them before moving on. She seemed satisfied. That had to be a good thing. At least she wasn't calling for a doctor or changing anything on the machines. He seemed to be stable, that's all she said.

The young doctor, dressed in a white coat and wearing a pair of dark framed spectacles, had told Alexandru that Bogdan had taken a blow to the back of his head which had fractured his skull. The skull was repairable he said, but what they didn't know was the impact of the blow on his brain. It was a possibility that he could have brain damage, the scans hadn't been conclusive, and they would have to wait until he woke up so they could assess him then. There was no telling when he would regain consciousness but the doctor was hopeful it would be within the next twenty four or forty eight hours. Until then, there was nothing they could do except keep an eye on him.

There were also a few policemen at the hospital and a Detective Knight had approached Alexandru and started to ask him a few questions. Alexandru pretended he couldn't speak English and, after a couple of failed attempts, the detective had given up. She handed over a card and asked him to call her when Bogdan woke up. No way was he going to do that, Alex thought to himself and, after she had left, he threw her card in the metal bin by the bedside.

Since coming to England, the Romanians had made a point of having as little as possible to do with anyone official in their adopted country. And certainly not the police, considering some of the things they were mixed up in. They'd learned it was best to stay as anonymous as possible. The less anyone in authority knew about you the better.

On his way back from the hospital, Alex had called two more of his cousins and arranged to meet them in an office building they used for a couple of their businesses. It was set up as an Insurance Agents office, but that was really just a front for their main business of drug smuggling. The two cousins, Cristian and Benedikte were brothers and, like Alex, they'd adopted shortened versions of their names after they'd moved to England. They were now known simply as Cris and Ben.

Alex told the two other men about Bog's situation, as far as he knew. Bog was still unconscious and so they didn't know exactly what had happened, but it appeared that the two bodyguards had been attacked first, while Bog was inside with his hairdresser friend. Then when he'd come out of the salon, their leader had been attacked from behind, presumably bundled into a car, and then dumped in a field a few miles away.

'Was that not where we took the Scott man?' Ben asked. Ben was the big Romanian man who had slung Scotty over his shoulder and carried him out of the snooker hall.

'Well yes it was near there, the same area,' Alex replied. 'I think that probably means something. Some sort of message. What you can do, we can do also. Something like that. We do it to one of them and they do the same back to us.'

'Except they've done more, no?' Cris said. 'He was on our territory, in the snooker hall, looking for trouble, no? They've gone and attacked Bog, our leader, and they've left him with more serious injuries, no? The Scott man wasn't that badly injured, I am thinking, and he deserved it. He was in our place.'

'Yes, you are right,' Alex replied. 'They've escalated it by attacking Bog. I know Bog didn't want us to have an all-out war with the English. He was happy with the progress we were making. A bit at a time he said, until we are ready to take over everything we want. Well I am thinking the time has come now. They haven't given us any option. They can't attack Bog and just expect us to sit back and do nothing. What would that say about us? That we don't care? We are cowards? No way. We need to take our revenge and we need to make it count.'

287

'I agree,' Cris replied and his brother Ben also nodded his head in approval. 'I'll get everyone together this evening in the room at the snooker hall and we can make our plans.'

Chapter 40

Scotty was feeling very satisfied with himself. Everything had gone well. Just as he'd predicted it would. And why wouldn't it? He was good at this sort of thing. He'd been doing it practically all his life. It was pretty simple really. In Scotty's view, most times you just had to get on and do it and not get caught up overthinking things. What if this happens, what if that ….who cares? Just take control of the situation and do it!

He'd lain low for a day or two afterwards, just to make sure there were no immediate repercussions from what he had done to the Romanian guy. They might have been looking for him. For a quick revenge. But it was all quiet. That was good. Either they didn't know it was him that had done it, or they didn't know what to do without their leader. In his mind he preferred to think it was the latter. He assumed Bog would be incapacitated for a while and he hoped the rest of the Romanians realised it was him that had attacked their man. He'd deliberately left Bog near where they'd dumped him before, so they'd get the message. He hoped they'd realise that. Don't mess with Scotty. That was the message.

289

Scotty was on his way now to meet with some of the other guys at the club. He hoped all of the gang would be there so he could tell them all together. He guessed they would know that something had happened to the Romanian leader, you couldn't keep something like that quiet, but they wouldn't know all the details. They wouldn't know what Scotty knew, what he had done. How he had sorted out their problems for them. He had kept it simple, no need for fancy technology plans. Just simple violence, he laughed to himself. He couldn't wait to tell them. The guys would be so pleased with him. He imagined they'd probably spend the rest of the day just celebrating and getting pissed. What could be better!

As soon as he arrived at the club Scotty went looking for Ally Bolton. He found him in the dance hall talking to one of the barmen. He waited until the conversation finished then walked across to his boss.

'Ally,' he called out as he approached with a big smile on his face.

'Hi Scotty, you okay?' Ally asked. 'What you looking so happy about?'

'Aye, sure,' Scotty replied, still smiling broadly. 'Are the lads all here?'

'Charlie and Chopper are in the back office. Eddie and Smithy are out checking out some of the other clubs,' Ally replied.

'Okay, dae ye have a minute? There's somethin' I want tae tell ye aw,' Scotty replied, unable to stop himself from smiling.

290

'Okay, sure, I'm heading back to the office now, let's go there and catch up with Charlie and Chopper,' Ally replied.

Scotty nodded his head and walked smartly alongside his boss. He couldn't wait to tell them all what he'd done.

Chapter 41

To say it hadn't gone quite as well as Scotty had been expecting was an understatement. He'd walked into the room, still with a big smile on his face, and sat down at the long table with Ally, Charlie and Chopper alongside him. He couldn't hold himself back and launched straight into it, proudly telling them exactly what he'd done to Bog and his two bodyguards.

When he'd finished talking he was surprised to see that no-one seemed to be smiling, they all had blank faces. Scotty had expected them all to be pleased with him. He'd done what they'd all been talking about doing. What they'd been planning, except he'd done it more quickly and with less fuss. Surely that was a good thing?

Apparently not. There was no celebration, no pats on the back, no "well done Scotty" from any of the others in the room. Ally and Charlie were furious. Charlie couldn't stay seated and began pacing the room. Chopper just sat there shaking his head. Scotty was shocked by their reaction. He couldn't understand it and he tried to explain how it was a good thing, what they'd all discussed doing, but he'd done it for them. But Ally and Charlie had a different view on it. They were insistent that he shouldn't have done it without their say so, without them knowing. These things needed to be planned and things put in place for afterwards. Had he thought about the repercussions? How the Romanians were going to react, they asked him?

He hadn't really. Scotty had just wanted revenge for the beating they'd given him and that's what he'd done. But he also thought it would be good for the Boltons. Teaching the Romanians a lesson. He knew they might come for him, which is why he'd stayed hidden for a few days. He hadn't thought any more than that. But who cared what the Romanians would do next? If they wanted a big fight then he was fine with that. He was ready for them. Ally had moved seat to the top of the table and he began to speak.

'Okay, in some ways Scotty is right. He's done what we were going to do, largely. He's taken out Bog. We just need to get our act together now for what we do next. And what they might do. We need to get everyone together, call everyone in,' Ally said. 'If I was them I'd be looking to hit back at us quickly with something bigger than what they've been doing up to now. I'm guessing something at one of the clubs, more violence, maybe some damage, a fire or something like that, that would be the easiest thing for them to do. Something that really disrupts our business.'

'Okay, I'll up the security on the clubs, double the team, at least for the rest of this week,' Charlie said. 'We'll keep a close eye on who's coming in to the clubs. If they try something we'll be ready for them with good numbers.'

'We should find out what the current position is with Bog too,' Ally said. 'Is he still alive? Is he in hospital, or what? Chopper, can you see what you can find out, someone must know.'

Chopper nodded and made a mental note to himself.

'Whit aboot we take the initiative and hit them first, attack them in their snooker place?' Scotty suggested, keen to try and get back in the Boltons' good books.

'No,' Ally replied immediately, shaking his head. 'Let's find out about Bog and wait for them to come to us. We'll be better prepared on our own premises and I don't think we'll have to wait long.'

Chapter 42

DC Knight and DI Strong were sitting at the long table in Strong's office. Knight had told Strong about the attack on Bogdan Popescu and her attempted questioning of another of the Romanians at the hospital.

'I couldn't get anything out of him,' Knight explained. 'He pretended he didn't speak English but I overheard him talking with one of the nurses earlier and his English was perfectly good. I don't suppose we'll get anything out of them though, even if Popescu does wake up. They don't like talking to us.'

'No, I think you're right,' Strong replied. 'I guess we can assume it was Boltons' mob that carried out the beating. We knew they were planning something, we just didn't know when.'

'What do you think we should do?' Knight asked. 'Go and see the Boltons? I don't suppose they're going to own up to anything, but we could warn them that we're watching them.'

'No, I don't think so,' Strong replied, shaking his head, 'but we need to keep an eye on things. Especially with the Romanians. The Chief is getting very twitchy about this gang war stuff and we need to make sure it doesn't escalate and get out of hand. If the Romanians can get themselves organised without their leader they might want to get their revenge for this attack. Do we know who might take over from Popescu?'

'We're still gathering information on them, but from what we know so far the most likely successor, at least while Bogdan is out of action, is a guy called Alexandru Ola....Olarescu,' DC Knight replied. 'I think that's how you pronounce it. It could have been him I saw at the hospital, that would make sense, but we haven't got a recent photo of him. He's supposed to be Bogdan Popescu's cousin and he's got a record as long as your arm back in Romania. Why we let him come here, I don't know. He likes a bit of violence which obviously isn't the best thing. At least with Bogdan he seemed to be working his way in gradually without too much serious aggravation. Just a bit of hassle in the clubs, disrupting the Boltons' operation, but nothing too bad. We might have a different situation on our hands now.'

'Yes, you could be right,' Strong replied, leaning back in his chair and stretching his long legs out in front of him. He ran his hand through his hair, scratching his head and thinking what best to do next. How much to discuss with Knight?

'We could do with knowing what the Romanians are planning,' Knight said. 'Are they going to seek their revenge or carry on as they were? What about your man you used before to get inside the Boltons team. Could you use him with the Romanians at all?'

DI Strong grimaced at the memory of Jack Wilson and the Bolton mob. It had started well. He'd got in there easily enough and planted the listening device and Strong had got a lot of good information on what they were planning to do, which of course was to attack Bogdan Popescu, which it now appeared they'd gone ahead and done. But then they'd found the device and guessed it was Jack Wilson who had planted it. Jack had told Strong about how they'd picked him up at the sports centre and asked him who he was working for. Thankfully they hadn't hurt him, Strong guessed that knowing he was working for the police, they didn't want to take the risk of giving the police an excuse to crawl all over them. But knowing that the police knew their plans, they obviously changed their tactics and seemingly successfully carried out the hit on Bogdan without the police having any idea it was imminent.

If the Romanians were going to take revenge for the attack on their leader it was likely that they would do it quickly. That would mean he would need to get Jack Wilson in straight away, which would be a greater risk for him. The more he thought about it though, he supposed it might be possible. They knew that the Romanians main hang out was at the snooker club and so if he could get Jack in there to plant a device, they might just have a chance to find out what the Romanians were planning to do.

'Yes, that's a possible,' Strong concluded. 'Let me have a chat with him and see what we can do. The trouble is I don't think the Romanians will

hang around. If they're going to take their revenge I
think they'll do it soon. Maybe even this weekend.
They may already have decided what they're going
to do. Keep an eye on Popescu in the hospital, as
soon as he is awake we need to try and see if he will
tell us anything. Maybe see if you can have another
go with his cousin too. If they know we're watching
them, that might put them off doing anything for a
while, which could buy us the time we need to get
more information.'

DC Knight returned to her desk in the main
office, a little dispirited. It felt like the calm before
the storm. She was sure that the Romanian gang
were going to cause more trouble, exact their
revenge for the vicious assault on their leader,
Bogdan Popescu, but there was nothing she could
do to stop it. She doubted that Alexandru Olarescu
would agree to talk to her and she also didn't think
that whatever the police did would have any impact
on whatever the Romanians were now planning. It
was out of her hands and all she could hope for was
that it would be quick and decisive, putting an end
to all the trouble and giving the police an
opportunity to get some of the key figures behind
bars.

Back in his office, DI Strong called Jack
Wilson. He knew getting Jack to plant a bug in the
Romanian's meeting place was a long shot but he
couldn't think of anything else to do at the moment
that would give the police the advantage they
needed. After a few rings, Jack answered the phone.

DI Strong gave Jack a bit of background on
what was happening with the two gangs but taking

care to avoid any reference to the assault on Bogdan Popescu. He didn't want to scare him off. Instead he explained he just wanted Jack to do a similar job to what he'd done previously, planting a listening device, but this time in the Snooker Club. Strong told Jack he would provide him with plans of the building and the location of the room where the bug would need to be placed.

'Okay, that all sounds fine,' Jack replied. 'Is next week okay? I can do it after I come back from the Lake District.

'The Lake District? What are you doing there?' Strong asked.

'Well, remember you told me I should lay low for a bit after those guys abducted me?' Jack replied. 'Well, me and Lucy and the kid have come up to the Lake district for a week to get away. It's lovely. I should be back Monday though if that's okay. Maybe I could meet you then?'

'Yeh, okay lets do that,' Strong replied and he ended the call. Shit, he thought. Monday might be too late. His police detective gut was telling him that something was going to happen this weekend. He hoped he was wrong.

Chapter 43

Campbell looked at his notes on the screen again. Three pages of them. He knew most of it by heart now, he'd gone over it often enough, but he also knew everything he had was just circumstantial. But taken together as one, it could read pretty conclusive. Couldn't it? At least he thought it was. But would the Chief Constable think the same way, he wondered, and what would it mean for his own career in the police? Being known as a whistle-blower on his boss? DI Strong was well liked in the police force. He had a lot of supporters at all levels. He knew the Chief Constable rated Strong highly and even Campbell himself was a huge fan of Strong, at least he had been until he had found out some of the things Strong had been doing. Things that just weren't right. Not by the book. Being a police officer meant you had to do things correctly. In Campbell's eyes you had to be whiter than white and be seen as being that too. No matter how hard it was. No matter how the system seemed to be working against you and in favour of the criminals. Yes, it could be very frustrating at times but Campbell believed that the right way always succeeded.

And what he had in front of him now indicated that DI Strong didn't always play by the rules. In Campbell's eyes he didn't even just bend the rules, it looked like he just ignored them. Campbell had become convinced that Strong would do almost anything to secure, what he saw as, justice. He had been very good at covering his tracks, getting rid of anything that linked him, but he'd made a few mistakes, too many for Campbell to not pick up on. And when you put them together the overall picture became clearer and even compelling. Strong had been involved in too many things that he didn't need to be. It was all too suspicious and as Strong himself had often told Campbell in the past, he didn't believe in coincidences.

From what Campbell had been able to piece together, it had all started with Andy Austin, the Anniversary Killer. Although Strong may have been doing the same thing before that, but Campbell hadn't uncovered anything to show that. With Andy Austin, at the time a wanted murderer, it appeared DI Strong had some sort of secret connection. He seemed to have been in contact with Austin and used him to carry out attacks on people who Strong thought deserved it. Granted they were criminals, but that wasn't the right way to do it. He even had Austin staying at his place in Leeds after he'd attacked Kyle Smith, the estate agent. That was a strange one, Campbell didn't know why Smith had been targeted but all the evidence indicated that Strong had a hand in it.

Then there was the time when Campbell had almost caught Austin, but he'd fallen and knocked himself out. It was Strong who had called the ambulance and given them the correct address. That had been suspicious and Strong's explanation that Austin had called him with the address, although possible, still seemed unlikely. Unless they already had a connection. Thinking back, Austin always seemed to have been one step ahead of them. He'd escaped from the farmhouse before the police got there. He'd left his partner Lucy in the park just before Campbell arrived. It was as if someone was tipping him off and, the more Campbell thought about it, that person could only have been DI Strong.

The final thing connected to Andy Austin was a strange one. One that Campbell hadn't been able to work out yet. Austin had been killed in a hit and run and it had been a few months before they'd identified the body as actually being him. Not long after that positive ID, Strong had asked DC Harris to go and talk to Jack Wilson, put some heat on him was what he had said. There was definitely history between Wilson and Austin but was that enough for Wilson to have killed Austin in the hit and run? And if it was, why had Strong not taken it further? The only possibility Campbell could think of was that he was using Wilson in some way, like he had used Austin before, to help in his approach to solving crimes and getting convictions. Could he be blackmailing Wilson to help him? Campbell didn't have any evidence of that and it was something they would have to investigate further if the Chief

Constable agreed with his findings. At least Wilson was still alive to be asked.

Then, more recently, there had been the Tony Fleming and Dylan Hughes deaths. Again DI Strong seemed to have been more involved in the whole thing than he needed to be. And he was keen, too keen maybe, to wrap the whole thing up as a double killing, even though it was likely that wasn't the case. And Campbell couldn't help thinking that Strong had got hold of Dylan's diary and tried to dispose of it. Marsha hadn't shown him it, she said it was too personal, but from what she had told him there was nothing in there to incriminate Strong. But maybe Strong thought that there might have been and so he took the diary to check and then, not having a plausible excuse for having it, he just decided to dump it. Marsha had also told Campbell about Dylan's laptop and when he followed that up with Jason in I.T., it appeared that Strong had told him to wipe everything from it. He'd told Jason that it was to protect Marsha and Campbell could understand that. But what if it wasn't for that reason. What if it was because Strong was frightened there might be some incriminating stuff on there? Campbell didn't know what, or what his connection with Dylan was but he was convinced there had been something and that Strong was keen to ensure it didn't surface. It might be possible to get an expert to retrieve what was on the laptop if the Chief went along with Campbell's theories.

DI Campbell looked at the clock and was surprised to see that it had just gone eleven pm. He'd warned Femi he'd be late home as he'd wanted to get this finished, as best he could, but he hadn't quite realised how long he'd been working on it. He took one last look at the file on his computer and hit the print button. Most of the team had knocked off for the night with only a few still sitting at their desks. The Serious Crime Team had a commitment to maintain a twenty four hour staff and so some of those still remaining would be there throughout the night, while others would be at home, but on call. Campbell walked across the office to the corner where the printer sat to collect his document. As he approached the device, he could see a red light flashing on the front display screen. He looked down at it and pressed the corresponding button. A message appeared on the screen,

"Error 453. Remove paper jam in tray 1"

Campbell pulled tray one out and looked into the gap it had left. There was nothing to see, no paper, no paper jam. He felt inside with his hand but again there was nothing. He looked at the paper in tray 1, it all looked okay. Half full with what appeared to be flat white sheets of paper. Nothing wrong there. He put the tray back in, pushing it firmly home. The red light was still flashing so Campbell switched the machine off, waited a few seconds and switched it on again. That often did the trick. He waited until it fired up again and then he was disappointed to see the red light was still flashing he pushed the button and this time the display read,

"Error 14. Call operator."

Campbell gave up and walked back to his desk thinking it would be too late to get anyone to fix the printer now. He'd have to try again in the morning, or maybe if he just took his laptop to the Chief Constable's office, they could print it off there. Campbell guessed the Chief would have his own personal printer, one of his many perks.

As he was unplugging his laptop to go home, he sensed a commotion in the office and he looked up to see DC Harris walking across the floor towards him.

'We've just had word that it's all kicking off at Club Extream. It seems that the Romanians are taking their revenge for what happened to Bog and they're smashing the place up, some sort of big fight,' Harris said excitedly. 'We're going there now, you coming?'

'Yes, sure,' Campbell replied, shutting down his laptop and grabbing his jacket from the back of his chair. He wasn't going to miss this.

Chapter 44

Outside, in the police car park, there were a number of people running towards their cars, a mix of uniformed and plain clothes policemen and policewomen. Almost everyone on night shift. Campbell was jogging along behind DC Harris.

'You want to jump in with me?' Harris asked as he stopped beside his car, a black Audi.

'Sure,' Campbell replied and he opened the passenger door and slid inside, pulling the seat belt around his solid frame.

Harris started the car and they drove out of the car park, in convoy with two other cars, both with their blue flashing lights and sirens on. Harris drove along carefully, staying in line with the two other police cars. As they made their way to the club, the other traffic moved out of their way, pulling into the side, and in no time at all they were all coming to a stop outside the doorway to Club Extream. There were already a few police cars there and Campbell saw two or three uniformed police enter the building as other people spilled out onto the street, mostly young women in brightly coloured dresses. He opened his car door and turned towards Harris,

'Come on, let's go see what's happening,' he said, but Harris didn't move.

'Shouldn't we wait a bit? Maybe we need an armed team? We don't know what's happening in there yet,' Harris replied.

'Exactly,' Campbell responded. 'We need to get in there and find out.'

Campbell closed the car door and started jogging towards the club entrance. As he entered, he was almost knocked over by a mass of people coming the other way. The majority were women, but there were also a few young men too. All of them, men and women, had a look of shock on their faces as they stared straight ahead, eyes focused on the club exit.

Inside the club, Campbell edged along the corridor wall, regularly bumping against fleeing customers, until he reached the doorway to the main hall. He stepped inside and stood still for a second trying to get his bearings, and to let his eyes get accustomed to the dim lighting. It was a long time since he'd been in a club, not since he was a young man, before he married Femi. But the clubs he used to go to were a lot smaller than this. This one looked huge, and chaotic. It was very noisy with people screaming and running in all directions. On top of that the music was still playing, a deep bass beat that Campbell could feel rising up into his legs and body, through the soles of his feet. He tried to get a sense of what, and where, people were running from and for a brief second he saw through a gap in the mass of people to the middle of the dance floor where there seemed to be some fighting taking

307

place. He started to make his way towards it, easing past people coming the other way.

Outside the club, DI Strong pulled up and jumped out of his car leaving the document he'd just read lying on the passenger seat. He made his way into the club. There were still people coming out, but in lesser numbers now and he soon made his way to the entrance to the main dance hall. He stepped inside and, like Campbell before him, he stood for a second until his eyes adjusted to the light. The music had stopped, but there were still multi coloured strobe lights flashing away to a now, non-existent beat. There were a lot of people in the big room but most of them had moved to the edges, huddled together in small groups, leaving a core of people fighting in the middle of the dance floor. There were a few upturned tables and chairs scattered around and pools of liquid on the floor where drinks had been knocked over. Strong estimated there were about twenty five men now involved, including a couple of uniformed police who he guessed must have been first on the scene.

Suddenly there was a loud bang which echoed around the room, followed, after a pause, by more screaming. A gunshot. This was getting serious and as Strong made his way towards the fighting group, he could see them thinning out as several more men stood back following the gun shot. Strong couldn't see if anyone had been hit and he guessed it might just have been a warning shot. A message to say "back off, I've got a gun." There was still some sporadic fighting going on around the edges of the group, not even the gun shot had stopped them, and as the noise of the gun shot faded, the fighting started to spread more widely again. Strong was now just a few paces away from the edge of the group and, to his surprise, he saw DI Campbell in the midst of the fighting, throwing a few punches. In his younger days Campbell had been quite a good boxer and he was demonstrating those skills now.

DC Knight had just entered the room and she stood watching, trying to get a better idea of what was going on, and what her next move might be. Thirty minutes earlier, she'd been at home, lying on the couch, watching some late night trash TV. When the call had come in, she'd jumped up quickly, grabbed her police badge, and made her way to the club as speedily as she could. She was excited, this was what she'd joined the police for, a bit of action.

Standing at the doorway, the light wasn't good, flashing on and off, but Knight thought she could glimpse DI Strong in amongst it all. He was a tall man and his silver hair stood out among the younger men. The man had his back to her though and in the melee she couldn't be certain it was him.

DI Strong was now at the edge of the group. The man immediately in front of him was shouting, mainly obscenities, which seemed to be directed towards some of the other men on the opposite side of the dance floor. Strong caught a glimpse of the side of the man's face as a light flashed on him, and he recognised him as being Ally Bolton, the leader of the Bolton gang. Strong gave him a hard push in the back and Ally Bolton couldn't resist, his legs propelling him forward towards the men he had just been shouting at. There was another loud bang and Ally Bolton suddenly stopped. He took a step backwards, looking down, his hands automatically moving to his chest. Time seemed to stop, no-one was moving, everyone just standing watching Ally Bolton. Strong reacted quickly, taking advantage of the mass paralysis, and he soon worked his way around until he was behind the man who had fired the shot. The man still had the gun in his hand and Strong grabbed his wrist, smashing it down onto his knee to try and dislodge the gun, but the man was strong and he managed to hold on. He threw his elbow back and caught Strong in the face and for the first time Strong realised he was up against a big man. The man shouted something, in Romanian, Strong guessed, and he tried to elbow Strong again. But Strong was ready for him this time and he ducked to one side.

Meanwhile, across the floor, DI Campbell threw another punch, successfully connecting with the side of a man's head and he fell to the floor. Campbell was enjoying this, it felt like he was back in the ring again. As the man fell, Campbell saw through a gap to two men fighting on the far side. He immediately recognised one of the men as DI Strong and it looked like he was struggling. Campbell stepped through the gap left by the fallen man and moved towards DI Strong.

Strong still had one hand clamped on the big Romanian's wrist and he kicked him hard in the leg, behind his knee. The man's legs gave way and he sunk down to the floor. Strong brought his elbow hard down on the man's head and felt him crumble slightly more. Over the man's head, Strong caught a glimpse of Campbell heading towards them, sweat shining off his forehead and a determined look on his face. Strong moved his hand down the man's wrist towards the gun, determined to get a hold of it and suddenly there was a third loud bang. Another gunshot.

DC Knight had made her way to the edge of the group. She caught sight of a couple of men she knew were part of the Bolton gang. The fighting seemed to be getting less and less as more men went down and on the latest gunshot only a few men carried on fighting. She could now see Strong and Campbell for definite. Strong was grappling with a large man who she recognised as the Romanian she'd met in the hospital, Alexandru Olarescu. The man who had apparently taken over the leadership of the Romanian gang while Bogdan Popescu lay in a hospital bed. Strong was behind him and both men appeared to be on their knees. Campbell was in the middle of the group, seemingly throwing punches at anyone that got in his way. Knight remembered someone telling her that he used to be a boxer.

Knight transferred her focus back to DI Strong. Suddenly there was another loud bang, another gunshot, and DC Knight involuntarily flinched. She resisted the temptation to step back and as her ears began to recover from the noise of the gunfire, she began to hear more shouting and screaming. DI Strong was still holding on to the big Romanian and, for the first time, she could see a gun in the big Romanian's hand, with Strong's hand overlapping the Romanian's fingers. She looked back across the group, but she couldn't see Campbell any more. Where was he?

At that very moment, there was a sudden influx of armed policemen, dressed in black flak jackets with the word "POLICE" emblazoned on the front in large, luminous silver letters. They surrounded the group, pointing their guns inwards and shouting aggressively. The armed police ordered everyone to lie down on the dance hall floor. DC Knight complied and as she sank down she saw DI Strong and his Romanian opponent do likewise, the gun falling and bouncing away from them across the floor out of Knight's sight. The armed police were now in control and they were systematically ordering people to stand up again, a few at a time, their guns still carefully trained on them as they moved them back towards the wall. While DC Knight waited her turn, she saw two of the armed policemen go down on their knees to apparently look at something on the floor. The policeman standing nearest to her motioned with his gun that she should now stand up and, as she did so, she took out her warrant card to let him see that she was also with the police. She moved towards DI Strong who was now also on his feet, giving him a little smile as she approached her boss. Knight reached out and touched Strong's arm.

'Are you okay?' she asked him, but he didn't react and she realised he was staring at the two kneeling policemen. They were giving CPR to a body lying on the floor. As DC Knight looked over, she saw that the man lying prone on the floor was DI Campbell.

Chapter 45

Femi Campbell woke up groggily from her sleep. There was a noise, what was it? It wasn't the baby crying, she would have recognised that straight away. She'd heard it often enough. Been woken up by it often enough. No it was a harsher sound than that. Something urgent. As she became fully awake she realised it was someone banging on the front door. She turned in the bed to face Joe, but he wasn't there. Femi sighed and turned, pushing back the duvet, she swung her legs out of the bed and put on her slippers and dressing gown. She looked at the bedside clock. It showed two thirty a.m.

Femi left the bedroom and switched the hall light on. The banging at the door stopped. She made her way down the cream carpeted stairs and stopped at the grey coloured front door.

'Who is it?' she called out.

'It's the police ma'am. Can you open the door please?' a female voice replied.

Femi looked through the frosted glass window on the door and could make out what she thought were two dark shapes. Two people. She had suggested to Joe that they get one of the doorbells with a camera in it, for safety reasons. It would be good to know who was at the door before you opened it. But Joe had said that they were a waste of money.

'Why do we need to see what the pizza delivery man looks like?' he said, telling her that they got so few visitors that the battery would have run out before they ever used it.

But Femi wished she had one now. At two thirty in the morning, she wanted to see that these were real police officers before she opened the door. They could be anyone.

Sensing her hesitation, the female voice called out again.

'Mrs Campbell, I'm going to pass my police identity badge through the letterbox so that you can see who I am.'

Femi watched as a flat, black, rectangular wallet holder slowly appeared through her letterbox. She took hold of it pulled it fully through. She held it up and looked at it. It seemed real. It was similar to the one Joe had. There was a photo of a woman with dark hair and the name beside it read "Laura Knight," with the title Detective Constable underneath in official looking black letters. That name seemed to ring a bell, there was a Detective Knight, she was sure she'd heard Joe mention her before. She decided to open the door slowly, ready to close it again if she needed to. But nothing happened and she soon had the door fully open. Femi could now see two police officers standing on her doorstep. One was presumably Laura Knight and the other was a young male officer in uniform. She handed the identity card back to Laura Knight and invited the two police officers into her house. They walked along the hallway and turned right into the living room. Femi turned the light on and beckoned to them to take a seat on the sofa. Femi sat down on the armchair across from them, leaning forward with her hands clasped together on her knees.

'We're sorry to disturb you at this time of the night Mrs Campbell,' the woman police officer began, 'I'm Detective Constable Knight and this is my colleague Police Constable Addison. We both work with your husband, Detective Inspector Campbell.'

Femi nodded, wondering what these police officers were doing here and if she should be offering them a cup of tea. She hadn't quite woken up yet and was feeling a bit confused. She hadn't realised it was so late, or early. After she'd got the baby to sleep, she'd lain down on her bed and must have just fallen asleep. Sometimes that happened.

'I'm afraid there was an incident at a night club and your husband, DI Campbell, has been injured. He's been taken to hospital but he is said to be in a stable condition,' DC Knight continued. 'Would you like to go and see him? We can take you there.'

'A night club, you said? What was he doing in a club?' Femi replied still feeling confused. 'He doesn't go to clubs any more. We have a baby.'

DC Knight leaned forward and put her hand on Femi's knee.

'I know Mrs Campbell. DI Campbell was on duty there, at the club. We all were,' DC Knight

316

replied, talking softly, still with her hand on Femi's knee. 'There was a big gang fight at the club and someone had a gun which unfortunately went off and hit DI Campbell. He was attended to straight away and taken in an ambulance to St. Johns hospital. As I said he is stable but you maybe want to come and see him. We have a car waiting outside.'

'Shot?.. shot, oh my god!' Femi said, standing up and pacing the room. 'I knew this would happen one day. I knew it. I told him. Is he....is he badly injured? Where was he hit?'

'He was shot in the chest, but as I say the doctors say he is stable. Do you want to get ready and we can take you to see him?' DC Knight replied, keen to get going.

'Yes, yes, sure....give me a minute...I'll just...' Femi replied as she left the room.

DC Knight and PC Addison sat in silence while they waited for Femi Campbell to reappear. Both were deep in thought, thinking how they would react if the police knocked on their door in the middle of the night to tell them a loved one had been shot. Not well, they both thought. Shocked certainly, but also a bit of disbelief and anger. Who would shoot someone they loved?

Femi stepped back into the living room, interrupting their thoughts and both police officers stood up. She was dressed casually, wearing a yellow sweat shirt and grey leggings, carrying a small bag and a baby.

'I'll have to bring Rosey,' she explained. 'I can't wake up my mum or anyone else at this time of the morning. It's too early.'

'Yes, I understand,' DC Knight replied. 'Let's go. We have a car waiting.'

'I knew this would happen one day,' Femi said as they walked along the hallway. 'I told him not to be a hero, but that was always him, wanting to be the one to…' her voice faded and she began to sob quietly.

Knight, Addison, Femi and the baby all left the house and got into the waiting police car outside. Knight sat in the rear of the car along with Femi and the baby, ready to do anything needed, but not knowing what to do. Femi continued to sob quietly. PC Addison slid into the driver's seat and they set off to St. Johns Hospital, Addison switching on his blue light although there was very little traffic at this time of the day.

They were soon at the hospital and Addison parked the car behind two other police cars at the side of the road, near the hospital entrance. DC Knight and Femi got out of the car, Femi still carrying baby Rosey. Luckily the baby had stayed asleep throughout the journey and Femi had now stopped crying. They entered the main, brightly lit, hospital entrance and Knight went up to the reception desk. They were directed to a corridor on the left, signposted "Accident and Emergency." Knight led the way and they soon reached a busy waiting area with people occupying most of the space, some standing, some sitting on plastic seats and some in wheelchairs. Knight went to the reception counter and explained why she was there. The woman on duty directed her to a door behind the desk which led to a number of curtained bays. Femi followed her through the door and they found DI Campbell in bay number four. Knight pulled back the curtain and the two women stepped inside. Femi's hand immediately went to her mouth and she let out a gasp on seeing her husband lying there, in the hospital trolley bed.

DI Campbell had a clear plastic mask over his mouth and various tubes and cables attached to it, and other parts of his body. All around him there were pieces of hospital equipment seemingly feeding stuff into his body, or recording how his body was performing. Despite all of this, Campbell looked peaceful. He was lying perfectly still, on his back, arms by his side with only the normal rise and fall of his chest demonstrating any sign of life. Knight looked at his chest for a few seconds and thought his breathing looked normal. Regular. That must be a good sign. Femi had moved to the side of DI Campbell's bed.

'Would you like me to hold the baby?' Knight asked and Femi turned around and handed her baby to the detective without replying.

Campbell's wife stood by the side of his bed, leaning over it, looking at the face of her husband, what she could see of it, not sure what to do. She wanted to hug her husband, hold his hand. Something. She wanted to do something. Most of all she wanted to wake up and find out this was just a bad dream, that it wasn't real. It couldn't be. But she knew it was.

Femi wanted to talk to him and tell him how much she loved him. Most of all she wanted him to wake up and smile. One of his big famous smiles, just for her. There was too much equipment, she didn't want to disturb anything, knock something out. She reached tentatively forward with her right hand and placed it on his arm. It felt warm. It wasn't much, but it was all she could think of to do. And warm must be good surely. Not cold.

DC Knight stood at the back of the bay, watching Femi, while carefully holding the baby. She was still asleep but Knight could see that she was a beautiful little girl, there was no doubt about that, and Knight could see bits of both parents in her. Her mother's hair, her father's nose. Femi was still holding DI Campbell's arm, standing beside the bed in silence and Knight could see tears rolling down her face as she began to sob again. Knight wished there was something she could do, or say, that would help her.

Just then, the curtain opened and a man in a white coat stepped inside, almost bumping into DC Knight as he entered. He stood for a second, taking in the scene, before walking to the opposite side of the bed to where Femi stood, picking up the clipboard from the end of the bed as he passed.

'Are you Mrs Campbell?' he asked Femi and she nodded, sniffing at the same time and wiping tears from her cheeks with the back of her hand. 'I'm Doctor Wright,' he said, introducing himself. 'As you probably know your husband came in with a gunshot wound to his chest area. He also took a blow to the back of his head, probably the

320

force of the gunshot knocked him backwards and he hit the floor. We're keeping an eye on that too. He is in a stable condition at the moment and we'll be taking him up to the operating theatre soon to have a proper look at him. We'll know more after that.'

'Is he.....is he going to die?' Femi asked, looking directly at the doctor, her eyes wide with fear and Knight could see that she was trembling. Knight felt a shiver run down her spine.

'At the moment all I can tell you Mrs Campbell is that he is stable,' the doctor replied. 'We'll do all we can to help him and I can assure you he is in good hands, but we won't know any more until we've had him in theatre. I'll come and talk to you after that. Meanwhile, I'd suggest you have a seat in the waiting room. I'll ask one of the nurses to come and take you there.'

And with that he was gone, back out through the curtain and Knight could hear him talking to someone outside in the corridor. Femi hadn't moved, still looking as if she was in conversation with the doctor, even though he was no longer there. The curtain opened again and this time a nurse entered the bay. The nurse was dressed in a blue and white uniform with a white hat. She approached Femi and put a hand on her arm.

'Would you like to come and have a seat in the family waiting room?' she said gently.

Femi looked at her, frightened to leave Joe on his own, but knowing she should do as the nurse said. She slowly let go of Joe's arm and turned to go with the nurse. DC Knight pulled the curtain open again and the three women and the baby walked down the corridor towards the waiting room. To wait. But for what, none of them knew.

Chapter 46

DI Strong walked through the office until he reached the desk DI Campbell had been using. The whole area was very quiet, although there were quite a few people in, no-one was talking. No-one was in the mood to talk. It just didn't seem right. One of their team had been shot and was lying in a hospital bed with an uncertain future.

Strong pulled out the chair and sat down at Campbell's desk. Alexandru Olarescu was in a cell downstairs and Ally Bolton was in the morgue. Strong had decided to make Olarescu wait for a while before he questioned him. The Romanian had asked for his lawyer, but Strong was confident that they would soon be charging him with the murder of Ally Bolton, and the attempted murder of DI Campbell.

But Strong had another important job to do before he started on Olarescu. He looked at Campbell's desk. The only things on the desktop were a biro pen, an orange stapler, a phone, a screen and an attached cable. Nothing personal, no documents. It hadn't been Campbell's permanent desk, just one he had been using while he had been seconded back to the team and Strong guessed he'd not adopted it fully as yet.

Strong opened and closed the desk drawers one by one. They were all empty. It appeared Campbell wasn't one for collecting stationery items or keeping any sort of printed documentation. At least not here in this desk. He stood up and turned towards the rest of the team sitting at their own desks.

'Does anyone know where DI Campbell's laptop is?' he asked generally. There were a few negative murmurs and general head shaking before Strong saw a hand go up. It was DC Harris.

'Yes, I've got it Guv,' Harris said. 'I was going to go through it to see if there was anything outstanding that we needed to pick up and action while Campbell is in hospital. I was going to let you know.'

'Okay. Have you started looking yet?' Strong asked the detective.

'No, not really. I was just starting to when I had to take a call. I was going to do it later when things were a bit quieter and we knew a bit more about Joe's situation…,' Harris replied.

'Okay, well, can you give it to me?' Strong requested. 'I think with it being DI Campbell, it's probably something I should do. As you know we worked pretty close together and I owe it to him. There might also be personal stuff on it and I'll be going to see his wife tomorrow so I can let her know then.'

'Okay Guv, no problem,' DC Harris replied and he picked up a laptop and cable from his desk and handed it over to DI Strong.

Strong took the device and walked back to his office. Inside, he closed the door and plugged in Campbell's laptop while sitting down in his big leather chair. He switched the machine on and the screen fired up. Strong scanned the various icons on the laptop screen and stopped when he saw a file icon with the name "Strong". He clicked on it and the file opened up in front of him. It was a Word document and as he skimmed through it he recognised it as being the same document he'd seen before. The one he now had in his briefcase.

A few hours before, just as Strong had been getting ready to go to the incident at Club Extream, young Jason from I.T. had come to his office.

'I was working late tonight and saw the office printer was jammed. I've managed to fix it,' he said to Strong as the detective started putting his coat on. 'I found this on it, I guess it must be yours, I saw your name at the top of it,' he said, handing a document to DI Strong. It was DI Campbell's notes, his thoughts, on his colleague DI Strong.

As he quickly scanned through it, Strong could see that most of the content was correct and he couldn't help but admire his colleague's detective skills. He'd certainly done a good job piecing it together as much as he had been able to over the years. Each individual part on its own wasn't significant, but when taken all together, Strong could see that it could be interpreted as something bigger, which of course he knew it was.

He sat back in his office chair for a few seconds, just thinking, before leaning forward again and closing the Word document on Campbell's laptop. Strong clicked on the file icon once more and selected the "delete" option. The icon disappeared. But Strong knew that didn't mean the file had disappeared completely. He clicked on the "Recycle Bin" icon and it opened up showing a list of files. He selected the one entitled "Strong" again and deleted it.

"Do you want to permanently delete this file?" the computer asked and Strong selected the "Yes" option.

He would have to talk to Campbell when he woke up and was strong enough to have a sensible conversation. Somehow he would have to convince his fellow detective that what he had done over the last few years had been the right thing to do. That it was the only thing to do to ensure that justice was served. He hoped Campbell would see sense.

Chapter 47

Femi Campbell, DC Knight and baby Rosey had been sitting in the relatives' waiting room for the last two hours. Nobody had come to see them and Knight had gone looking for a nurse a couple of times to find out what was happening, but she had just been told there was no news yet.

Apparently DI Campbell was still in theatre and the doctor would come and see them as soon as he was finished. Knight had also managed to find a café and had returned with two coffees. Femi hadn't touched hers, leaving it on the small wooden table set in the middle of the room, and Knight had felt somewhat guilty at eagerly drinking her own coffee, but she'd needed the caffeine kick. It had been a long night.

The detective had tried starting conversation a few times but Femi was not for talking. She just sat there, on a beige coloured padded chair, holding the baby, head bowed, staring down at the floor. DC Knight could only imagine the pain she was going through, wondering what the future held for her and her family.

At one point, Knight had also managed to leave the room to make a phone call. She'd phoned

DI Strong to see how he was and if there was any further news on the incident. She was relieved to hear that Strong was okay. She had worried that he might have also been injured in the struggle at the club, he'd been in the thick of it, but he assured her he was fine and that he was back in the police station.

Strong told her that Ally Bolton had died at the scene and they were holding Alexandru Olarescu in the police cells downstairs, pending interrogation. He didn't have anything to add about Campbell that Knight didn't already know. Strong told Knight to stay at the hospital with Femi and to let him know as soon as there was any further news on DI Campbell.

'What did you see at the club?' Strong asked, but before Knight could reply Strong carried on talking. 'Did you see what happened? Did you see Bolton running towards the Romanian and getting shot by him and then the same thing with DI Campbell as he made his way through the crowd towards Olarescu? I tried to knock the gun out of Olarescu's hand but he had a tight grip on it and I couldn't stop him firing.'

'Well, I was at the edge of the group and it was pretty dark and chaotic, there was lots going on, but I think that's what I saw too,' DC Knight replied.

'Ah, that's good Laura. I was hoping that you would have seen the same as me,' Strong replied. 'We may need to rely on your testimony to back me up and get a successful prosecution on Olarescu. Two respected police officers saying the same thing will be much more convincing and give us a better chance of putting him away and finally ending this turf war. I'm sure he'll have all sorts of alternative stories to try and get away with it.'

The line went quiet for a few seconds and Knight wondered if they'd been cut off, but then DI Strong spoke again.

'I'm glad I've got your backing Laura. You're a very good detective. I always know I can rely on you' Strong added and then he ended the call.

Back in the relatives' waiting room, Knight's thoughts wandered back to the club. She was relieved that nothing had happened to DI Strong. He seemed to be right in the middle of the fighting and could easily have got injured, but thankfully not. Although she had been there, on the edge of it all, Knight hadn't really seen that much of what had actually happened. She'd only been able to see snippets of what was happening in the gloomy light, and as people moved in and out of her line of sight. It was like she was watching an old black and white movie that kept cutting out and then coming back on again, a few seconds missed each time. What had happened during those few seconds?

But how Strong had described the incident to her largely fitted with what she had been able to see. It was a plausible description of the bits that she'd missed which could explain the whole story, and she was happy to back her Guvnor up on it if required. They needed to make sure Olarescu was put away for a long time and, despite what had happened to DI Campbell, this could be the

329

breakthrough she needed to end the current turf war. Which, in turn, could also be the key to her getting promoted to the role of Detective Sergeant.

Femi was still sitting in her seat. She hadn't moved at all since they'd entered the room, but now it looked like the baby was beginning to wake up. Knight could see little movements from the bundle of white blankets Femi was holding on her lap. The movements were followed by snuffling sounds. Femi awoke from her trance like state and stood up, rocking the baby back and forwards while making gentle, soothing noises into the bundle. The baby seemed to settle down again, oblivious to what was going on, that her father had been shot and was seriously ill in an operating theatre. She would never have any memory of this day, which was probably a good thing.

Knight asked Femi if everything was okay and she just nodded in reply. The detective had an urge for another coffee and asked Femi if she wanted one, briefly glancing at her untouched cup on the table, but Femi just shook her head. Her grief had seemingly taken away her ability to speak. Knight felt too guilty to get another one and so she just decided to sit down and wait. At this point in time there was nothing else she could do.

Chapter 48

Back at the police station, DI Strong and DC Harris were sitting in the large conference room, preparing for the interview with Alexandru Olarescu. There were various notes scattered on the table in front of them. The Romanian's lawyer had turned up at the police station thirty minutes ago and he and his client had been in deep conversation since then.

'I usually don't like going in blind to interrogations,' Strong said. 'I like to know who we are dealing with, how they might act, what they're likely to say. But we don't know much at all about these two do we?'

'No, not really,' DC Harris replied. 'We were just starting to gather some information on the Romanians but it's been pretty difficult. They tend to keep themselves to themselves and so we haven't been able to get that much inside information at all. All we know is that this guy, Olarescu, is Bogdan Popescu's cousin. He has a record in Romania and seems to like a bit of violence. He was prosecuted a few years ago in Bucharest on firearms offences but it didn't stick and he got off. I think it wasn't long after that when he came to the UK. As for his lawyer, he's not someone I've come across before,

331

but must have some sort of connection to the Romanians.'

'No, I've never met him before either, but hopefully that won't matter too much,' Strong replied. 'It seems pretty straightforward, what happened in the club. I know what I saw and DC Knight told me she'd seen the same. The two of us saw Olarescu shooting both Bolton and DI Campbell. I tried to stop him shooting Campbell but he had a firm grip on the gun and well…. I'm sure we'll be able to find other witnesses too, after everyone has been processed. There were a lot of people still there in the club when it happened. You didn't see anything did you?' Strong asked Harris.

'Emm, no,' Harris replied. 'I was just coming in to the club when I heard a shot go off and the armed response team were just arriving, so I waited for them and then followed them in.'

'Ah, okay, that was sensible,' Strong replied, thinking that was typical of DC Harris, safe and sure, a bit of a steady Eddie. Strong was happy though, he had Knight on his side and he was confident that would be enough.

The two detectives spent another ten minutes agreeing on their approach for the interview before picking up their notes and leaving the room.

'Did you find anything useful on Campbell's laptop?' Harris asked his boss as they walked along the corridor to meet Olarescu and his lawyer.

'Not really,' Strong replied. 'From what I could see there wasn't anything new from what he'd reported at the last team meeting. He was focusing on the Bolton gang, gathering information specifically on Ally Bolton, and of course with him dead now that's all a bit less relevant. There wasn't anything personal on the laptop. I'll give it back to you later and you can check his emails, make sure I haven't missed anything. After that we'll see how Campbell is doing, but I think he'll be off for a while recovering.'

Back in Club Extream, the remaining members of the Bolton gang had got back together. Charlie had been to identify his brother's body and had felt guilty leaving him in the morgue, but he knew it was important that they all got together and got their stories straight before the police started asking questions.

He was now sitting in the meeting room at the rear of Club Extream with his cousin Eddie, Smithy, Chopper and Scotty. With the killing of Ally, his brother Charlie had naturally assumed the lead role, at least in the short term. The rest of the gang respected that. After what had happened the previous night in the club, they had a lot to discuss.

'So is everyone clear on what we tell the police?' Charlie began. 'The story is, we were all here in the back room, talking about the business when one of the security guys, let's say it was Billy, I'll tell him what to say. So Billy comes into the room and tells us there's some sort of disturbance going on in the club. Some foreign crew starting a fight. We all go to see what's happening and we get attacked by this mob. We have to fight back, self-defence obviously, then some guy starts firing a gun. Then the police arrive and that stopped it all. Nothing else. Okay?'

'Did they take everyone's name?' Eddie asked.

'No mine,' Scotty replied. 'Ah managed tae sneak oot the back door and legged it after the fighting was finished. Ah got some good hits in afore that though.'

'Okay, well I guess they won't want to see you then,' Charlie replied. 'It'll save them having to get an interpreter in I guess,' he added laughing and the others joined in. Charlie was relieved Scotty might escape being interviewed by the police. He was a bit of a wildcard and couldn't be fully trusted not to say something he shouldn't.

'I didn't actually see the Romanian guy, Alex, I think he calls himself, shooting Ally or the other bloke but from what I understand it seems pretty clear cut that he did, so I guess he'll be in for a long stretch unless the coppers mess it up,' Eddie said.

'Actually I had a good view of it all, I wasn't that far from him,' Chopper said. 'There was a bit of a stand-off and then I saw Ally suddenly running towards the Romanian and then the gun went off and Ally fell to the ground. The next thing I see is somebody on the Romanian's back trying to wrestle the gun from him. They both had a hold of it when it went off again and hit that other bloke, the black guy. I don't know who he was but he was getting stuck in before he got shot.'

'Okay, but what we need to say is that none of us saw anything. Okay? Is that clear?' Charlie said looking around the room and the other men all nodded in response.

'Right,' Charlie continued. 'We'll close the club for a couple of days in respect of Ally and I'll have his funeral to sort out, but other than that let's carry on as normal. We don't want anyone, the Romanians or anyone else, seeing any weakness. We need to stay strong and keep the businesses going. Let's do it for Ally.'

The other four men nodded in unison.

Chapter 49

Without any warning the waiting room door suddenly opened. No knock, just a man in a white coat breezing into the room. DC Knight recognised him as the doctor who had spoken to them a few hours earlier at DI Campbell's bedside. The two women had stood up when he came in and he motioned to them to sit down again. The doctor took the seat across from Femi. He was leaning forward, elbows on his knees and hands clasped together in front of him. DC Knight tried to read something, anything, from his body language. She realised she couldn't remember his name and so tried to see if he was wearing a name badge, but she couldn't see his coat lapel without standing up and making it obvious that was what she was looking for. What was it again? Was it White? Something like that. He looked across the way at Femi.

'Mrs Campbell, I'm Doctor Wright,' he began.

Of course that was it - Doctor Wright, never wrong, DC Knight thought, silently chuckling to herself, somewhat inappropriately, as the doctor carried on speaking.

'We met a few hours ago, you may remember. and I've been with your husband in the operating theatre since then. So, the good news is he is still stable, but he is still unconscious. But that's not a bad thing. He still has a bullet inside him, but it is too dangerous for us to remove it at this point. For now it is best to leave it where it is until his body starts to recover and he gets a bit stronger. We can have another look at it then. He also took a bump to his head when he fell and there is some bleeding with that, but again the best thing for now is to wait and keep an eye on that too. I can assure you Mrs Campbell, your husband is in the best hands and we will let you know as soon as anything changes. Do you have any questions?'

Femi sat still and started to sob.

Chapter 50

It was a few weeks later and DI Strong was sitting in the Chief Constable's office. His PA had brought in two cups of coffee, china cups and saucers, with coffee from the Chief's personal coffee making machine. No vending machine rubbish here.

The Chief seemed to be in an agreeable mood. That was a good thing. He'd been pretty grumpy over the past few months with the pressure he had been getting from above. Those damned politicians.

'So Mo, everything seems to have quietened down again, thankfully,' the Chief said. 'I haven't heard from Ms Gordon, the PCC, for over a week now. And that must be a record. Between you and me she was becoming a right pain in the arse,' the Chief smiled and winked conspiratorially, before taking a sip of his coffee.

'She was practically calling me every day,' he continued. 'I was talking with her more than I was with my wife! I wouldn't mind if she was helping in some way, but.... Anyway that one incident in Club Extream seems to have finished it all, do you think?'

'Yes I think so,' Strong replied, smiling. 'It was a shame that it had to happen how it did, particularly with what happened to Joe Campbell, but I think it was inevitable. It had become like a pressure cooker and something had to give. It needed something like that to sort it all out.'

'So what's the situation now then?' the Chief asked.

'Well, the Bolton gang have receded somewhat without Ally Bolton leading them,' Strong replied. 'His brother Charlie seems to be in charge, but he's a bit quieter than Ally was, and Tony Fleming before that. We've got them pretty much under control now. Of course we're never going to stop the prostitution and drugs completely but I'd say it's in a manageable state now, which is good. We know who's doing what, and it's better that it stays like that.'

'And the Romanians…have they all gone now?' the Chief asked.

'Pretty much,' Strong replied. 'Bogdan Popescu, their leader is still in a bad way, but he's been transferred back to a hospital in Romania, so I don't expect we'll see him again. The guy that took over from him is Alex Olarescu and, as you know, we have him locked up, awaiting trial. As for the rest of them, I don't think many of them had the stomach to carry on trying to take over from the Boltons. From what we know, a lot of them have moved back home to Bucharest, and those left behind don't seem to be intent on causing any more trouble.'

'Mmm…that's a good result,' the Chief Constable replied, nodding his head. 'And the case against Alexandru Olarescu is pretty watertight?'

'I think so,' Strong replied, nodding. 'He's not talking to us, but his lawyer has issued a statement which claims self-defence for the killing of Ally Bolton. He says Bolton was charging towards him and he was fearful for his life. He claims he meant to just scare him off, but Bolton had thrown himself at him and couldn't avoid what he called the warning shot. And for the shooting of Joe Campbell he says the gun went off accidentally during the struggle with me. Of course that wasn't what happened and we've got a few witnesses, including myself and DC Knight, who saw it differently, so we should be pretty solid in both cases I'd say.'

'I can't see any jury going with his version of events,' Strong added, 'so I'm confident we'll get the right outcome and he'll be locked away for a long time.'

'Good, good,' the Chief nodded.

'By the way,' Strong carried on, 'I'll shortly be putting DC Knight forward for the vacant DS role, I think she's done enough to deserve it and it'll be good to have a woman progressing up the ladder. It'll send out a good message.'

'Yes, I agree. So, all in all Mo, overall it's been a good result,' the Chief Constable said, 'with the exception of Joe Campbell of course. Hopefully he will make a full recovery.'

Strong nodded and both men picked up their cups and saucers and took a drink of coffee as they thought of Campbell still lying in his hospital bed. The Chief put his coffee back down on the table and started talking again.

'But the stats are all looking good. We have one of the best regions in the country now, even better than Greater Manchester and you know how they like to blow their own trumpet! Dave Cairns, their Chief Constable is never reticent at telling everyone how good they are when we all get together at conference. Well this year I'll be able to get one up on him,' the Chief said, laughing.

DI Strong laughed along with his boss before picking up his cup of coffee to take another drink. Strong didn't like the whole stats and political side of things in the police. He tried to stay out of it as much as possible, but he recognised how important it was to the Chief and to the politicians who set their budgets, and so he knew that meant it was important to him, and the rest of the police force too. But Strong just wanted to get justice for the victims of crime, that was all that really motivated him.

Perhaps sensing that Strong didn't want to discuss the statistics, the Chief Constable changed the conversation topic back to their injured colleague.

'How is Joe Campbell, have you heard any more about how he's doing recently?' the Chief asked.

Strong replaced his cup in the saucer on the table before replying with a frown.

'He's still in a coma, but the doctors say that's not necessarily a bad thing,' Strong replied.

341

'Apparently it helps to let his body heal in its own time. He seems strong and stable and the doctors say there's a possibility that he could wake up at anytime. His wife said she thought he'd moved his hand one day last week when she was visiting him. So we're all just hoping it will be soon and that he'll be okay.'

'Yes. Are we doing all we can to support his wife and family? Femi isn't it?' the Chief asked.

'Yes, Femi. I believe so,' Strong replied. 'They've got a big, close knit family anyway, and I think they are all helping out where needed. I've gone to see Femi a few times and she seems to be coping. She's a strong woman and with the help of her family she seems to be getting through it.'

'Good, good,' the Chief Constable replied. 'Well let's keep up with the good work and keep on top of everything Mo,' he said and he got up from the table and, carrying his cup and saucer, he returned to his desk. Strong knew that was his signal that their meeting was over.

Chapter 51

It was three months after the incident in Club Extream before DI Campbell began to come out of his coma. It had been a gradual thing, over a period of a few weeks. Firstly there had been the hand movement. Had it moved or did Femi just imagine it? Did she simply want it to move? Willed it to? But then it happened again and a nurse saw it. It was definitely moving. Just an inch or two, but it was there. Then his foot and his legs moved. Definitely. You couldn't imagine that.

The medical team said it was a good sign but they warned Femi not to get too hopeful. It was too early to tell whether he would continue to progress or not. Or whether he would return to some sort of normality. How his brain might be. They warned Femi that he might not be the same Joe Campbell as he had been before he had got shot. But as the weeks passed the movements became more regular and seemingly stronger. Then one day he opened his eyes when one of the nurses was turning him in the bed. A few weeks later he was able to move his head and smile. The first time he smiled at Femi it took all her strength to hold herself together. She could feel her legs starting to buckle but she held on to the edge of his bed and somehow managed to stay upright.

'Hello you,' she said, smiling back at him, while holding back her tears.

He continued to progress and soon he was beginning to talk again. Just the odd word to begin with. The doctors were very pleased with his recovery and their mood seemed to change from one of caution to one of optimism. Now there was talk about him potentially making a full recovery. Or something close to that.

As he began to improve, DI Strong started to visit him regularly, just like a good boss should do. Each time he saw him, Strong would chat to Campbell about past cases they had worked on, testing Campbell on his memory, but it was apparent he couldn't recall much at all about the last couple of years. Although he still couldn't talk much, it seemed he couldn't remember being in Leeds and he seemed to have very little recollection of Andy Austin, the Anniversary Killer, not even recognising the name when Strong first said it. Just a shake of the head.

The doctors had advised Femi and DI Strong that Campbell's memory of that period might never return. On the positive side, he appeared to have a good recollection of the period before his shooting, his life with Femi, and his brain seemed to be functioning perfectly well now, so they should be thankful for that at least. Some people lost their memories completely and that was tough for everyone. Strong was thankful.

A month after that first smile Campbell was back on his feet, working hard with the physio team, learning how to walk again. His speech was getting better every day too. He couldn't put full sentences together yet but he could say a few words and the doctors were sure it would only be a matter of time before he was speaking fully again. Strong continued his regular visits and Femi was grateful to him for that. It gave her a break and let her do something else other than continually visiting the hospital. It also gave Campbell a sense of purpose. She knew that he wanted to get back to the job of being a detective, it was his passion and always had been. Strong kept Campbell up to speed with what was happening at work and he was able to remember everything that Strong told him, but still not anything that had happened in the previous two or three years.

Ten months after being shot in Club Extream, DI Campbell was ready to come home. The doctors were pleased with his recovery and were optimistic that he would continue to improve to the point where he should be able to lead a fairly normal life. Maybe even return to his job with the police, but the doctors warned him that could still take some time and effort. His memory was still patchy and the doctors thought that it was now unlikely that it would ever return completely.

Campbell was desperate to get out of the hospital, to get back home, and he was also itching to get back to work. He hadn't lost the passion to be a detective. To solve crimes. That was what he wanted to get back to. And he wanted to do that as soon as possible.

DI Strong had been a regular visitor while he had been in hospital and had kept him up to speed with what was going on in the police world and Campbell was keen to hear about it. He looked forward to his boss's visits. It made him feel he was, in some small way, still part of the Serious Crime Team. Some of his other colleagues had also come to see him in hospital, but usually making just the one visit out of a sense of duty.

The man who had shot him, Alex Olarescu, had been found guilty of the murder of Ally Bolton and the attempted murder of Campbell. He had been sentenced to life imprisonment, which was the right decision, and Campbell was pleased by that, but in a strange way he couldn't get a full sense of satisfaction at the verdict because he couldn't remember it actually happening. It was like he was reading about someone else in the newspaper, not himself. Strong had told him what happened that night in the club, but to Campbell it just seemed like a story about someone else. How could it have been him if he couldn't remember it, or feel it in some way?

When Strong visited him now, he would occasionally refer back to cases the two of them had worked on together in the past but, frustratingly, Campbell, as hard as he might try, just couldn't remember any of them. None of the detail, none of the names. Strong was very supportive though and told him not to worry. The main thing was he was well now and almost ready to start work again on current and future cases. Those were the main things. What's happening now. The past wasn't that important, Strong told him, and he began to believe it. Besides, Strong was filling him in on all the important details he'd forgotten so he was effectively restocking his memory banks.

'What about my work laptop?' Campbell asked him. 'Could I get it back so at least I can read through what's happened before and start getting emails and the like, work my way gradually back into things?'

'Your laptop's been re-assigned,' Strong replied. 'It's standard procedure, with you being out for so long. Got to make use of what we have resource-wise,' Strong explained, smiling. 'You know how it is. You still remember that! I'll see what I can do in terms of getting you another one soon though. Maybe when you get home.'

'Okay, thanks Guv. I really appreciate all you've done for me,' Campbell replied. 'I know other guvnors might have just given up on me, put me out to farm. But not you. You've really helped me, encouraged me all the way, both before and during all of this, and now I just can't wait to get back to the job again.'

Chapter 52

A few weeks later, Campbell was released from hospital, finally being allowed to go back home. It had been a frustrating time. He was ready to leave earlier, but it had taken the Social Services team three weeks to ensure that the necessary support services were set up to enable Campbell to safely live at home again. Campbell accepted this. He knew they had to do things properly and not cut corners. It wouldn't have been fair on Femi to have to do everything that he needed, especially with her also having to look after little Rosey. But Campbell was also determined to keep improving as quickly as possible so that they soon wouldn't need any outside help. He was the man of the house and he was keen to get things back to that position. Campbell was a proud man.

Physically, he was improving all the time, and every day he made himself walk a little bit further than he had the previous day, no matter how tired he felt. It seemed to be working.

Mentally he was fine. In fact in some ways he was enjoying the challenge of getting himself back into a fit state again. Some days he felt frustrated, but he knew it was a long game. A marathon, not a sprint. The only thing that wasn't improving still was his memory, or to be more specific his memory of the last two to three years. He'd begun to get used to that now though and Femi had filled him in with all the important points, the bits he'd missed. Strong had also been a regular visitor and done likewise with the main cases he'd worked on over the years.

So the whole lack of memory thing wasn't really bothering him. He was living in the now and making new memories for himself. DI Strong had been a great help, a great mentor to him over the last year. He'd told him to forget about the past, what was important was now, today, and the future. They were all that mattered and Campbell had come to believe that too.

Strong had been keeping Campbell up to speed with the cases the Serious Crime Team were currently working on and, although he wasn't officially back at work yet, the two of them would often spend an hour or so talking through the cases, allowing Campbell to have some input, easing him back into the job again, but slowly. Campbell was still rehabilitating and he would get tired sometimes and so Strong was careful not to overload him.

However, with a lot of hard work, Campbell was getting more and more healthy, and he was keen to get back into his police work, in an official capacity as soon as he could. DI Strong understood that and so on his next visit he told Campbell what they were planning for him.

'I've spoken with the Chief Constable and he's agreed that you can come back to our team for now and work on a part time basis, as little or as much as suits you to begin with,' Strong told Campbell as they sat together in Campbell's living room with cups of coffee.

'When you're fit and healthy and able to return full time, then of course we'll look to get you back into a proper DI position again as soon as there is one available. I think with all you've been through you should have a very good chance of being able to get something fairly local, which of course would suit you and your family better.'

Strong had already discussed that with the Chief Constable and they'd pencilled in a role for Campbell as a Regional Detective Inspector in an area not far from where he lived. That should suit everyone. Now that Campbell had forgotten all his doubts, and even the notes he'd made, about Strong, he was no longer a danger to him. Of course Strong would continue to do all he could to help his colleague, he knew Campbell was a good detective.

Strong had brought a laptop for Campbell to start using while he was at home, just to gradually ease him back into work.

'You better just check it all works, while I'm here,' DI Strong said. 'It should be okay, but just in case I have to take it back.'

The two men walked through to Campbell's study room. Campbell hadn't been in here for a while, there hadn't been any need really. It had been the room he used anytime he wanted to do a bit of work at home. It was somewhere where he could get a bit of peace and quiet, somewhere to think. It was fairly sparse in terms of furniture, just a desk and a chair. There was a shelfing unit on one wall which Strong noticed contained a variety of police and legal books. At one end of the lower shelf there was a framed photo of a younger Campbell standing in a boxing ring, smiling and holding aloft a boxing belt, which Strong assumed he must have won. He picked the photo up and looked at it.

'When was this taken?' he asked Campbell.

'Oh…I cant remember exactly,' Campbell replied. 'Probably fifteen years ago. Maybe twenty? It was some regional competition I won. I didn't go much further than that though, police work took up too much of my time. I couldn't train as much as I needed to.'

Strong put the photo carefully back on the shelf and waited as Campbell sat down on the leather office chair, self-propelling it up to the edge of his desk. Strong stepped around the desk and stood beside him. Campbell switched the laptop on and while he waited for it to boot up, he opened the top right hand drawer of his desk. It was largely full of pens and other stationery items, but at the front he noticed a small silver flash disk. He picked it up and looked at it. There was something written on it and he looked closely, reading out what he could see.

'DI Strong,' he laughed. 'Ha-ha that's funny. I assume this must be yours,' he said. Shall we see what's on it?'

'What? No, better not. I think I remember giving you that,' Strong replied. 'Its got some old case data on it. It'll be well out of date, I'd better take it back,' he said and he held out his hand for the disk.

Campbell wasn't looking at him though, he was too busy rummaging around in his desk to see if there was anything else of interest. He still held the disk in his left hand, away from Strong.

'Might as well check though,' Campbell said and moved to insert the disk into the USB port on the side of his machine, but before he could do that Strong leaned forward and took it from him.

'Best I just take it,' he said. 'It might corrupt your machine with the new security software they have on them now,' and he popped the disk into his jacket pocket.

'What? Oh, okay …I guess so,' Campbell replied, slightly taken aback by his boss's uncharacteristically forceful attitude. 'The laptop seems to be working fine, at least it's started up okay, let's see if I can get into my emails all right.'

Strong smiled to himself. He had no doubt what the disk held. Since he'd found the file on Campbell's laptop, he'd always wondered, had a fear, that Campbell might have kept another copy of it somewhere. He'd looked in Campbell's desk at the police station of course, but there was nothing there. But here it was now. He'd kept it at home, but thankfully he no longer knew what it was, and now it was in Strong's possession. How lucky was that? This time he'd make sure he destroyed it properly, he wouldn't make the same mistake that he had with Dylan's diary. In his mind, he decided he would smash it up and then flush it down the toilet. That would do it.

This last year had been a tricky one for Strong, but now everything was back under control. Under Strong's control. His way of delivering justice had worked well and, in his eyes, proved that it was the right way. Sometimes you just had to do what was necessary to get the correct result. The gang war was now over and Olarescu was locked away for good. What could be wrong with that? Everything had worked out very well indeed. Just then his phone rang.

'Hello, what's up?' Strong said.

'We've found a body guv, a middle aged man. Looks like he's been stabbed,' came the reply.

Strong recognised Detective Sergeant Knight's voice, following her recent promotion, she was now his second in command.

'Okay, I'm on my way,' Strong replied, smiling to himself. He enjoyed the thrill of the chase. The chase to get justice, and it looked like a new one had just begun.

Two Wrongs

Acknowledgements

There are a few people I'd like to thank for helping and encouraging me to write this latest book. As always these things are a team effort and their support has been invaluable. Firstly my family and friends, especially my wife and daughter, Gill and Megan, for just letting me get on with it - and supplying teas and coffees….along with the occasional biscuit as I sat writing. It's a lonely task!

I'd also like to thank my regular team of first readers and editors, who have all helped with the final draft – (Wee) Jean Farrell and Jim Anderson. Thanks to both of you for your extremely helpful input and suggestions.

Now that it's all done, it's time to start writing the next book….

Due for release in late 2022

The next book in the DI Strong series. Following on from Two Wrongs. Find out what happens next with DI Strong and his quest for justice.

Two Wrongs

Other books by Ian Anderson:

Jack's Lottery Plan

This is the funny and moving story of Jack Burns. One day he finds out that a friend has secretly won the lottery and he embarks on a clandestine plan to get a share. But his plan goes hopelessly wrong impacting Jack and his friends in ways he would never have imagined.

Jack's Big Surprise

Jack Burns is planning a surprise proposal for his girlfriend Hannah. But as is usually the way with Jack, his plan doesn't quite go the way he was hoping it would. Instead he finds himself hopelessly involved in a series of hilariously funny, and sometimes, unfortunate incidents. This is the sequel to Jack's Lottery Plan and finds Jack just as chaotic as he always is.

The Anniversary

In the first book of the DI Strong crime thriller series, Andy Austin's family are killed in a road accident. With a sense of injustice, he becomes obsessed on seeking revenge. He befriends DI Strong and uses him to help carry out his plan. As the police get closer to catching him it becomes clear that not everyone is without a guilty secret.

The Deal

Detective Inspector Strong hatches a plan to use Andy Austin, a wanted murderer, to help him deliver justice to serious criminals the police aren't able to convict by conventional means. As Strong gets more and more confident with his scheme, he begins to make mistakes and leave himself exposed to a greater risk of being caught and ruining his career. This is the second great book in the DI Strong crime thriller series, following on from The Anniversary.

Loose Ends

This is the third book in the DI Strong Crime Thriller series, following on from The Anniversary and The Deal. DI Strong has been bending the law to get the justice he can't achieve through conventional police methods. But is Strong taking too many chances and arousing suspicion? Too many people are becoming involved, too many loose ends, which Strong knows he will have to do something about.

For more information, please visit my website at:
www.ianandersonhome.wixsite.com/ianandersonauthor

Or find me on Facebook at:
www.facebook.com/IanAndersonAuthor

Printed in Great Britain
by Amazon